MEMENTO

MEMENTO

A Novel in Dreams, Thoughts, and Images

Cordelia Schmidt-Hellerau

International Psychoanalytic Books (IPBooks)
New York • http://www.IPBooks.net

Published by IPBooks, Queens, NY

Cover Design by Karola Schmidt-Hellerau and Lawrence L. Schwartz
Layout and typesetting by Noel S. Morado

ISBN 978-1-956864-49-6

For my sister
Karola Schmidt-Hellerau
with gratitude and affection
everlasting

To run against the window and, weak after exerting all one's strength, to step over the window sill through the splintered wood and glass.
Franz Kafka

There is no end. There is no beginning. There is only the passion of life.
Frederico Fellini

… the distinction between past, present and future is only a stubbornly persistent illusion.
Albert Einstein

Contents

Who is who on Sine's mind?
Sam is Sine's husband
Mikki is Sine's daughter
Lukas is Sine's father
Marlene is Sine's mother
(*Lilli* is Marlene, Sine's mother, whenever she is coquette
Lenchen is Marlene, Sine's mother, when she was a child)
Enna is Sine's sister
Jules is Sine's student
and other unnamed persons

ARRIVAL

In the late afternoon, Sam and I arrive at our hotel. It's a big old castle. A plaque announces its opening in 1895. The walls in the lobby are paneled in wood, and the floor is carpeted with oriental rugs. Brass chandeliers with small flame-shaped bulbs spread almost no light onto the various desks, behind which men in black suits serve their customers. Sam stands in line with the other newly arrived guests and waits for his turn to register. I sit down on a sofa. Marlene and Enna are standing nearby. Marlene complains about something, I cannot hear what it is. Enna looks over to me, her eyebrows raised. When Marlene is gone, Enna comes and sits down next to me. Mother wants to open a gallery here, she says, she can't accept that she's eighty-five! Enna sighs and shakes her head. I move a bit away. I don't want to talk with Enna. I am tired, and my eyes keep falling shut.

Sam comes to me with the keys and says, let's go upstairs. But that seems impossible! I ask him to give me a minute. I'm so tired, I explain. Okay, he says, I'll go ahead. Our room is 859.

Don't forget: 859! He leaves. 859, I murmur, and can't keep my eyes open. Enna tells me how she brought our mother all the way to this hotel. I have no idea what she's talking about. Finally I manage to get up. With one hand I grab my bag, with the other I rub my eyes in order to force their lids open—to no avail. I almost walk into a pillar. Then I find the elevator, but I can't make out the call button, because now my eyes are firmly closed. When I manage to open them a bit, my vision is blurred. I'm so tired. The elevator door opens. Behind me a family with kids and luggage and a stroller, all rush to the open door. I let them pass. I'm the last to squeeze in. My eyes are still closed, thus I can't find the button for the eighth floor. When I finally discern the number 8 on the brass board it turns out that there is no button next to it. This elevator doesn't serve the eighth floor. Am I dreaming?

On the tenth floor the door opens, the children push me, run out, and chase each other through the hallway. Their little white dog is running after them and barks like crazy. I hadn't noticed the dog in the elevator. The father drags the luggage into the corridor, and the mother bounces the baby. Ba-ba-ba she sings. The baby cries. I think I'd better take the elevator down to the lobby to find another way to the eighth floor, but before I can get back in, the doors have closed. Maybe I can find some stairs to walk down? I fumble along the corridor trying to read the numbers on the doors, which is hard, because my eyes won't open. I'm so tired. Was the room number 858 or 885 or actually 585? I can't find the staircase, but somehow I can see that Marlene has stretched out on the red sofa under a blanket. She seems to be sleeping. I'm mystified: she decided to sleep in the lobby? Then a door opens next to me. There is Sam. Sine, he exclaims, his voice soaked with relief, where have you been? How can I explain? This is all so confusing. I must be sleeping. I couldn't open my eyes, I say, I couldn't find the right elevator. He lets me in. Finally! I'm so glad I found him!

Sam had opened our bags and thrown everything on the bed. I'm searching for this thing…he says. What thing, I ask. Impatiently he growls: the monitor, remember? The monitor! I crawl on the bed, lie down between the suits, shoes, toiletries, and everything that's spread out as if floating on the open sea. The monitor…I say, before I doze off, losing myself in the dark. When my eyes finally open, I see Sam next to me, sleeping. His head rests on my new sweater, which still has the price tag attached to its collar, his hands are buried under my thighs. Night must have fallen, because there is no light coming from the window. Tomorrow Sam has his presentation at this congress, I remember, but I've forgotten the subject of his paper and the theme of the meeting. What was it about? The monitor, I think, he needs the monitor for his demonstration. Warily I sit up, careful not to awaken him. Had I packed his monitor or had he? The last time I saw this little device, it was sitting on the kitchen counter, a heavy silver metal clump, not bigger than an apple or a hand grenade, with nothing but a plughole on one side and an on-off switch on the other. What is it, I had asked, what does it do? It's too complicated to quickly explain, Sam had declared, briefly lifting it up and putting it down with a thud as if to make his case. It's complicated.

White light from the open bathroom ventures into our room. On the carpet I will do my exercises, I decide, and at the desk I can grade my students' papers. They have internet connection in all guest rooms. I can do research for my next book while Sam is at his meetings. We'll see. I dive into my bag. Sam had emptied it only halfway through. He must have gotten tired during the search. We'd spent two days on this trip. Our original flight had been delayed, then it was canceled, then moved to a different airline, then this one too got delayed; finally we could board the plane, detached from the gate, moved towards the runway, then stopped, waited, and had to return to the gate and get out: some problem with the engine, they said, a different plane would come in the morning. We received a voucher for dinner, but at this point the airport restaurant had closed. The only food and soda vending machine nearby was out of service. We had to go to the restroom to drink water. Sam and I had stretched out on the floor with our heads on our bags. We wanted to sleep so badly, but couldn't get comfortable. Finally we'd sat up and played cards till 4 AM. I won. Sam felt guilty for putting me through this. I reassured him that I considered it an adventure. He smiled sheepishly.

The window sash slowly swings open as if gently pushed by invisible hands. The wind, only the wind. I step towards the cool air flowing in and look out into the wafting dusk. A man is sitting in the big oak tree opposite the hotel entrance. He crouches on a lower branch looking through some chunky binoculars straight at me. He reminds me of a photo: Todd, my strange little brother, sitting on a branch of our chestnut tree. I tentatively wave my hand, and the man waves back. Hi there! An oak leaf is floating into the room, hovers for a bit over Sam's sleeping hand, then sinks down settling right next to it. I close the window, firmly. It's time to go to sleep.

At night Marlene played hide and seek with her thoughts. There was someone she would follow. She would find him in a different country. Who knew? At night Marlene came into my room, dressed in her chemise, a ghost, like a ghost, silently she moved only to check on her daughter. Was she sleeping? She sat for a while on the small mattress right next to my feet and stroked the comforter as if in displacement. The alarm clock's second hand softly throbbed, tack, tack, tack, tack, so calming, a rhythm hypnotic and suggestive, pulling her in and over to these strange places of yore. There she rose and started to dance, all alone yet as if in front of stunned eyes. She lifted the veil of her nightgown that lagged behind her at every turn and threatened to wrap around her like a noose. Her big bare feet palpitated the floorboards in search of a safe place to stay. None was ever found. Her legs, tight and strong, wouldn't rest. They seemed to float through the moonlight, as did her bare arms, rising and falling like a penguin's wings. Was she happy or desperate? Was she acting in a trance or secretly crazy? It happened, it always happened that her nightie dropped, if not on purpose, slipped off her shoulders to the one or the other side, got hung up for a moment at her full breasts before the whole curtain skidded down and crumbled around her feet. But the music in her head never stopped. Her beautiful hands lifted her hair up over her head, and freed from all restraint she now danced, cooing with closed eyes and a luscious smile, all longing, wailing: huu-huu, you-you! who-who...? Through the grate of my lashes I saw the ugly scar that slashed her back from her right buttock to her left shoulder.

When I awaken, Sam is already dressed. He looks crisp: white shirt, gray tie, blue suit, and a fresh scent of aftershave around him. Did you find your thing?, I blurt out, because I feel so bad about not having known where it was. Good morning, my love, Sam responds, and gives me a bright smile. Yes, I found it. It'd snuck into your sneaker! He chuckles and lifts up the silver ball or bullet, and it hits me with a sharp flash of sunlight. So glad, I whisper. Sam has already turned around to stuff his little items into the various pockets of his suit jacket. He does this always in the same order. That's how he does it, he knows what he does. Why don't you sleep another round, he asks me while checking his phone for messages or something, I'll just have a quick coffee in the lobby and go to my meeting. Okay, I say. When will you be back? Don't know, he responds, but certainly by six or say eight at the latest. I'll call you, should something change. He smiles at me. I wish him good luck and he leaves.

As soon as he's gone I feel wide awake. How to start the day? Breakfast first. I quickly jump into some clothes, brush my hair, grab the key and leave the room. The hotel is built like a hollow tower, I now realize. From the balustrade I can see all the way down to the lobby. Maybe I can see Sam having coffee? I search through the sparse light, and then I see him. A coffee cup in his hand, he sits with Marlene on the sofa. She's just spreading her blanket over both of their knees. I'm surprised. What are they doing? My heart is pounding. I decide to take my time. I want to compose myself. Slowly I walk down the stairs with my hand sliding along the rail to steady my thoughts. The carpet on the steps is thick and soft, muffling all noises. It's almost as if I'm gliding down. When I reach the ground floor my hand is covered with dust.

Through a heavy curtain I enter the lobby. A few tables are set up for breakfast. Sam is gone and so is Marlene. Her woolen blanket, neatly folded and decoratively thrown over the backrest of a chaise longue, exudes innocence. I pick one of the small tables and sit down. The waiter brings coffee and a basket with a roll, a croissant and a muffin, butter and jam on the side. I order orange juice in addition. The coffee is good, really good, and the muffin is sweet. I look around. This place is so different from where we live. Our house is modern, open and light. The hotel is as dark as Dracula's castle, its guest rooms probably holding the count's daily blood supply. Nonsense, and currently I'm anemic. I'm here because I needed a change of scenery after my mother's passing.

But I'd rather have gone to Tuscany… Via Ciampolo da Panzano is lined on both sides with small old houses closely hunched together, slightly bulging beneath the weight of time, yet well taken care of, as is the custom—earthy colors for the facades, the shutters dark green and brown, flowerpots on the window sills—and all is quiet, so quiet, breathing the assurance of home for generations to come. Here I walked with Marlene a few years ago. When we met people on the street we would greet each other and smile, as if we weren't strangers. *Buon giorno!* Now Marlene is gone—and everything seems different. Will I return to Panzano once in a while, or was this the last time ever? Noontime and nobody on the street. A cat on a doormat squints its eyes as it looks at me. An old woman on the second floor waters her garden pottery; when the water starts dripping down to the street, she firmly closes the window and disappears. Lunchtime spreads silence. In the country Italians eat and take a nap. Work rests. All slows down. Take a breath! Then: a scream—a scream loud and shrill, a piercing yell trembling through the alley, a woman's pain, cutting through stone, through the walls of privacy, the home of this house, bursting out, this scream, crushing the muse, slicing my heart, still slicing it, ever and anon…Is it rage, despair, delusion? Nothing moves, nobody looks or wonders, all is silent. I'm paralyzed, prey to the shock. What a moment! The cat has fallen asleep.

For five years we'd taken care of our mother, my sister and I. Enna provided most of the care during daytime. In the evening, when I came home from school, she left, and I took over. I did the night shifts. At night Marlene called: a pillow had slipped off her bed, she'd heard someone talking to her, she needed to go to the bathroom, or wanted a glass of water—not the water, which was next to her at the bedside table, no, fresh water, but not too cold! I got it for her. Maybe she was anxious at night, maybe she felt lonely. Her calls broke into my sleep, invaded my dreams. Sometimes I dreamt her call and got up, only to find her fast asleep. But the water was cold and delicious. It ran down her throat, and she liked it. She lifted herself up, and when I wanted to support her, she fought off my hand. I just had to be there. She drank, and she did it all on her own. She smiled to herself. Seeing her submerged in her secret pleasure, my mouth got dry. Her long hair, charged with some electric power, radiated off her white face like a coral's tentacles, freely moving into space while she remained stuck on her bed's reef.

We both witnessed her slow demise, Enna and I. Sam sort of watched from afar. Mother was weak but her mind was clear. Occasionally she was a bit off, but when she noticed, she had the wits to hide it with some excuse. In the evening, Enna would tell me what had happened during the day, if anything. She had a good way to deal with her. She would tell her this and that, stories she'd read in the newspaper, or things she'd noticed in the grocery store—whatever seemed to be entertaining. Mother would listen, say something, but rarely would it amount to a real conversation. She was involved in her own thoughts and wouldn't let us in on them. But once in a while she would squint her eyes and come up with something surprising, even unsettling. Out of the blue a thought would detach itself from her lips, catch up with the soft sound of her whisper and then linger for a while. She would say: We give birth to death enhancing our demise. Where did that come from? Mother seemed to enjoy when we looked puzzled.

I felt worn down. Sam was concerned. He said I should try to recapture my good old self. We hadn't made love for months. Our life had been stopped in its tracks while my mother was ambling towards her end. We had taken her in when she couldn't manage on her own any longer. I felt grateful but also upset that Sam immediately accepted this option. And when I asked our daughter Mikki if she would allow me to rearrange her room for her grandmother, she said: Do whatever works best for you guys. I tried to plead with her: but what about all your stuff? She just laughed. Box it up, she suggested. It's not my room anymore. I live with Hank in Bedford now. She was right, but I felt abandoned by both, Mikki and Sam. My mother moved in.

How confusing these times were! Marlene in the prime of life was almost always exhausted. After a long day of work, ten hours at her desk, getting through half of the company's list of holiday greeting cards, for which she had to handwrite the addresses on the envelope—to make it look more personal, as her boss had stated—and with nothing to look forward to for the rest of the night, not even the prospect of a some-what satisfying meal—at home she had just half a package of a processed cheese, but no bread to go with it—Marlene had decided to save on the train ticket and walk all the way back to this fringe area, where she'd rented a cheap room that matched her meager income. What a cold winter night it was! She'd walked over an hour, hoping to get so tired that she would just fall asleep upon arrival. Seven trains had already passed, ablaze with light, their windows fogged from the crowd densely packed along the ride, when she finally reached her street, which lay unmoved and ordinary between its rundown tenements. Not a single soul around. Marlene sighs. Everybody's having dinner with their families. She pushes open the door to the entrance hall. Unsuspectingly looking around while rummaging through her purse for her keys, she notices a dim shine on the floor near the basement door. Believing it to be a rumpled cellophane wrapper, at first she wants to disregard it and save on the few additional steps to the end of the hallway, where this mute glimmer comes from; but its yellow-brownish shine does stir her curiosity. So she walks over, bends down to what is partly hidden under a dirty rag, and lifts up a golden brooch! Marlene immediately recognizes it: it's her landlady's brooch. Ms. Mack always wore it right in the middle between her humongous breasts, where it had to keep the two wings of her blouse together. She must have lost it. Her breasts blasted it off, Marlene thinks, indulging for a moment in her malice. She holds it in her hand, weighing and scrutinizing it, guessing that it is made out of real gold. The hall light goes off! Too bad! Marlene slips the brooch in her pocket, and as she cautiously feels for the switch, she hears Ms. Mack open her door on the second floor and turn on the light. Marlene stiffens. Her heart is pounding. Slowly she starts climbing up the stairs. Even though she vaguely pictures herself giving the brooch to her landlady, she can't quite think about it, not now. Ms. Mack, wrapped in her raccoon coat with her poodle on its leash, approaches. Hello, Marlene, she says, coming home late? Lots of work? Yeah, good evening, Ms. Mack, Marlene says, lots of work! A few steps above Marlene, Ms. Mack stops and says: I've put a little pot with goulash soup in front of your door, just some leftovers, and it's best when it's fresh. I thought you'd like it. Marlene feels herself blushing. Oh, how nice of you, Ms. Mack, she says, thank you! I'm glad I won't have to cook tonight! Ms. Mack nods complacently. I thought it was the right thing to do, she says, and follows her poodle down the stairs.

Nobody is having breakfast anymore. The waiter has cleaned off all the other tables and is parading his impatience back and forth in front of my idle eyes. I decide to take a walk to explore the area. When I leave the hotel, a chauffeur opens the door of his black limousine. Where can I bring you, he asks. Oh thank you, I say, I just want to take a walk. He shakes his head. There's nothing to see, he says, nobody walks around here. Well, then I'll take some fresh air, I defend my idea.

Maybe later you could bring me to Watertown. He nods. We're here till 5 PM, he lets me know. I wave at him with all five fingers stretched out.

Do I really want to take a walk in a remote place like this? Small shrubs, mossy fields, vast stretches of heather and wild rocks, that's it. First I stroll along the street that connects the hotel with the rest of the world. But soon I veer off and trudge across the field, just ahead. It's not possible to get lost here, one can see the hotel castle from far away. It's the only building for miles and miles. The wind is blowing softly, two rabbits run away from me, a hawk is hovering high above. I feel calm but slightly nervous. Why did I come here?

Suddenly I hear a noise coming from behind a rock. It sounds like the call of a gray goose or some other bird. They are breeding on the ground, I think, maybe I can see the nest? My arms stretched out to balance my moves on this treacherous terrain, I step over heather and low growing pinewood, or maybe I'm flying. Five flaps into the marsh I see my mother sitting on the ground leaning against the rock. She's holding her left leg. I got caught in a root, I fell, she whimpers, I think I broke my foot! I look at her foot which sticks out of a red ballet flat split open along its sole. She has muck all over her hands, clothes and even on her face. Oh, I'm sorry, I say, and for a moment I see her sitting with Sam under the blanket. I'll help you up, I suggest. It'll hurt, she whines. Well, you cannot stay here, can you, I return, a bit harsher than planned. I'm Lilli, she offers, we know each other from last night. Mother, stop that nonsense, I say, I'm not in the mood. I reach out for her hand to pull her up. But she insists, I first have to know your name. She wants to play for time—or has she lost it? Angrily I say: I'm Gesine, your daughter. Ah, Sine, she marvels, I don't know anybody who's called Sine. Let's try to get you up, I say, and I think of all the times when my mother fell, because she was too proud to use the walker or let us support her. I can do it, she insisted, then her legs buckled, and she fell to the floor. How heavy she was when she couldn't or wouldn't help to get back on her feet!

Lilli accepts my hands under her axles, and I pull her up. I'm surprised how light she is. Only skin and bones under her bulky jacket. Have we not fed her well? As soon as she's up, I loosen my grip, and she slides down again, falls on her behind with a thud. Ouch, she moans, I can't stand, my other foot hurts as well, I can't walk! Expectantly she looks at me. So you'll have to sit here, and I'll send someone from the hotel to get you, I suggest. No, no, she wails, don't leave me, carry me to the hotel! She's crazy! I'm not Hercules, I retort. You can do this, she insists, I'm only 42 kilos. I bend down to check on her other foot, because I don't want to be taken for a ride, and just then she suddenly throws her arms around my neck, grabs my waist with her legs, opened and snapped shut like a scissor, and scoots up my back, clinging there like a wretch, ready to strangle me rather than let me go. Sam, I think, where are you!

Once Mikki demanded to be carried that way to Kindergarten. She stomped her little feet and wouldn't move, since I had refused to let her ride on my back. She was a cowboy, she declared, and cowboys don't walk, they ride on their horses! I'm not a horse, I defended myself. Yes, you are, she claimed, tightly folding her arms in front of her chest and pinching her lips to show that she was done arguing. So I was her horse, and actually I loved to carry her and feel her little warm body snug at my back. Sometimes she screamed: gallop, and then I jumped and ran for a bit before I slowed down again to a trot. When we finally arrived at the entrance to her Kindergarten, she slipped down and ran to join her friends in the courtyard. No looking back at her brave horse.

Lilli's bones push at my back, thin and sharp-edged. A nasty spider has lured me into her trap. Ouch, she squalls when I make an abrupt move to steady my steps on this uneven ground. Watch it, she yells, I'm hurting! I'm furious. Sam, I think, help me! When we finally arrive at the hotel, the black limousine is still there. The chauffeur leans at the fender smoking a cigarette. Can you please open the door, I gasp, you have to bring my mother to the nearest hospital. He looks at Marlene and says, She's dirty, she'll soil my seats. At the end of my tether, I drop her down on the trunk of his limousine. The chauffeur frowns, leaves and comes back with a large plastic panel, which he wraps all around Lilli before he hauls her into the back seat. She looks like a mummy; only her head sticks out of the plastic wrap. She implores me to come with her, but I shake my head. The limousine drives off.

My cheeks are cold, my hair is moist, and earth crumbs peel off my boots as I walk back to our room. I feel refreshed and relieved, as if I had escaped a great danger. I am alive. It's almost ten. I call room service and ask for a hot chocolate. Then I settle at the desk. I have to grade thirty papers in these next few days. Thirty papers! The desk chair is a bit too low. I get up to find a pillow to put on it. Nothing in the closet. The chest of drawers contains a bible, a shoehorn, some broken coat hangers, and a folder with the hotel's stationery. But fortunately just then my hot chocolate arrives, and the server shows me how to raise the seat by pushing a handle upwards. I hadn't noticed it. This is a piano seat, he explains. Oh, I say, and am glad my problem is solved. Just to finish up, I open the last drawer—and there is Sam's monitor. He didn't take it? Did he forget it? What is it doing here? I take it out of the drawer and weigh it in my hand. It feels nice, not too heavy, and the surface is smooth. The metal warms up as I'm holding it. It gets warmer than my hand's temperature. Soon it's so warm that I drop it on the desk. Ah, I splutter and the monitor says *hmmm…* What kind of device is this? What does this monitor monitor? I look at it more closely and discover that the power switch is turned on. Maybe I accidentally did this when I lifted it out of the drawer. I turn the switch off, and the monitor hums *hmmm…*

There is a knock at the door, and when I open it, Marlene stands in front of me. How could she be back so fast? I'm sorry to disturb you, she says, and casually walks past me into our room. My leg is not broken after all, she declares. I feel much better. On our way to Watertown the driver got a flat tire. While he was working to change it, I could wiggle myself free, get out, and walk back to the hotel. Here I am, exhausted! I need to rest, she says and walks towards our bed, uninvited. I sense a tornado approaching. Why don't you go to your room and rest, I challenge her. Marlene gives me an indignant look. My daughter is my home, she puts forth. Besides, I'm waiting for my friend, he hasn't arrived yet. He's the keynote speaker at this conference, and they've put him up in a suite here. But they won't give me the keys. I can't wait for him any longer. Last night I had to camp out on that crappy sofa in the lobby. I'm aching, I need to rest. And throwing herself on our bed, she says, Never mind, I'll just lie here for a bit. I won't disturb you. Brazenly she smiles at me. I'm speechless!

But as if in a contest of wills I decide to ignore her. I sit down at the desk and open the folder with my students' essays. The subject I'd given them was deliberately open: *An experience*. It mustn't be an experience in the real world, I had told them—write down whatever you think of, because that's an experience as well. They had looked at me pensive or puzzled. How would Jules have worked with this task? He didn't like writing assignments, but he complied and always found an interesting way of making them his. I close the folder. I don't feel like reading these papers now. But I have to start grading them. I don't want to. I open the folder again. I notice the monitor on my desk. Its silver surface is a mirror, showing me Lilli lying on our bed. Is it really her? To reassure myself I turn around and briefly glance at her. Already in her fifties she still looks glamorous! It seems she's fast asleep. Her hair is flowing over her shoulders, her hands are holding the pillow in front of her. She has replaced her broken ballet flats with black stilettos, which are now piercing our comforter. How could she walk in these high heels after having moaned in pain only half an hour ago whenever the slightest move seemed to unsettle her? She's a malingerer. Turning away from her, I accidentally touch Sam's monitor. *Hmmm…* it utters and reflects me and Lilli bent together on its surface. This is annoying. I don't want to see myself so close to Lilli.

But there she is, and the winter sun is shining warm on her face. Unsure of what to think about, Marlene can't quite grasp how she'd gotten to this place where she has been for so long, forever, her whole life. Something is going to happen, someone is going to come. But she can't figure what that might be. Ought to be. In a tentative gesture she stretches the fingers of her right hand, and since there is nothing to touch, she bends them again into their usual curled-up position. Somewhere downstairs she hears Enna patter around the house. It is good that someone is there – there and not here where the space is all hers. Lukas passed away. He died while she was having tea. She had missed the moment! If she could she would bring him back to life, just to be present when he would die again. How was this – dying…? Marlene feels slightly excited thinking about it. This moment, this transition…How much could one grasp of this move from life to death? Just a glimpse? Death itself didn't seem interesting. But this moment when she would detach herself from her life…She'd also missed her father's death. He died far away at home while she was trying to find a new place to stay and start over. They said her father had been shot. A Russian killed him. While the bullet had torn through his chest, he couldn't have been able to steer his thoughts, instantly they would have surged out of him, then perhaps for a little while trailed above looking at him as he lay on the ground, one arm over his dying dog—an amazing picture until all would have darkened and disappeared. Night in the middle of an afternoon. Then the Russian inspected the place. Listlessly he roamed around the empty house. To him it didn't mean anything other than a bunch of wild boar sausages hanging in the kitchen cabinet and a chunk of cheese wrapped in a moist napkin, so it wouldn't dry out. The Russian wiped his penknife on his pants and cut a good piece of cheese off the wheel. Now bread would be good, but there wasn't any. He just didn't know that the bread was kept in a closed pot below the windowsill. A tank rattled past the house. The Russian sat down at the kitchen table and stretched his tired legs. The cheese stuck to the roof of his mouth. This damned war! Marlene shrugs her shoulders and shivers. Enna had mentioned that Lukas felt cold, and that she'd wrapped a blanket around his shoulders, but the cold wouldn't go away. Why does death come with a chill? Maybe it mutes the ache when the organs fail. I want to die by myself, Marlene thinks, nobody watching me. It'll be my death, mine alone.

WATERTOWN

I put the essay down. I can't concentrate on it. I feel anxious.
When Sam is working on something, he often sits at the
piano and plays – usually he starts out with Variations by
Beethoven because that's just there on the music stand or
because he knows most of them by heart; then he veers off
to freely improvise, it seems, muses on the keyboard like
others might draw doodles on paper or knead figurines
out of the soft parts of bread. He thinks by hand, his finger
strikes a key, then another one and repeats it when he likes
what he hears – or so it seems to me. Our house is quiet
while his tones wander around. I watch him. He looks calm
and patient – or is he sad?

There is the long trail of refugees moving towards an uncer-
tain future. Word had gotten out that there would be barracks
with running water or at least stable tents, enough for everybody, electricity, and the basic medical care needed for the
youngest and oldest amongst them. They had already lost
most of their belongings. They had been misled and disappointed more often than not. But what could they do? They

held on to the promise of salvation. Few countries were still willing to take people in. That's what they dreamt of when they weren't crushing their exhaustion into a deadened sleep. And each time they woke up with a startle, scared of having missed something essential while asleep. Rarely Sam's father had spoken of his longwinded way East in order to finally arrive in the West, all by foot, for miles and weeks on end. But Sam had pictured him on his trek, still sees him walking with all the others yet alone, silent and vigilant. And then one night his father had split off from the group, had made his way through a large forest, which took many days and almost his life, but in the end he had reached the border river, had crossed it by night with his clothes and passport strapped to the top of his head, and had left his mad country for good.

I wish Sam would play for me now. I like to grade essays while he lingers at the piano. But what distracts me now is my peripheral view of Lilli reflected on the monitor's surface. Lilli hasn't moved. I don't even hear her breathe. Maybe she quietly died. I need to get some fresh air! I grab my coat, sneak to the door and open it without making any noise. The hallway is dark, but when I step over the doorsill the lights automatically go on, and I see the chauffeur sitting on the carpet opposite my room. Is the lady with you?, he asks. No, I almost reflexively say, why would she be here? The doorman said so, he responds, he told me she asked for your room number, and he gave it to her – he wasn't supposed to do that! Can you bring me to Watertown, I ask him. Fifty bucks, he answers. Sure, I agree, even though I find his price outrageous. It's only for one way, he explains, if you want me to wait and take you back to the hotel within an hour, it's double with a ten percent discount, that's 90 for the round trip. I nod. He gets up, and still haltingly he asks: Are you sure the lady isn't in your room? Yes I am, I say, let's go. He walks ahead of me to the elevator.

On the back seat of the limousine there is still the ripped-up plastic canvas Marlene had been swathed in. I feel reluctant to get in, but to my surprise the chauffeur gives me a shove, and I almost fly onto the backbench of his car. Hey! I scream, shocked and outraged. He immediately apologizes saying he only wanted to be helpful. I let it go. It's uncomfortable to sit between these huddles of plastic, which cling to me and sizzle at each of my moves. The radio sings ob-la-di, ob-la-da, life goes on, bra-la-la. Driving with his left arm hanging out of his side window, the chauffeur watches me via his rear mirror as I try to fight off the sticky plastic wrap. His eyes are as gray as the land to the right and left of our dead straight street.

Without premonition Lukas grabs my hand and flings me into the back seat of his car. His clothes are piled up next to me. On the passenger seat sits his computer. The car smells of cold smoke. Where are we going? You'll see, he simply says and ignites the motor. The street is bumpy. We dash over potholes. Lukas pushes the engine to speed, speeds faster and faster. My heart is racing. I know we won't come back. I left my diary behind, no time to snatch it from the shelf. Where's mother? You'll see, he snorts. A chewing gum wrapper sticks to the back of his seat. Monterey, it says. Monterey…? I must have fallen asleep, started dreaming a dream in a dream. Lukas shakes me. He's opened my door. Out! He shouts. I stagger out. Someone is pounding against the hood from inside the trunk. What's that? I ask. You'll see, Lukas growls. He lights a cigarette, burns a wisp of his hair that's hanging over his furrowed brow. Shoot! The place is bleak, just barren land, dry earth and rubble all around. Lukas opens the trunk. Marlene jumps out, furious! How dare you!? she yells. Ha, Lukas sneers, you see? I told you! He shrugs, turns around, sits down in the car, and drives off! Drives off? Oh god! He's dumped us, dumped us at this place where there's nothing, nobody, nowhere. Mother is beside herself, totally loses it, goes mad! She kicks a rock, *there!*, howls in pain and holds her foot, then starts sobbing, sobbing. I don't know what to do. Mother wails and whines. I go over and put my hand on her shoulder. Oh go away, Marlene screams, it's all your fault, yours! Shocked, I flinch back. At some distance I crouch down. Cold winds are ripping over land, whipping the shrubs. Here we have to live, huddled in a dirt hole, covered by the crown of a fallen tree.

Once in a while some aborigines come by. At first they only look at us, curious from afar. Then they approach us, touch our skin, probe it, scratch it. Marlene and I. We are scared. Do you have food, any food? And water, any water? We can only whisper, dried up as we are, seared by fate, frail as dead leaves. The aborigines laugh and leave. Later they come back with two leather bags, one filled with water, the other with grain. They place it in front of us and watch us eat. We eat like pigs, Marlene and I, voraciously shovel the grains into our mouths and swallow it, barely chewed up. Later we sit around an open fire waiting. Waiting for what? You'll see! Father is gone. His trace is lost. The fire dims and goes out.

Would Sam come up to our room during a coffee break? At the earliest possible moment he might sneak out of his conference to check on me. I feel bad that I hadn't left a note for him about my trip to Watertown. But he'd figure it out. Sam is a man of reason. He's not prone to panic. Time and again his sanity has calmed me down in these past three years when I was about to lose it with my mother. She could needle and provoke me – but she could also be sweet and even funny, and then again sad about all she'd lost in her life: her home, her friends, her freedom, her plans to become a glider pilot…When I was 18 or 19, she would say, I was so happy, it was the best time in my life. But aren't you happy with father? I once asked. I may have sensed some tension between my parents and probably hoped my mother would confirm that her present life was a good one. That's different, she'd brushed me off, and then she had marveled again about these times long ago when her afternoons were filled with her friends, when they would gather at one of the big lakes near her hometown to play tennis, listen to music, and dance – all that, a promise that remained unfulfilled, a yearning she treasured forever.

Lukas comes home—home is it, isn't it? He hangs his coat on the rack. He shakes the rain from his hair. Home. Through the open kitchen door he sees Enna kneeling on a chair, bent over a book on the table, studying it seems. In the living room Marlene is speaking on the phone, her back a shield against him and everybody else. Hi, he says to no response. The evening has darkened the place. Only Enna has a light shining on her book on the kitchen table. Lukas wavers, lingers in the hallway. For some reason he can't bring himself to march in as if making a statement: I'm here! I'm home! He looks over to Marlene who keeps talking into the receiver with a lowered voice, like she's speaking to a secret confidante. Does he still mind? Lukas isn't sure. His sense of home has been slipping away for some time, deserting him in subtle ways, which he's been noticing with an indifferent sense of guilt in his heart and no vim to do anything about it. He is almost beyond it. One day he may leave. He drops his briefcase on the floor and goes to the bathroom as if to a different continent. What if he'd start anew—somewhere else? A weary smile shows up on the mirror in front of him. Will he take Enna with him? And Sine? He isn't sure. He sees himself in a hacienda somewhere in South America where he could build a new wallpaper factory – just like his grandfather, long ago. A woman comes in—young, gifted and black…She says something to him, but he can't understand a word.

In Watertown the chauffeur parks his limousine at the Farmers Market. It's an old brick building with big archways, through which small trucks carry in crates filled with potatoes, apples, vegetables and other goods while empty trucks trundle out to a nearby holding area. The market hall is filled with voices, vendors yelling, shoppers talking, radios playing…I want to buy apples, pears, oranges and bananas. It's always good to have fruit in a hotel room. Walking past a butcher's shop I see a flattened pig with its pink head sitting upright on a shelf as if still alive, its tongue poking out in defiance. The meatman asks me if I want to try his liverwurst. I decline. I can't think of eating anything under the watchful eyes of this pig. Sparrows are flitting through the air and chirp from the wooden beams, which crisscross the hall and prevent the roof from falling down. On the soapstone floor pigeons are marching along the aisles, nodding with every step until they come across something that has fallen off a food stall and can be picked up. Flies are swirling over the fish display. Children jump and stumble around their mothers. I sit at a small coffee bar in the middle of this buzzing crowd and watch the activities around me. A mutt sniffs at my leg, then expectantly looks up at me.

Suddenly I feel a hand on my shoulder, turn around, and there is Sam! I am surprised and so pleased. Sam I say, what are you doing here…? He gives me a kiss. The opening speeches were not so interesting, he explains. I came back to our room, I wanted to see how you are doing. When you weren't there, I asked about you at the reception. The concierge told me you went to Watertown. So I took a driver to look for you. I'm glad I found you. He puts his arms around my shoulders, and it feels good to lean on him. Was Lilli still on our bed when you came up? I ask. Lilli, he wonders, who is Lilli? Marlene, my mother, I say slightly, and feel annoyed that he doesn't remember. Sam looks at me in utter surprise. Then he says: there was no Lilli or anybody in our room. Your mother passed away. It must have been a dream. But I noticed that the monitor's battery had run empty, so I had plugged it in to recharge. Actually, why did you put it on the desk? Why did you turn it on? His question sounds as if I had done something off-limits. I feel embarrassed. I don't know, I say. It's no big deal, Sam gently reassures me, but you shouldn't do that.

And then we stroll hand in hand out of the market hall, walk through the main street, past the church and the cemetery, and the monument of the Fallen Heroes, which throws its shadow on the parking lot of Watertown's modern shopping mall. Maybe I can get a replacement battery here, just in case the other one runs out, Sam says. We approach a group of people huddled in the front of a big entry door that is closed. Do they open so late, Sam marvels. It's already past noon. One of the shoppers, a short sturdy man with a corduroy cap, turns around and says: they're having a power outage. Everything is automatic here. So they can't open the doors. People are locked in, and we are locked out. He seems to enjoy knowing about these things.

Right at this moment the sun breaks through the clouds. Sam and I stroll out of the parking lot, past a schoolhouse and along a creek lined with willow trees and ducked down mulberries. Hordes of croaking frogs seem to give us a friendly welcome. The whole time I wonder how Sam can be here with me instead of attending this conference with his colleagues. But I don't want to remind him, I just want him to be with me. Finally we sit in the grass, and Sam splits up a turkey-breast sandwich and opens the soda bottle he'd bought in the market hall before he discovered me at the coffee bar. I'm so glad you're here, I mumble. He smiles. Do you want to come with me when I give my paper? he asks. Yes, I say, I'd love that. Will you explain the monitor? He nods and smiles. I'm happy to see him happy. Finally he gets to present his invention.

Having shuffled, mixed, organized and regrouped thirty short stories (a selection out of over fifty) time and again, one day the collection seems to be perfect. Lukas writes a letter: Dear Editor…folds it, pins it to the manuscript, slips everything in a large envelope carefully addressed and sends it off. Leaving the post office he feels like he's already accomplished something. When would the manuscript reach the publisher? Three to five business days, the postal clerk said. And with this time frame in mind, an anxious hope in his heart, he returns home trying to imagine a positive response. He will have his own book. Not a bestseller, but a nice present for friends. He'll hold it, look at it, open it sometimes, read through it, and like it. His book! At first waiting feels like a pleasant anticipation. It is reasonable to assume that his envelope is on its way, reaches the publisher, and is sitting on a pile waiting for the editor in charge. So far so good. Lukas is patient, has to be. But the weeks grow long. With not even the shortest note coming back to him, his confidence starts to wear thin. Eventually he finds himself sitting at his desk, unable to think, unable to write or even to turn on his computer. A hawk is flying by his window. The leaves of the chestnut tree are turning yellow. He berates himself for his aspirations. He has to run the wallpaper factory. Writing stories is for idle hands. What was he thinking? With a forced smile he tries to convince himself that this isn't a big deal.

When I open my eyes I find myself surrounded by a horde of white geese. They look straight at me. I feel threatened. Where is Sam? He must have gone while I was sleeping. Only the rest of our sandwich, wrapped in plastic, is sitting where he was just a moment ago. I get up and throw the sandwich to the geese. Immediately they start fighting for a bite. Gingerly I cleave through the crowd. The afternoon light has turned hazy. How strange that Sam would leave me sleeping unprotected in this open field. I guess he needed to return to his conference, but why wouldn't he have taken me with him? Have I lost him? For too long I made my mother a priority in our evening hours. Often he went to bed without me, reading for a while and falling asleep before I finally came to slip next to him under our comforter. It was a lonely way of going to sleep for both of us. He seemed so far away. Hearing him steadily breathe felt even lonelier. What could I do? In the evenings my mother was most awake and demanded my company. With her I've seen every documentary and most of the discussion and quiz programs available on TV. Around 11 PM when I tried to start the end-of-day routine, putting the washbowl, the glass for her dentures, the extra moisturizer, and the hairbrush on her bedside table, she would protest, claiming it was much too early for her to go to sleep. Sometimes she just ignored me as I was standing next to her, the dripping washcloth in my hands. While I tried to suppress fits of yawning she was chipper and enjoyed playing with the remote control. The next day she would sleep almost all morning and in addition she took a long nap after lunch. Meanwhile I had to teach my classes. She didn't care. It's only 11:30, she would say, no adult person goes to bed that early, don't be a baby! It stung.

When I get back to the market hall, my driver is gone. I am not surprised, because it's more than three hours ago that he had brought me to Watertown. So he must have left and put fifty dollars on our hotel bill. Maybe he brought Sam back to the hotel. Sam probably thought I would take a cab. But as it turns out, there are no cabs in Watertown. Everybody here has a car or two, and the hotel runs its own limousines. I can't possibly walk these more than 5 miles back. I could call the hotel and ask them to send me a car, but I resent the 90 dollar fee it would cost. But then I have an idea. I enter a bookstore, and to make myself worthy of an answer, I pick a collection of best American short stories, go to the cashier and ask her if she has any idea how I could get to our hotel. She thinks for a while with her eyes closed. I look at her shivering eyelids, her innocent face, which is pink and clean, friendly features, and I think she may never have gotten out of Watertown, nor ever wanted to leave, but that's probably an exaggeration. Finally she looks at me and suggests that I could rent a bike at Randy's Roadrunner Rentals a few blocks away from her bookstore. A bike, I marvel, I haven't used a bike in decades! But I can do this!

Randy is the man with the corduroy cap we'd seen at the mall. Oh hi, I say in recognition, and he immediately tells me that the mall continues to be out of power, but they'd managed to manually open the door. You can go there, he suggests, but now I want to rent a bike. Hmm, he says scratching his neck with his oil-smudgy fingers, I just rented out the last adult bike. Now all I am left with are fairy cycles and one tandem, which you certainly could drive single, it's just a bit heavier, that's all. I look around his shop, where all kinds of vehicles are lined up: baby buggies, three-wheelers, kids' bicycles in all colors, the tandem he mentioned, and even a couple of wheel chairs. In a corner I discover a motor scooter. Can I rent the motor scooter? I ask, and he asks back, Do you have a driver license for it? No I don't. Critically he looks at me as if to ascertain my driving capacities. Then he shakes his head. I can't give you the scooter, he says. I understand. So I settle on the tandem.

Meanwhile the day's been dimming down, even though it's only 4 PM. I strap my bag on the carrier and start riding along Tappan Street, whose small buildings duck down under the weight of conformity, block after block all the same, which feels uncanny, like in a dream. Peddling on I start worrying that I'm only treading water and won't make any headway, but finally I get out onto this vast flat land that stretches its unforgiving monotony all the way up to the hotel castle. I can see it in the far distance, illuminated for the big conference. If I remember correctly, the main presentations will go until 6 PM, and by then, I'm sure, I'll be back.

Riding against the wind as if straightaway to heaven, I feel a sudden surge of happiness. Here I am, free, relaxed. Yes, now I can do what I want! I can ride on this tandem, which is heavy, but Sam sits behind me and helps me pedal, so it's actually okay. Sam has this way of supporting me without wanting much credit for it; he's always there when I need him, and as soon as I get on with things he steps back. He is so good with this that I sometimes wonder if I take him for granted and don't pay enough attention to what he himself needs or wants. But he doesn't complain, he just pedals behind me. The road to the hotel is slightly rising, and the longer I ride the more I feel strained in my legs. Will I make it all the way back? I want to take a rest, but I worry that night is falling faster than I thought, and it could be dark before I reach the hotel. This thought makes me uncomfortable. But then I see someone on a bike riding before me, and I immediately think that this person got the last adult bike at Randy's. Who would be in the same situation that I'm in? I hurry to catch up with this person to see who it is. Breathlessly I come closer, and then I realize that it's Enna. Enna, I shout, and the person in front of me turns around, and it's really Enna! She stops, gets off her bike and waits for me to come right next to her. I didn't know you went to Watertown, I say, what were you doing there? I went to see a doctor, she says, I got a rash; it seems to be a food allergy, that's all. And looking at my tandem she says: that's quite a vehicle, do you plan to take a ride with our mother? We both laugh. Do you want to ride with me, I ask. I've never been on a tandem, she responds, it may be fun. Quickly she pushes her bike under some shrubs and swings her leg over the back saddle behind me. Let's go, she says, and we start peddling, now together.

That's what I wanted, but I didn't say it. I was unprepared for what was coming. Or was I? Maybe we should break it off…My friend said it only tentatively, but he repeated it: Maybe we should break it off…He was sitting on his bike, one foot on a pedal, the other on the walkway, and he seemed to waver. I knew he had been feeling sad and lost for some time, nervous about the paper he had to write, listless with regard to the whole semester, and not knowing what to do after his final exams. Would he stay in Dartmouth? Should he go back to Sweden? As the winds ballooned his rain jacket, he seemed to shrink into a shell of doubt and regret. You don't know what you want either, do you, he asked. I hadn't anticipated his move. The shock hardened me, strangely so, as if this was about losing face. I just shrugged. Not true! Why hadn't I hugged him on the spot? Time and again I returned to the impulse of doing it, but something held me back. We remained standing in front of my dorm, both silently waiting for the other to say something. The ache, this ache in all of me...Okay then, my friend said, be well! He pushed off the walkway and biked away, slowly as if still waiting for me to call him back, yet I didn't—why didn't I? I remember thinking that I would have to go home and take care of Todd. I looked at him, still in reach yet trailing off, softly blurring, the outline of my friend, the last I saw of him.

When we finally reach the hotel, most lights have been turned off or dimmed down. The glass front door is locked, so we have to ring the bell. The night porter looks up from his small TV screen, squints his eyes and seems to ponder whether he should let us in or not. Finally he gets up, pushes his bare feet into a pair of sneakers, takes a gun and comes towards the door. His attitude shows annoyance, distrust, and some pride in his nightly authority, which he would exercise on everybody without exception. In front of the closed door he stops. For a few moments he seems to gaze at his own reflection in the bullet-proof glass, because he twitches at his hair and rearranges some of its strands before he shouts at us: What do you want? We don't really hear it, but we can read his lips. We are guests here, we scream back in tandem. What room are you in? he seems to counter, and I am quick to say 858, showing the three numbers with my fingers. The porter scuffles back to his desk, searches around for a while, and then returns with an envelope that reads "For Sine". He shows me the envelope, and when I eagerly nod my head he takes a key out of his pocket, unlocks the door, opens it the width of a slit, so that I just barely can get through without touching upon his protruding belly. We are actually closing at midnight, he growls as he hands me the envelope. I'm sorry, I whisper, but he has already turned away from me to lock the door anew. Good night, he says, seeming somewhat mollified now, and returns to his desk shaking his head. Having spent all my energies on the ride I slowly creep up the stairs. Suddenly a thought jolts me: Enna! Did she make it in? Enna, I call, and a soft echo multiplies my wish for her to be here. Yes, she responds from somewhere above me, I'm here, I'm already at my room. Good night! And I nod to myself and mumble good night as well.

MARGUERITE

Marlene grabs her typewriter, her most important possession, randomly throws a few items in a bag, undies, a sweater, pants, her wallet, and runs with the others. Panic has erupted since word spread: *the Russians are coming, they are only a few miles away, hurry, leave, now!* They hop on the open loading space of the mayor's truck, crouch down, huddle together in their winter coats, and as the crammed-full lorry lumbers through the night, they look back, their burning eyes attached to their small town that lies dark now amidst snow-covered fields, aged, empty and without protection—and will they ever see it again? Their homes grow small and smaller, the church shrinks to an inconsequential stripe, soon the whole settlement only a mere dash on the horizon and gone after their first bend south. But Marlene's father is missing. He'd made a short trip to a nearby farmer when the news broke. Had he left from there? Will they see him at their next stop? He shouldn't have gone, her mother mumbles. He's on his way, for sure, Marlene asserts. He may've been worried about the dog, Odile cautions. Neither looks in the other's eyes. The night is cold, the journey long, and their hope anxious with his life at stake. Later they learned that he'd gone home after all. He'd told his friends he'd have to look after his family, make sure they'd get out. He didn't. Still later, much later, the last person who'd left town on a motorbike wrote Marlene that he'd seen her father through the open yard gate. He was walking towards the house with his terrier by his side. Hey, he'd yelled at him, go, leave! But her father hadn't turned around, had only lifted his hand to gesture some soft salute as he'd crossed the plot. What was he thinking? On one side he hears the Russian tank-chains rattling in, on the other the motorcycle wheezing off. The roar of war imposes itself in its perverse failure. Yet he feels calm and almost relieved. His family got out. That is good. Nothing more to do. Across the courtyard he sees the door to the barn half open. No point in closing it now, he thinks. He hears the steps on the gravel behind him—a voice, a Russian order, and a rifle's short click. He doesn't turn around. It's alright, he thinks, it's over. A sharp noise, his dog howls, and as he looks down to the dying creature, his life simply stops before the bullet can touch his heart.

Nine o'clock, Enna states as soon as I open my eyes, don't you ever want to have breakfast? She sits at my desk, holding one of my students' papers, and seems to be amused by seeing me so puzzled about her presence. Oh, I say and feel ashamed and defensive. How did you get in? The door wasn't locked, she responds and continues reading. Do you want to grade the essays for me? I challenge her. Hurry up, she urges me, adding that she's been sitting here for more than an hour. Startled, I get up and seek shelter in the bathroom. I take a long shower; the warm water is so relaxing, I feel like staying here for hours. But breakfast isn't a bad idea either.

When we come down to the lobby the waiter is just about to collect the unused plates from the tables. Quickly we sit down and grab the empty cups to prevent them from being cleared away. Alright then, he grudgingly concedes, because breakfast officially goes till ten o'clock, thus he's obliged to serve us for ten more minutes. We are glad we made it in time and lean back. It's strange, Enna says, since mother passed away, I feel a bit useless or just lazy. I thought I would feel free and energized, but now it seems I have to first relearn how to be on my own. Yeah, I say, it's been three arduous years... We dip our croissants into the coffee. And then I ask her what I always wanted to ask her: Has mother told you about your father...? Enna shakes her head. Not much, she responds, at least nothing new... Have you asked her, I want to know. Enna smiles. Not really, she concedes, mother always seemed so uncomfortable about it.

But she did tell us that it was hard to find work after the war. Everything was broken. Some people were ready to help. But many were distrustful of these fugitives and resented this interference with their orderly lives. As if anything still was orderly at this point. Where to go? Where to start? It was a chilly day when Marlene got her job, and barely had she been able to suppress shivering like a stray dog while waiting to see the boss. The winds had messed up her hair, which she hadn't thought of, because when entering his suite and seeing all the marble and wood and brass, she'd felt kind of honored and immediately thought: if I get this job I'll move up and will be recognized and valued! So she'd lost sight of the damage the wind had done to her hairdo, which was meant to look as proper as would befit a chef's secretary, but this inadvertent twist had turned out to be a stroke of luck, she later thought, much later, when her boss whispered into her ear that what attracted him most about her that morning was her tousled hair; it looked sexy, he told her, like she'd just come out of bed after a passionate night. But on the morning of her job interview he hadn't hinted at any of this, instead he was polite, friendly and forgiving. When she, nervous as she was, had put her wet umbrella on the leather couch in his office, he'd simply removed it with a smile and put it where it belonged, in the umbrella stand. And when she, in a hurry not to waste too much of his time, had dropped her purse while trying to wiggle herself out of her coat, he had picked it up for her and placed it on the coffee table next to her chair. She had, though, crossed her legs, remembering that men often complimented her on her beautiful legs, and she wanted to put forward this additional asset she would bring to the job. Why not? Her boss was gentle. He first asked her about her previous positions, none of which was noteworthy. He wouldn't press for specifics. He listened and empathically nodded when she tried to explain her lack of credentials. He seemed to be impressed when she told him that she'd been the best in her class in stenography and second best in typewriting. When she confided that she had fled from East Germany and now lived alone in a small rental on the outskirts with no family around and no knowledge about their whereabouts, he ordered an office aid to bring in coffee and cookies, which seemed to show that he understood the hardship she was experiencing. She liked him. She'd felt totally safe in this job interview, she told Enna many times as if still marveling about something so pleasant being at all possible. It went very different from what she had anticipated. But the room was warm, the light soft, his voice deep, and his demeanor so gentlemanly – all of which had made her feel good about herself, as if she was going to be resurrected from the many offenses her life had already aggrieved her with. It was cold outside.

Obviously annoyed with us for sitting past the official breakfast time, the waiter switches off the light over our table. In
response we don't leave him a tip, knowing that our revenge
may set us up for a hostile atmosphere in the days to come.
But together with Enna I feel emboldened. During breakfast
I had noticed a big door at the far end of the lobby. Let's go
this way, I suggest, maybe there is something worth discov-
ering. The door is heavy, made of solid oak with black iron
fittings, like a church's portal, and it needs our joint strength
to be pried open. A sharp draft almost blows us away but
immediately dies down when we are on the other side and
the door has shut behind us. To our surprise we find ourselves
on some kind of square lined with small shops. This must
be the giftshop area of the hotel, but it looks more like a
postwar village. The walls seem to be in a state of decay, the
paint has peeled off from the façades and shutters, and only
a few items lie in the shop windows. In the middle of the
square stands a meager brown cow in front of a trough with
hay; it stops chewing and stares at us. How strange, I whisper,
and Enna anxiously takes my hand. Maybe we'd better go
back, she suggests. But I'm too curious to follow her advice.
Come, I softly say, and pull her with me to inspect what's in
the showcases. As it turns out, the stores seem to be second-
hand and pawn shops, the items displayed in the windows
look old-fashioned, odd and even dusty as if they've been
lying there forever. The display of an antiquarian bookstore

is dark, a sign in the window reads *CLOSED*. If only the sun could reach all that's stranded here...

Once when I was on my way to my seminar, I saw Jules sitting in the grass with his back and head leaning against the trunk of the big oak tree next to the library's entrance. It was in the fall, and big heaps of leaves surrounded him like pillows on a quilt. Jules' eyes were closed, and he wore a headset. I thought he was listening to music, maybe Bach, his favorite, as he had told me, and just walked by. But when I returned, two hours later—dusk was already falling, a cold wind had come up and the air smelled of rain—Jules was still sitting there in the same position, his legs now covered with leaves. I was shocked. I thought he was dead, had unexpectedly died, alone and unnoticed. Anxiously I approached him and touched his shoulder, and when he didn't react, I vigorously shook him and called him: Jules! He opened his eyes, startled and seemingly confused. What...? he asked, and pushed his headset down to his shoulders. Then he recognized me and jumped up. Sorry, am I late? he stammered. I don't know, I said, because he wasn't registered for my seminar. Have you been sitting here all afternoon? Seemingly embarrassed Jules brushed some leaves from his jacket. I've just been thinking about something, he replied, grinding out a faint smile, and walked off.

Let's get back to the lobby, Enna again urges me with a mix of fear and determination. Okay, I respond, but first we'll get a soda in the bar over there, and then, I promise, we'll go back. Reluctantly she follows me. The bar door squeals as we open it. We enter a small room with four tables to the right and left of the door and a bigger round table in the middle. Good morning, the innkeeper calls from behind the counter and adds, I just opened, and here you are, my first guests! We sit down at one of the small tables and wait for her to come over. Enna studies the photos on the wall next to our table: movie stars from the fifties and sixties. Pointing to a small black-and-white picture she says: Look, Paul Newman, our mother's favorite — I liked him too. The innkeeper comes and places two glasses of milk in front of us. Actually, we wanted some soda, I explain, do you carry coke? The innkeeper shakes her head. No, this is a milk-bar, we only serve milk—fresh milk from Maddy, our cow out there. If you wish I can give you some instant chocolate, or coffee to mix in. Mystified, I decline. What a strange place this is!

Enna slowly pushes her glass over to me. She finds milk disgusting and doesn't even want to sit near it. I'm not crazy about it either but I try — milk fresh from a cow? It smells sour and is body-warm…yuck! I manage to control my facial expression, or else Enna would just run out. From a back room behind the counter a man shuffles in, grumbling something and oddly gesturing to the innkeeper. In response she smiles but shakes her head, as if she were flirting with him. The man grins and waits. The innkeeper continues to clean the counter while whispering to him and pointing with her head towards us. Maybe she tells him to behave because there are strangers in the room, but after briefly glancing over to us, he presses forward, pushes the innkeeper towards the counter and starts manhandling her behind while bringing himself into position. Hey, she bursts out, but he doesn't stop. Abruptly Enna gets up and walks towards the door. I hurry to catch up with her. The innkeeper yells after us: It's ten dollars for the milk; I put it on your hotel bill! But how would she know our room numbers?

From there I must have run all the way back home, because I am out of breath when I arrive. Marlene is gone. Nobody there. The door stands open, the water in the kettle has evaporated, and with the flame on the stove still burning the air smells of singeing steel. Maybe she's just picking apples in the yard? But when I check, she's not. I call for her: Mom? Silence echoes back. No reason to worry, but I'm anxious. The hut we've rented for the summer is surrounded by forests – would she go into these woods, looking for blackberries, would she – and get lost? Marlene is unconventional. She lacks caution. She does things. She walks straight ahead, here and there lightly bending branches to the side while slipping through the wilderness. She feels great. The sun's flickering through the fir and beech trees, swarms of bees are buzzing around the bushes, dragonflies crisscross her way. Fabulous! The forest floor softly springs under her feet. Marlene discovers a patch of dry moss and sits down. Gets out of her shoes. Wiggles her toes in the warm air. An almost dizzying happiness grips her head. She lies back and closes her eyes. It's almost like it was long ago. Like she could be young again – free and on her own…Three soldiers step in. Old stuff. Go away! She hadn't heard them coming. They step closer, one by one, surround her. One clicks his tongue. All alone, sweetie? They laugh. Marlene wants to sit up, but one holds her down with his rifle pressed on her shoulder. Ouch, Marlene screams, you hurt me! Uh oh, one says, we don't mean to do that, do we? They snicker. One strips her skirt up. Stop it, Marlene shrieks. She tries to struggle herself free, but one kneels on her arms and grabs her breasts, one holds her legs. They open their flies. They grin and pant, they smack of dirt, they do it, one after the other…and leave her there, alone, besmirched and hurting. The woods turn gray and grim. A wild dove wails, ou-ouh, ou-ouh…Marlene crawls to a nearby rock to sit up. Her shoes trodden down in the mud, a heel broken off. Oh no, no-no…She feels crushed, ashamed. The bees are humming. Not far Marlene sees some blackberry bushes. She walks over, heedlessly plucks the berries. Their thorny branches scratch her arms. She doesn't like blackberries. Lukas does. She'll serve them for dinner. When she comes home she carries the berry-filled box like a piece of evidence. All is good. Where were you, I anxiously ask? Just picking berries, she snubs me, breezily, angrily, what are you staring at me for? Her red hair glows in the evening sun.

I understood mother, Enna recently asserted as if to defend her against me. Yet Marlene insisted that we had no idea. Had we not? You've no idea, none! Or had we? Never did she get tired of telling us about the hardship of her post-war years, a fixed set of stories, from which she wouldn't veer off, however much we tried to nudge her to shed more light onto some of its inconsistencies. Her secrecy made us wonder. Maybe she savored our ignorance as part of her power. In her last years, when she was still mobile, Marlene used to go through her things, carefully deciding what to keep and what to destroy, so it would not fall into the hands of her curious children. When she was alone, she would unlock a small lumber-room next to her bedroom where she hid her photo albums, letter collection, old passports and documents, as well as her jewelry and other objects she felt attached to. Once I came home sooner than she'd thought, the door to the lumber-room was open, and she was on her knees in front of an open bottom drawer. What are you looking for, I asked, and visibly shocked she pushed the drawer closed and muttered: nothing, nothing! If she cast things away on such occasions, we never noticed.

But after she'd passed away, we finally opened her lumber-room, entered with some trepidation, and found it almost empty. The few items it still contained didn't seem of much significance.

Her boss desires her. Marlene can see it in his eyes. It flatters her. Deliberately she turns towards the pile of correspondence she's been going through, dividing up the serious from the frivolous bidders. She feels his hand on her back. You work too hard, her boss says. True, it's half past lunchtime, everybody is gone (Want to come with us, her colleagues had asked, but Too much work, she had declined) and now all are out. She'd guessed he would come to see her, and sure enough he had. She knows she can make him come. It excites her. She doesn't show it, looks at her papers. I want to get this done, she says pretending to keep things professional. It's part of the game. It tickles her. Look, he says, I got you a little something, and he pulls a marguerite out of his jacket pocket. Instantly she feels the pang of disappointment; she'd rather have a chocolate bar, like last week, or at least a rose. A marguerite, what does that say! He's cheap! She smiles. You look beautiful, her boss says, you always do! Why not spoil me with a brief pause, work can wait, he suggests. Marlene moves away, just a bit. First you heap all this stuff on my desk, and then you want me to fritter away my time, she sulks. Oh come on, he says, and runs his hand up and down her back. He knows her special spot. He goes right there, softly massaging it. What do you want? she pretends. Oh you know, he coos. He's thirty-three years her senior, bald and married, and has three adolescent children. His belly stretches his dress-shirt and bulges over his belt. He owns the company. He has a knack for lonely girls lost in their longing for father figures. He winks at her. Would you please get up, Ms. Marlene, he formally orders, and reluctantly she does. Bending towards what is about to happen she sheepishly looks at the door, which isn't closed, just ajar, but she doesn't say a thing. Much better, her boss compliments, much, much better, and stepping closer his hands move to feeling her up, kindly at first, and when she seems to meekly try to extricate herself from his embrace, faintly protesting, he more forcefully pushes her, then sits her down on her desk, there, now piggishly panting and grabbing all over her with his big paddle hands as his belt slips off its loops and falls down with the buckle briefly clanking on the floor, and her desk starts squeaking and jiggling, and one of her dangling feet topples the wastepaper basket, and she barely manages to get some hold of the heavy typewriter on her desk while he's working himself off on her. Her phone rings. Let it ring, he gasps. He's not yet done. Marlene hears Ms. Fest walk past her door. She doesn't know if she's peeking in. She feels a run tickling down her nylons. She thinks of what she could ask him for, and that he should at least compensate her for her nylons. Now he's done. Oh, what you do to me, he says, shaking his head while rearranging his suit. Marlene hears her colleagues laughing in the hallway. Well, well, he deadpans, our company's lunch breaks are much too short, I will have to bring this up at our next board meeting. He pinches her cheek. Good work, Miss Marlene, he says, and while she is still fixing herself up, he hastens away leaving the door gaping wide open. Marlene stares at the flattened marguerite on her desk, and on the spur of the moment she picks it up and swallows it down.

The afternoon sun shines through the lobby's arched windows. I meant to grade another essay but strayed off course when I saw the New York Times Book Review hanging on a newspaper hook. I couldn't resist. Was there anything new worth reading? How often have I felt intrigued by a review, ordered the book, and ended up disappointed. I am a peculiar reader. I hunger for literary oddballs with humor and psychological depth. I thought my father could be such a writer. He never published a book. He was a wonderful storyteller with a knack for the absurd. Sometimes at night when he couldn't sleep he would get up, and just following his thoughts he would walk through the house, here and there, until an idea snuck up on him with enough urgency to make him sit down and try it out. Often it ended after a few lines, and he would return to bed. But once in a while a vague thought unfolded its mysterious wings and flew into an amazing story to be written by him before sunrise. And now I wonder: Where have all his stories gone?

Sam and another man enter the lobby. Sam seems angry, he's agitated while talking. The other looks like he wants to assuage him, placing his hand on Sam's arm. But Sam shakes it off. I know Sam. When he is annoyed, he needs space to thrash out. What makes him so furious? I go over and say: Can I join you for a bit? Sure, Sam responds and briefly introduces this colleague as Dr. Paul Peacock, who'd just presented a paper drawing on major parts of his, Sam's, most recent research results as if they were his own. Well, well…, Dr. Peacock tries to qualify his alleged malefaction, but Sam's not having any of it, and his voice gets sharp enough to pierce Peacock's ears: You feathered your nest with my ideas, you're a plagiarist! Dr. Peacock looks at me and licks his lips. We know what you did, he mumbles, as if deliberately vague, and adds: tomorrow you'll present and – if you feel you have to – you can correct the record. Yet this doesn't seem to be enough for Sam. How did you even get your hands on my design, he challenges him, I put it in the Institute's safe, and only the department's secretary has access to it…Haha, Peakock laughs, ha-ha-ha, that's so funny! Sam looks startled. Oh that's so good, Peacock screams and snorts with laughter while holding his belly. He turns around, faintly waves goodbye, and still laughing he staggers to the lobby's exit, where he, still all consumed with laughter, accidentally bangs his head on the door before he finally lurches out. This Peacock is crazy!

Sam, what was that about? I ask, but Sam only shakes his head. His eyes and lips are pinched to small slits, his face muscles twitch, he looks like a firedrake…We are still standing where Peacock left us, being of two minds about what to do next. I would like to give Sam a comforting hug, say that I love him, but this wouldn't be right, because Sam's just feathering Peacock and isn't in a lovey-dovey mood. Finally he says: It may have been a mistake to attend this conference. In fact, I regret it. But since we are here, I want to say my piece and not have this Peacock…He takes my hand and pulls me to the elevator. Let's go to our room, I need a break! And we take the smooth ride up to the eighth floor. It's about the monitor, I softly suggest and he confirms: More precisely, the monitor's software! I nod and leave it at that, trusting that Sam will tell me more when he wants to.

Housekeeping has already drawn the curtains in our room for the night, it's darkish when we enter, but Sam likes it that way right now. He tells me that he wants to take a short nap, and lies down on our bed. I sit next to him with my laptop on my knees and read the New York Times online. Once in a while I look over to Sam. Sleep has relaxed him. He's steadily breathing. His wrinkled cheeks caving, his beard stubble shooting up like mini dirks. We are aging together. First I noticed it in my face and disliked it. Then I saw it in Sam's, which made me feel okay again. And I even felt vigorous when I supported my old parents in their final years, when they were so weak that they needed a hand. But mentally they stayed strong. Sometimes my father was anxious about dying, wanting to hasten yet simultaneously dreading it. Once I asked him what he was afraid of. I don't know what's ahead, he whispered. I think death is like a long dreamless sleep, I suggested, hoping it would make him more comfortable. His eyes were straying through the night.

When I was little I declared to my parents that I wanted to be a writer and marry a man who would let me write. My father smiled. It was a wistful smile, unwittingly betraying some disappointment with his own early aspirations. He had told me that he too wanted to be a writer. Instead he took over his father's wallpaper factory. There is a photograph showing my father as a young man with my grandfather. Both are standing in the courtyard of the factory, the big chestnut tree behind them. My grandfather looks old and frail, but his eyes are as sharp as an eagle's. My father has linked arms with him, maybe affectionately or supportively. The photo was taken at the end of the war. Nobody else is in the picture, none of the factory workers, drivers, secretaries or designers they had employed. The wide open site looks empty, and it seems that even though my father is standing close to his father, so close that their shoulders touch, they both wouldn't dare to talk with each other. The awareness of all the war's destruction and the ensuing economic breakdown weighs heavily on my grandfather. His factory is about to shut down. His life's work a pile of shards. He wants to set his son free, but my father has just declared he would rebuild the factory, and my grandfather is tempted by the idea that his son would follow in his footsteps. He is mindful of the fact that his son's passion is literature. This is what he always wanted: study literature, be a writer, and make a living as a teacher. Could he accept his son's offer? They silently stand, surrounded by the wallpaper factory. Father and son holding together, both firm yet anxious, close yet apart, and the presence of this moment is as short as the camera shutter's click and as long as their life's meandering paths. Decades before this picture fell into my hands, history had dispersed their dreams and left them parting, my grandfather to the graveyard and my father to a life in the factory.

Sam looks at his watch. Oh, it's already five o'clock! I think I should go to the late afternoon presentation. Want to come with me? And we go together, ride the elevator all the way down to the basement floor, where hundreds of people, coffee cups in their hands, briefcases clamped under their arms, mingle, chat, and push or block each other from getting anywhere. The babble of voices is so loud that Sam doesn't hear me when I ask him what we are going to hear before I yell at him, and then he finally responds: The title is *Perilingual Detection of Hidden Agendas in Memory Clusters*. This sounds monstrous! I'm afraid I won't understand a word.

The auditorium looks like an Amphitheatre with a big arena, from which many rows of seats steeply rise in circles to where we, hustled and jostled by those behind us, enter. Let's take a seat up here next to the exit, so we can leave at any time if it gets boring, Sam suggests, and I agree – even though I usually prefer front-row seats, which allow me to study the presenter up close. We file into the last row. Sam sits down, and immediately starts a conversation with the person next to him, obviously someone he knows, while I struggle with the folding chair: whenever I want to sit down it snaps back up. Sam doesn't notice, but a woman behind me gives me a hand. I thank her and she settles in beside me, sinks her backpack between her legs to the floor and places a big paper bag full of popcorn in front of her on the small drop-leaf table. These are tricky chairs, she says and rolls her eyes. We laugh a bit. Want some popcorn? she asks, grabbing a handful for herself. I decline. Are you from the artificial intelligence group or one of the cognitive psychologists? she asks, munching popcorn. Oh, I'm just a guest, I'm here with my husband, I explain, and point to Sam's shoulder. So what's your profession? she wants to know, and inexplicably I feel a bit challenged. I'm a teacher, I say, I'm teaching creative writing. Ah, finally a half-decent person, she comments and ironically adds: Well then enjoy the presentation—you'll hear a lot about cybernetics, statistics, neural networks, information engineering and the like.

The lights are dimmed, the audience falls silent except for some nervous harrumphing and the sound of popcorn crackling between my neighbor's teeth – how brazen to nosh on popcorn here! Through the back door a woman enters and behind her a man, both in dark suits, both waving their hands to an erupting applause, which they graciously accept and then modestly mute. They are the stars of this conference, Sam whispers in my ear, and obviously curious he leans forward and peers to the podium where both presenters now stand and exchange hushed words as if they were negotiating the proceedings. Didn't they have time to do this beforehand? Now the man steps up to the microphone, but the woman quickly snatches it off its stand and walks a few steps towards the middle of the room. What pretty high heels she wears! Hello, good evening everybody, she pipes and gives everybody a smile with her bright red lips. And then she takes a small silver something out of her jacket pocket, a something that turns out to be a pistol, a shot cracks the silence, the audience squalls, the man at the podium drops to the floor…Stupid! I look over to Sam who scribbles some notes on his pad while the presenter rushes with his pointer through some crowded slides and talks scientific Chinese. The woman meanwhile has taken a seat next to the podium, and leafing through her manuscript she scratches her left shank with her right foot. My neighbor digs down in her backpack and comes up with opera glasses through which she studies the female presenter. She wears Chanel, she comments to me, and offers the binoculars to me. Thanks, I say and look through the glasses, search for the presenters, but as my magnified focus swipes over the empty stage, I discover a black-and-white puppy sitting as if lost in the shadow of a big flowerpot, which marks the end of the podium.

I'm pregnant, Marlene states. Her boss groans: My god, how could that happen? Are you sure? Why didn't you tell me? I told you to be careful. Oh my god! He's really upset, scratches his head, clenches his fist. My god, Marlene, that's really not what we need right now. The annual stocktaking is coming up. Well that won't be interfered with, you can still work on that, I suppose. But we can't have this child, can we? I have my own family, you know that. With three children I have enough. That wasn't what we agreed to, was it? So you'll take care of it, right? Or what? Have you already gotten some information? I could help you with that. I won't let you down. I know someone who knows someone who did it somewhere. We have to be discrete. Hope you didn't tell anybody. Better you keep this under wraps. What would people think of you! On and on he goes, he's just so upset, and Marlene is sitting at her desk, strangely appeased for no good reason. It's so common, she thinks, like some ordinary movie, just the wrong movie. She notices how the sun is shining on her hand on her desk, this simple hand with no ring and no nail polish on its fingers, and she thinks for a moment that she could ruin her boss' family by coming forward, by letting everybody know, and then the sun disappears behind a cloud, and she realizes she doesn't want to do this and has to figure it out on her own. Another possibility would be, her boss now says and hands her the folder with the signed letters he wants her to mail, yes, another possibility – I mean, just in case you don't want to get rid of it – I know a couple, decent people, really, well off, catholic, former clients – he once confided to me that they can't have children but would like to – so they would probably be happy to adopt it, of course pay for all expenses and so on, I could ask them! Would you like me to do this? Or perhaps better first try out this person who knows this person, the other solution I mentioned? Just...and her boss interrupts himself because Olga, Marlene's colleague, enters. He straightens up and says: these letters should go out today, it's important! Once more he looks at Marlene, but cannot meet her eyes, because Marlene is looking elsewhere: she sees the elegant home of these catholic people, the lovely room they would set up for her child, light blue if it's a boy, or pink if it's a girl, and she sees the woman-turned-mother play with her child, Marlene's child, in her well groomed garden with rose bushes and a bright green lawn full of sparkling kids' toys. Marlene's heart aches. She takes a deep breath and sees herself going to a dark place, a district almost completely destroyed by war, but in its ruins there are people living, those who came fleeing the Russians, people like her, those who have nobody here to move in with, but needed to stay and look for work. Maybe in one of these ruins a witch runs an abortion shop, has pregnant women spread their legs and then pricks in with a bent knitting needle poking around to turn a fetus into a stillborn angel. But Marlene can't imagine spreading her legs in front of a witch. Are you not well? her colleague asks her. I'm fine, Marlene responds and starts folding the signed letters. Her boss' assistant, enters, and with a curious look at her but no comment he hands Marlene an envelope and leaves. Somehow she knows what's in there, somehow she doesn't, and somehow she feels totally indifferent about what's to come. That's why she can calmly open this letter and read the official notice of her work contract's termination.

With a jar Sam stops writing. I look over to him and then back to the stage. The presenter just shows the picture of a mouse with a clunky apparatus wired to its tiny head and explains: Dr. Peacock succeeded in monitoring the activation of three major mouse brain areas, the activation of which resulted in the mouse's motivation to jump. Whether the mouse ended up jumping or not—he could show that the mouse wanted to jump! Sam picks up his pad and pen, ready to go. I could kill him, he murmurs and indicates that we are leaving, right now! Quickly I get up, but unprepared for this sudden move I inadvertently push over my neighbor's popcorn bag, the golden bullets spill over and rain on the people sitting in the lower rows in front of us. What a mess! My neighbor grins and says: Well done! Apologizing multiple times we squeeze ourselves past the audience towards the exit door.

Marlene, the cancelation in her hand, turns away from her colleagues' mean thoughts about her. Pricking up her nose she leaves this snake pit, leaves her supposed friends, who will blame her, only her, for messing up their neat little lives, their order, their rosy world. Yeah! What do they know! Nobody will find fault with the boss, who stands there in his cheap suit, all insolence, who watches her leave, as she notices from the corner of her eyes, gawks at her, poised and unmoved, in fact he already pats her successor's shoulder, friendly, it seems, but what a sleaze! She will be his new secretary or whatever; she has already put her green purse on Marlene's desk, where it is sitting bulky, shiny, and stupid just like the rest of her. Oh, how long is this aisle from her desk to the door! Marlene suddenly thinks of her shoes, a huge image of their worn out heels comes to mind, these heels that are supposed to be black, straight, and shiny, but they are gray, bent, and dull. Marlene thinks of confronting her colleagues head on. What do they know, what! But as she is leaving, with a hundred black-hearted eyes gleefully following her, she knows that the girls are checking her out, assessing her ass in her tight skirt, damn, and then, quickly moving down along her stockings' seam, they will see the awful state of her pumps! What else! Any other offense ready to trample down her dignity? Marlene leaves through the swinging door, and only after she's heard it repeatedly bump into the frame, indicating that she's escaped her colleagues' gaze, does she allow her tears to come up. Where will she go, how, when and why? And all on her own, with no one to help and be there? In her skirt's pocket, right on her left thigh, she feels the stiff paper of her boss' letters, the termination of her work contract, and the other one that he'd discretely slipped into her hands before she left her office. She had quickly glanced at it before she'd grabbed her coat, but she wasn't prepared for what it said, namely that she should either go to a certain address to be cleared out, or leave town within a week, move to a boardinghouse, where her boss would make arrangements for her, where she could carry out her thing. In his letter her boss also committed himself to paying for either solution, provided that she would stay away from him, not show up at the office, and keep her mouth shut, point-blank. Marlene felt like scrunching and ripping this letter up. However, it was a document, she realized, a contract of sorts she now depended on, and that's why she could stop herself from immediately destroying his note of betrayal.

INTERIM

I know it bugs me too much, Sam says. By now I shouldn't care anymore. But I do. It's nothing new, and still I can't wrap my head around it. I put all my energy into my research, I work hard, and I enjoy it – this is all good. But I also want to be recognized for what I accomplish! I thought quality counts, the better will prevail. Shouldn't it be that way? It's not! I feel so naïve. Success is a social thing, first and foremost. Are you part of the insider group? Do you flatter or bow to the top cats? Guess I wasn't smart enough to do that. And I studied at a public university when it should have been an Ivy League like Harvard, Princeton, or Yale. That's where my colleagues come from, they are family, I'm not. Peacock is part of the ingroup. For years he twiddled with inserting electrodes into mice brains – these poor creatures croaked by the dozens – and nothing worth showing! He secured for himself the keynote at this conference – and has nothing, really, nothing to present. Somehow he must have gotten access to my files and looted them for his talk. And not even this did he do well. I could sue him for mental property theft, but what a nuisance, what a waste of time and money, and it would cost me the bit of good will that I still have with the dean and some of my friends – who after all want to be promoted by Peacock! That's how it works.

Sam is lying on our bed and tries to calm down, but he is so upset that he twists and turns and pounds the pillow with his fist and kicks the comforter at his feet. I've seen him like this before. It's like a thunderstorm, short and fierce. When his anger has blown over, calm sets in, and for a while he seems resigned or depressed. Then he returns to his research, clear, balanced, and curious, probing preliminary formulations, challenging, rejecting, and reconnecting them to the one question he has in mind until he finds a solution. This is who he is. He lifts the veil, he moves the pebbles, never is he far behind the light on his way. And I let him be. Sam has fallen asleep. His eyes move rapidly, he's dreaming. Maybe he's fighting Peacock, or he's developing his monitor. And I can sit next to him and relax.

Sundays are long and quiet. Marlene picks her cuticles. No work, no colleagues, no friends, and no money to spend. Meanwhile the boss is sitting in his brand-new car, a Ford convertible, as he said, sits there, proud ass that he is, and drives his family to his weekend house in the mountains. Ha! His wife looks through her fancy sunglasses adorned with fake diamonds; she chats with him and laughs; the red of her lips matches the polish on her fingernails. But what a stupid nose she has! And her tight summer dress divulges her considerable fat rolls. Yuck! Two of their three kids play cards in the back of the car, the third bailed out, had something better going on. The boss always wants to be center; only begrudgingly would he have let his oldest off the hook. How does he do this, family man on the weekend and Dr. Casanova in the office? Marlene feels so uncomfortable! She's itchy and angry. He's obnoxious. He never allowed her to call him by his first name, Harold. He fucks her, he says Marlene hop—and she has to say: yes, boss, and thank you, boss. But he fell for her! She didn't provoke it! And he certainly likes her. Maybe he'll love her someday. Goodness gracious! He's a responsible family man, oh yes, real responsible, stipulates that clearly and precisely. He could never divorce his wife, he said. And here they're driving the twisted road up to their house in the mountains. Fir and oak trees on their left, the steep slope on their right. Hmm…He knows this road so well, he once said, he could drive it with his eyes closed. What a bragger! Now he has this new car, delivered a few days ago, red like his wife's lipstick. Look how it accelerates, he says to her. They speed along. Won't you slow down a bit, his anxious wife cautions? Don't you worry, he says, and is annoyed with her for being such a chicken. Next week he'll show Marlene how fast he can go, he thinks. That's when he misses the bend, hurls the car off the road – it tumbles down the precipice, crashes and skids off the rocks, bangs away at the trees, one of which rips the boss' door open and he shoots out, the lucky guy, and gets pinned to some fallen trunk – while the others are shattered somewhere deep down at the bottom of the valley. Pretty bad! He survives. His family: gone! Poof! His fault. Stupid! Marlene cries. Her hands stroke the plump ball of her pregnant belly.

Sam opens his eyes and smiles. Oh, this was good, he says, I feel refreshed. He rolls to his side, supports his head with his hand, lovingly looks at me, and I feel like crawling into the crook of his arm and crying. But Sam is hungry, and we decide to go downstairs to find something to eat. The lobby is empty. There is nobody at the bar, and even the reception desk is unstaffed. The lights over the counters are shut off. Where is everybody, I wonder. Sam suggests that people are attending the congress' main panel. Even the doorman, I wonder to myself, but then I think that the staff may have retreated to their private chambers since nobody would request their services at this time. Sam's stomach rumbles. I know of a milk bar in the hotel yard, I say, maybe we can get something there. And we go to the back of the lobby, Sam pries the door open, and entering the courtyard we are surprised to find it filled with hundreds of people at what looks like a cocktail party. Women in fancy dresses and men in tuxedos, all with wine glasses in their hands, are cheerfully chatting while chewing artfully decorated canapés that waiters in golden suits pass around on big plates. We are flabbergasted! When a waiter walks by, Sam has the presence of mind to snatch a couple of smoked salmon sandwiches from his plate. He offers me one of them, and when I decline he swallows both in an instant. Let's get some more of these and some wine, he says, and we start pushing through the crowd. I follow Sam holding on to a corner of his jacket.

All of a sudden a band starts playing Viennese palm court music. People step back and aside opening a space in the middle of the patio, where Maddy, the cow, is still tied to the pole, now surrounded by wildly moving dancers, who seem to frighten her, because she starts to gut-wrenchingly moo. The bandleader ups the sound volume, and more couples rush to the dance floor. This is weird, Sam says. He takes my hand and pulls me behind him, apparently still determined to find us a glass of wine. But I let go of his hand because—albeit only out of the corner of my eye—I think I just saw Lilli in a skintight black sequined dress coming to waltz with Dr. Peacock from behind the cow's feeding trough. Is it really her? In an instant other dancers bar my view, but yes, it must have been her! Hadn't she told me that she's staying with the keynote speaker? Now I understand, she's in cahoots with Peacock! How embarrassing! He is certainly at least two decades younger than she. If Sam knew that my mother dwells with the Peacock, he certainly wouldn't want to ever talk with her again. But I'm not sure. My eyes search through the crowd to get another glimpse of the two, but in vain. When I finally look for Sam, I can't see him either. He must have proceeded to the bar. I fight my way through the crowd. The space seems to get more densely packed by the second, and only slowly can I make headway. When I reach the end of the courtyard, there is no bar and no food is served here either. Large piles of plates with leftover snacks, abandoned glasses, and dirty napkins are heaped up on small tables along the wall. The waiters are standing together in groups smoking cigarettes. Where is Sam?

At the atrium's end I find a door that leads into a garden. The door falls shut behind me with a bang, and the noise level abruptly dies down. The sudden silence is almost deafening. Nobody there. It's a mild night. The moon shines bright onto the white path that meanders through the carefully curated bush and flower sites. Sam? I softly call for him, but there is no answer. So I walk to the end of the path where I find a bench to sit down and rest. Why am I here? What am I supposed to do now or ever? Mikki always loved to sit with me on park benches. Dangling her short legs in the air she demanded a story. Tell me a story! And when I claimed to be too tired to tell a story, she declared that I may first relax, but then I would have to tell her a story, or else she wouldn't ever leave this bench! She thought that this was what I asked my students to do, tell stories, and she wanted to know the true promise of this storytelling. As she grew older, she sometimes made up a story for me, and then her interest in stories morphed into her psychoanalytic research of patients' narratives. What story could I tell her now? I don't even want to think of one. Farther down the hill I notice a tree, a branching sculpture in black with a strong stem, solid limbs, and delicate twigs, but no leaves – shouldn't there be leaves on it now? Instead I again see this man with binoculars squatting on a knag peering at the hotel. Is he still spying on our room? High up on a limb sits an owl. An owl!

One day an owl was sitting on a branch in front of Lukas's window. Quietly looking ahead and only sometimes turning its head the owl stayed for hours. Lukas felt in awe, honored, mesmerized. He watched it for a long time. Later when he looked up from his desk, the owl was gone. However, the next afternoon it came back. Maybe it was a young owl, because its feathers looked fluffy. Quietly sitting on this one branch, sprinkled by the late afternoon sun flickering through the leaves, the owl made its way into Lukas's heart. It felt as if someone had sent him this owl! And just when he took a closer look, another owl came, sitting down next to the first, and both started to do a little dance, bopping up and down, as if out of pure fun or trying to mate or expending their energy. How beautiful! And then another owl came flying up, and a fourth owl. They were all sitting in this same tree, using different branches, bopping and hopping – it was magic! Then they flew away. But the first one came back, every day around five-thirty. And so in the late afternoons Lukas was often looking out of his window waiting for his owl to come. For a while the owl was his friend. He named it Olly. After a few more weeks Olly didn't come back. Lukas was waiting and looking out for it. But Olly was gone.

Now I know that Marlene hadn't felt alone. Even having been sent away to an unfamiliar place, even not knowing how all of this could possibly go, Marlene wouldn't have felt alone – or not in the way she'd felt lonely when she still had her boss or her colleagues and friends around. Of course she wasn't alone, she was pregnant, but that wasn't it. She was with herself! She looked at the small rented room, which was scantily outfitted: a wooden closet, a table, two chairs, a bed and a sink with a round mirror above – almost as sparse as a prison cell, she thought. Yet she was free! Her days were long and slow. Her mother had always rushed them: get up, what are you lounging around for, there's work to do! And now there was no rush, nothing to do. Her father was different. He'd extricated himself from these kinds of demands by just going away. Once when she'd been late for school and was riding her bike on a shortcut through the fields, she'd seen him peacefully sitting on the ground under a tree smoking his pipe. She'd passed without calling him. He is with himself, she'd thought – and now she was with herself. With the big pillow at her back she was comfortably sitting on her bed, watching the sun patches move on the wallpaper, this up and down of light and shadow. She could be an artist, she thought. She always liked to draw and paint. She could go to Berlin and study painting, maybe not at the Academy, but with some painter who would teach her for chores she could do for him. She could buy his groceries, do his laundry, clean his apartment – provided he would teach her two hours a day, or three, better three, and he would provide her with materials, just the cheap ones to start, just paper and pencil. And Marlene took the envelope she'd just received with her weekly allowance and a brief note from the boss saying that he hoped she was alright, and turned it around to its blank back, and instead of throwing it into the trash she thought she could turn this envelope into a piece of art! It felt like a premonition.

But where is Sam? Sure enough he's searching for me in the crowd! Having received two glasses of wine he may have turned around and noticed that I'm not behind him. What would he do? Of course he would go back to where he saw me last. On his way he may have run into Lilli dancing with Peacock – a truly appalling sight! As he has finished his glass, and since I'm not around he'd just drop the empty one on a passing tray and start sipping on the other one, the one he got for me. Bring it to me, Sam, I'd like a glass of wine! But right then the hostess of the milk bar would pull at his sleeve and ask: Have you seen Maddy, our cow? She's a bit scared with all the music and dancing going on, but she's so brave, she just gave five gallons of milk! Sam would smile, he's polite but not interested in weird stuff. He would be looking for me and decide to return to our room, where I would most likely end up going as well. But I'm too tired to do that – or am I sad, but sad about what?

I sit on a high barstool watching the crowd. It's already close to midnight, and even though some people are still dancing like crazy, it's obvious that their energy level has dropped. The hostess of the milk bar is now raving with the man who Enna and I had seen coming at her behind the counter; long strands of her hair dangle in front of her red face as she stomps in fulsome devotion to the beat of some techno music, while his arms and legs jerk and twitch in a manner towards her that looks overbearing. Next to the cow the hotel chauffeur drinks champagne from the bottle. Two women sitting on the stairs to the band's stage have slipped out of their pumps and shamelessly wiggle their naked toes in the air; listlessly they stare at the dancers, their shoulders slumped, their hands hanging between their opened knees like withered fruit –

nothing seems like fun anymore. Did I look like this when I was young and spent long nights in discotheques? All was new at the time, I wanted to miss nothing. But what was I hoping for? When I came home in the early morning hours, just in time before my parents would get up, I felt exhausted—not excited, fulfilled, or free—only tired with a stale taste in my mouth from all the cigarettes I had smoked. Long nights. I fell into bed, barely throwing my shoes off, and hugging my pillow I plunged into a deep sleep. Yes, a good sleep, that's my calling! I decide to go back to our room.

The corridor leading to the main lobby is dead straight and empty. Along the walls frumpish ladies and old-fogyish men are watching my every movement from big oil-painted portraits. Who are these people? Maybe they present generations of owners of this hotel or the long line of honored guests who once lodged here. My steps softly squeak on the rubber floor. And then I discover a small recess in the wall to my right. I step closer and find a window offering a perfect overlook of the large auditorium where Sam and I had been just a while ago. All seats are still taken, the lights are dimmed, and far down on the illuminated stage I see Sam! He's obviously giving a lecture. Didn't he want me to attend his presentation? Why hadn't he told me that it was tonight? I can't hear anything, because the window is made of bullet-proof glass, but I can see that Sam is animated as he speaks. He points to a screen showing a slide with mathematical equations and then to other ones with graphics of switch panels – just the things he's constantly working on. I wish I could sit in the first row listening to him. Now Sam bends down to his briefcase, and out he pulls his monitor! I see this silver bullet sparkling like a fiery star. He holds it up, and there seems to be amazement in the audience, people crane their necks and slip to the edge of their seats in order to be closer to this new item, his exciting discovery! Applause erupts. I'm so happy for him!

But just as Sam puts the monitor down on the lectern, I see Peacock rushing up to the stage, in his haste almost tripping over the microphone cable, his red tie flapping in the headwind over his shoulder. What is he up to? Sam doesn't seem to have noticed Peacock's approach from behind. He has opened another slide and is pointing at the big screen, when Peacock launches ahead, grabs the monitor from the lectern and swings it high above his head, obviously in order to hit Sam over his head – *oh no!* – but fortunately it so happens that Sam just moves a bit to the side, and Peacock's strike lands on Sam's shoulder, hard enough though, it seems, because Sam's knees briefly buckle, but he can catch himself, turns around, and as people in the audience jump, scream, and throw their hands up in horror, Sam deals a heavy blow right in the middle of Peacock's face: boom! The attacker stumbles back, blood shooting out of his nose or mouth, the monitor drops to the floor and rolls around to the back of the stage sending brief sparks of light through the auditorium. There is a momentary freeze. Both men gaze at each other. Then Peacock picks himself up and again pumping his fists he runs into Sam. The two get into a brawl, Sam grabs a bunch of Peacock's hair and flings his head to the ground; Peacock holds on to Sam's throat trying to choke him, thereby knocking the lectern over with his foot; Sam's manuscript pages go flying, everything whirling through the air in this silent movie. The two roll around, pound their fists into each other, wrestle for the upper hand – until some colleagues get to the fighters and pull them apart. Sam's sleeve has detached itself from the jacket shoulder, he stands clearly shocked at the lectern, his hand holding on to the microphone. From Peacock's mouth or nose a fountain of blood is gushing out, freely spraying onto his white shirt; he has lost one of his patent leather shoes, revealing to everybody his toe sticking out through a hole in his sock – quite an embarrassing display of professional envy.

People are getting up from their seats—of course Sam's presentation can't go on, what a shabby win for Peacock! And with all these broad backs rising in front of my niche window I can't see anything any longer. I continue my way to the elevator, hurry as fast as I can through the hallway to meet up with Sam, swiftly move past two EMTs who come running towards me pushing an emergency stretcher to the auditorium's entrance, probably to remove Peacock, and I try to hold my pace and not lose direction as more and more people pour out of the simultaneously opening doors to the auditorium, filling the passage with their bulky bodies, their need to stop and exchange outrage with other colleagues, their indecision about where to go from here, or whatever they may feel like venting. All elevators are taken, so I run up the stairs, eight floors up, and breathlessly reach our room – but Sam isn't there. Of course, how could he be! Still I had hoped to find him sitting on our bed waiting to tell me what happened. He'll come later. He may need to wait until Peacock has been carried away. Or he may have to make a statement to the police for an official record of the events.

Lukas, the kid, kicks the ball around the corner where the wind blows and he's alone with thoughts of his own. His mother, leaning forward over the balcony railing, may just fly out to spy on him while he's having his private dreams. His father goes to work every day. Take me with you! I could work in the factory! Lukas maunders through the City Park, a small patch of plants around a mossy lawn surrounded by a wired fence. He's feeling weird lately, his bones aching, his stomach knotted, his skin itchy. Little Sue is playing in the sandbox. An old man is sitting on the only bench reading a newspaper. It must be Sue's grandfather, dispatched to watch the little girl. Lukas decides to sit down on the grass. He stretches his legs. His mother cowers on a branch of the chestnut tree, her eyes glued to him. A passing train howls. Three o'clock and nowhere to go. One day I will have my own family, he muses. I will do stuff with them, often, all weekends and some other days as well. First I'll travel around the world, go west, always west, by car, boat and plane. Maybe I'll never return. His father has rolled up his shirt sleeves; he's checking the speed of the wallpaper print machine: too fast and the paper would rip; too slow and the print would turn mushy, he'd explained to Lukas. He is into Asian design lately. How did this come up? – A noise in the bushes, a rustle, some giggles, then three guys standing around Lukas, looking down on him. Three guys! Hey weirdo, one says, preying on little girls? They laugh. One kicks Lukas's leg. I'm just sitting here, Lukas says. Just sitting, he–he, one of the guys apes him, slapping his hand over Lukas' head. Another punches his knee into Lukas's back. One spits on him...And in a split-second Lukas is up on his feet, striking one with his fist in the face, kicking another in his groin, and knocking the third off his feet. All scream and jumble, swear and thrash about. Lukas, rotator in the ravel, is flailing his arms like clubs, drubbing hard and fast, faster than ever, mowing down his attackers one after the other. So it goes! Ha! He did it! All right! There we go!—He's exhausted. He's hurting. He doesn't care. His head upraised, Lukas leaves the park. It's five o'clock in the afternoon.

For most of our childhood Enna and I had no idea that we had different fathers. We talked about our parents, shared what annoyed us about them and envisioned what we would make differently, once we moved out. Enna would have a big house where she would breed dogs, in particular collies, boxers, and golden retrievers. She would marry and have children, no less than two, no more than five. At the age of twelve she'd figured it all out. I wasn't so sure about children, because I wanted to be a writer. Had I picked this up from my father? But maybe my father didn't want to be a writer, maybe he just wanted to make note of what he'd lost along the way. And maybe my mother didn't want to be an artist, maybe she just wanted to paint a better picture of her troubled life. And Enna didn't become a dog breeder but a lawyer who worked and now still freelances for an animals rights organization; she married an anthropologist who, as it turned out, couldn't have children, but they lived a happy life and had various dogs until last year when her husband and their golden retriever were killed in a terrible car accident. And I—why didn't I pursue a career as a writer? I ended up teaching creative writing. I don't believe one can teach much about how to write. Even worse, I worry that fiction writing courses smother the writer's original still unformed voice by encouraging a certain scheme or fiction style, something common enough to be published for some time—and then forgotten. But I do like to encourage my students to develop and try out their ideas. I start every seminar by writing on the blackboard: *DARE TO WRITE.*

I was surprised when Jules stood at my door, shyly looking at me and apologizing for his late-night intrusion. It was 10:30, and I was still up. His visit was unusual. I hadn't seen or heard from him in three years. He had finished his master's in creative writing and two years later published his first novel with an indie publisher. He sent me a copy with a dedication saying *Please know I'm on my way. Thanks, Jules.* I read it, and I liked it, and I wrote him some thoughts about it. He responded a few weeks later with a brief note, which was quirky, just his original style. Since then once in a while I had googled him, wondering if he had published another book, but nothing showed up. I knew he earned his living giving private lessons in Greek and Latin, but I was sure that he would continue writing. I asked him in. Sam was watching a basketball game in the living room, so I took Jules to my study. He was in a dark mood. He told me that he had worked for many years on an epic text—he wouldn't call it a novel—a project he had started long before he enrolled into our writing program, a work that he felt was at the core of what his writing was about. There wasn't a day he hadn't worked on it, he said. He rewrote, revised, edited, and re-edited it a million times. Five months ago he decided to end it. It was done—even though he probably could have gone on forever. But at 1,328 pages it was all that would fit between book covers, he conceded. He was excited and curious when he sent it to the indie who had liked and published his first book. Simultaneously he also offered it to three other literary publishers, whose programs he appreciated, and a number of agents. He thought someone might consider it. After months of waiting, of the four publishers and the agents who had at least responded, all had declined. He had just received the last rejection from his previous publisher. Jules looked at me and said: I think they are right. What I tried didn't work. I was too obsessed with it to realize that it wouldn't work. I don't know what to do!

The door opens, and there is Sam. Finally! I jump up and give him a hug. He softly strokes my back and says hi, but I feel that he is completely exhausted. So I let him go, and he lies down on our bed. I take the shoes off his feet and sit next to him. How are you, I ask. He looks at me faintly smiling and closes his eyes. He's pale, dark circles around his eyes, he must be so tired! I pull the comforter over him, and he helps me with one hand. Then he falls asleep, a pained look on his face. He came back in his shirt, left his jacket at the scene of the crime, maybe a piece of evidence. Also his briefcase with all his personal things in it is missing. Where is the monitor? He always guarded it jealously, nobody except for me was allowed to even touch it. And now it's gone. But I saw where it rolled to a stop. Maybe nobody else saw it, and it's still sitting in this corner waiting to be picked up by me. I look at Sam who is fast asleep. He won't move for hours, he won't need me. I pick up the key and tiptoe out of our room.

The hotel is asleep. The hallway is dark, only illuminated by a big red EXIT sign, which leads me to the staircase. I don't want to use the elevator, I'd rather walk down. Crossing the lobby I see the night watchman slumped in his chair, asleep. Easily I find the auditorium, whose doors are still open, but there is no light either, the hall is submerged in black. I sit down on the top of the stairs waiting for my eyes to adapt to the darkness of this place, and as I stare into this black hole, I notice deep down, where I assume the stage is, a tiny twinkle. This must be the monitor, I think, and with my heart pounding fast, I get up, cautiously feel my way down, take step after step, and slowly approach this blinking. Even though I can't see it, I'm confident that it comes from Sam's monitor, because now I remember that it had rolled under this big radiator. I lie down, slip my arm under the heater, and can reach it, but it doesn't move, it's stuck between two iron bars. However, as soon as I touch the monitor it starts blinking faster, as if excitedly responding to my rescue operation. And thanks to its short rays shooting off at the speed of light, I eventually notice an opening behind the monitor and understand that I have to first push it way back, and then I can roll it sideways and pull it out of its trap. It works! I've retrieved Sam's monitor! I feel proud to be able to bring it back to him. He'll be so relieved, so happy!

But what kind of device is this monitor, and what does it do? I switch it on, and since nothing happens, I roll it back and forth between my hands—maybe I can reveal its secret? It is a beautiful object of perfect design, it is warm, smooth and heavy—and heavily it is lying in my hand, like Sam's head when he was sick and fell asleep with his cheek on my palm. He was hardly able to move, and I didn't want to wake him up by withdrawing my hand. He needed his sleep after those long nights of restlessness. Yet at other times when he seemed to slip away with his breath slow and labored, I got anxious and shook his hand, cooled his forehead with a wet cloth, or hummed a song he liked, just to get him back...Then he would utter something akin to a word, indiscernible in its meaning, or was it just the sound of pain that wrenched itself from his chest? He lay, all his senses turned inwards where a huge battle silently raged through his body. In the brief moments of respite when he opened his eyes, I wanted to be right next to him, I wanted him to know that I wouldn't let him go. Our life felt far from over, I needed him to survive...

The monitor has cooled down in my hand. Enough for today, enough! When I return to our room, dawn is breaking. I feel I've been running around all day for nothing other than escaping some strange truth, and now I'm worn out. I slip under the comforter, take Sam's hand, and close my eyes.

Baby won't sleep. She cries and cries. Good heavens! Mother has nursed her for hours, it seems, and still baby won't calm down. Marlene doesn't know why. Maybe her milk isn't good. She might as well get formula. She wants baby to fall asleep, wants it so bad, just shut up. The second hand of the clock on the wall is steadily hopping ahead. Everybody else parties, by now they've been dancing for more than two hours, celebrating and cheering—and baby's crying. Oh shut up! Why don't you! Though nothing she can do. How to get baby to sleep? This whole thing! Baby cries. She pushes her sore nipple forward towards this gaping hole, these toothless chops, this wet mouth. Baby's crying in despair. There, there! But baby is too upset to drink. I'm so nervous, she thinks, I can't calm her down. Too tense to nurse. For what feels to her like a long time, even a complete falling out of time, from which she would never be able to return, no, she stares at the door, which opens to the dimly illuminated corridor, stares as if to stare down her destiny. Baby keeps crying. She's moved her around, here and there, tapped her back, rattled her arms, changed her diapers—all to no avail. Well then we have to skip dinner, my dear! Abruptly she gets up and puts her baby down in the crib. Baby cries. Nobody will know. She'll survive one skipped meal. I can't stand it any longer, or else I'll strangle her. She looks for her keys, grabs her bag and turns off the light. Night, night, she shouts and closes the door. Baby cries. She leaves the apartment, a poor sigh of relief, feeling bad against her will. She'll fall asleep, soon enough. Marlene hurries through the dark street, soon reaches the bus station, and half an hour later, no baby crying, she rings her friend's doorbell. Hey, here you are, you made it! She gets out of her coat, gets her glass of wine, a seat next to her friend who is talking with an unknown man. Hi! He offers her a cigarette. She deeply inhales. Being in the world. Glen Miller. Ray Charles. Billie Holiday… She leans back. I'll never return, she thinks, and a strange smile escapes her guard. Baby cries. She wants to be free, wants to celebrate life, her life, not baby's life. This isn't my child, she thinks, I carried it—so what! She savors the wine, the music, the people, most of whom she doesn't know, which is fine. She is far away. She has no baby, no husband, no home. She's just she, just now, just here. Let me start over. Someone has opened a window. A thunderstorm rages over the city. Her house could catch fire and burn down, burn everything to the ground. And she, who has run out just for a moment, couldn't get back in, no, the police would hold her back: it's too dangerous, madam, don't go in there. But my baby, she'd cry. We do what we can, the fire marshal would say. But there'd be nothing they could do. All gone. Ashes to ashes. And she'd walk away, leave this city, go someplace else, and start over. Leave no address behind, no baby crying. The hours are wearing long. Nobody really takes an interest in her, nor does she see anybody she'd want to talk to. She's so bummed out, no milk, nothing. At one in the morning she leaves, walks all the way back to her house. The rain has stopped, the wind has calmed down, fall leaves coat the wet streets. What a life—and she somewhere in it. When she approaches her house, which is as dark as the night, pitch black, still outside in the front yard she hears her baby crying. Baby still cries for me, she thinks with surprise, how strange, she's still crying...

Sam left me a note on my nightstand: *Can I take you to lunch? Restaurant at the top floor, 12 noon.* I jump up, it's 11:30, and I don't want to be late. While showering and then putting on my best dress, I can't stop smiling. Today is our anniversary, for all this conference's brouhaha going on, Sam did not forget! When I enter the restaurant I'm almost shocked by the change of scenery: totally modern architecture, all glass and steel, with a ballooning cupola, flooding the space with abundant light even among today's deep hanging clouds. The floor in bright wood, the tables and chairs in chrome, bunches of black violas on white cloth—how exquisite! And there is Sam in his nice gray suit, light blue shirt and dark blue tie:

he looks fabulous! Thank you for dressing up for me, he says with a smile and leads me to a window table. The waiter brings two glasses of Champagne. Happy Anniversary, he says, and Many Happy Returns, I respond. 34 years and still in love, Sam marvels, and listening to him I know it will never end…But here we are, our time is limited, and before Sam has to return to his meetings, I want to know how he thinks about Peacock. Sam ponders for a while looking out over this barren land around the hotel and then says: It is what it is. I don't want to waste too much energy on fighting these kinds of battles. I will say my piece tonight, and I think some will hear me. Peacock didn't manage to grasp my research, and his presentation was lousy, they all noticed. I think eventually I will prevail—if only posthumously. What counts most is to get it right. Considering all of this, I'm good. At times I feel angry, like yesterday, but then again…I think I'm blessed with enjoying my work, finding things out, making progress. All the rest…Sam shrugs and smiles at me. Seeing him so calm and at peace with himself, I feel lifted by a wave of joy, so much so that I'm tearing up. I'm so in love with you, I say to him and he responds with: Me too. Again we clink glasses. If only we could stop time…The waiter brings our plates. A wild pigeon places itself on the windowsill, looks at us, and nods.

SWING

Luckily I'd left early enough to catch the only limo waiting in front of the hotel. Just behind me a group of men, probably participants of the conference, had poured out of the lobby's revolving door, all obviously looking for a ride to Watertown. Comfortably sitting on the soft leather cushion behind the driver, I briefly felt a sense of triumph when the car rolled past these stunned looking men. I had to suppress the silly impulse to wave at them like the Queen of England. Now they are stuck in this isolated place until one of the two hotel limos returns from its ride, which could take hours. I decide to have the driver wait for me in town until I feel ready to return.

This is a weird place. Why would anybody ever have thought of building a hotel out here, in the middle of nowhere? That's what I ask my driver. He scrutinizes me through the rearview mirror and then reluctantly says: that's a long story…But since we have a long ride ahead and I insist on hearing it, he tells me that at the end of the 19th century there was a family with a peculiar malady: when they reached middle age, they lost the capacity to sleep, their health deteriorated, and they died. It was a torturous end, the driver says; as they could neither fully fall asleep nor fully wake up, they lingered in a strange in-between state, filled with wild dreams and bizarre hallucinations. It drove them crazy. For brief moments they would find some rest in dozing off. But the slightest noise would startle and agitate them so much that they couldn't calm down for hours thereafter. That's why the head of this family, a wealthy hatter, bought some hundred acres of land up here, far from the noise of civilization, and built a home or rather a castle for himself and his children and relatives, whoever wanted to join him. But living here, these 'a-sleepers', as they called themselves, still felt shocked and revved up by the chirp of a bird, the crackle of a tree's branch, or the howling of a coyote. Thus in their desperate quest for quiet they had all trees and bushes chopped down and thereafter sprayed the ground with gray oil paint to make it undesirable and inhabitable for any living creature. With nothing growing anymore, the place was dead. The misery, though, continued for these poor people. They ended up being so noise sensitive that they couldn't even tolerate hearing their own breath. Thus the last descendants of this family decided to dispose of their shared agony once and for all. They sold everything and bestowed the proceeds and their own brains to a neuroscience lab that did research on this mysterious disease. Then they jointly committed suicide. Decades later a man bought the place, renovated it, and transformed the mansion into a conference hotel. In a gigantic effort he had a company excavate and remove the oil paint from the grounds to allow vegetation to naturally recover. He also succeeded in creating a nice garden and planting some trees around the hotel, and bit by bit some prairie grass and tough bushes have grown back on the land. Ultimately he wants to establish an 18-hole golf course here, but the costs of this project seem to have put it on hold for now. That's why he promotes this hotel for conferences. No one else would want to spend time here. The driver nods and falls silent.

In Watertown I get out at the market hall. Still puzzling over the story of these a-sleepers—how would it be to neither sleep nor be awake?—I stroll along Birch Grove Avenue and look at its shop windows without wanting to buy anything, and what I see doesn't appeal to me anyway. How are the residents living here? What are they doing? Is there a company providing work and income for the townspeople? Do they process meat or vegetables, produce machine parts, pharmaceuticals or clothing? The buildings lining the street are unremarkable. Is there anything worth noticing around here—besides this peculiar hotel castle? I enter a coffee shop and find myself in some kind of granny's living room. Old-fashioned chairs and tables, squiggly doilies, flimsy curtains, baroque porcelain figurines on dark wooden shelves and gilt-framed pictures on the walls resemble rather the hapless effort of some furniture company to stylize coziness and individuality than anybody's lived history. But I sit down and order a cappuccino and an almond croissant, which I see in the glass case next to the counter. The waitress, a young girl of barely twenty years, seems to be in a good mood. While the coffee machine is heating up, she goes through the room to freshen the small bunches of plastic roses on the tables with brief puffs of water from a spray bottle and humming a popular hit (which I can't quite identify). Then she brings my cappuccino, fortunately in a simple contemporary mug. With a friendly smile she tells me that the pastries haven't arrived yet; she thought they had, but when she looked at the back door where they are delivered, they hadn't. Can't I have the one in the vitrine? I ask. She laughs. These are only show samples, she explains, they're not real, just plastic, I'm sorry. She has a gracious way of saying this.

In a corner of the coffeeshop I notice an old couple sitting at a small table. They are holding hands while softly talking to each other. How nice! I guess they are in their eighties; both have white hair loosely falling onto their dark sweaters, his green, hers brown, perhaps hand-knit; two walkers are parked next to their table. If my parents were here right now, they probably would read the newspaper. They wouldn't hold hands—or would they? I know my father would have liked to do that, but my mother was prickly. Unreconciled with whatever injustice she felt she'd suffered in her life, she never quite relaxed into the good parts of her marriage. She felt people cut her off, never appreciated her accomplishments, focused more on my father than on her, or left her out altogether. She resented that and blamed it on my father. At times she was right. And she didn't have it in her to let slights roll off and look at the bright side of things. In her anger she could be provocative. Maybe out of a never quenched thirst for revenge or simply to hurt him as much as she felt hurt, she cheated on my father and justified it by accusing him of neglecting her. At one point my father moved out. But he came back, maybe because of the moral imperative that reigned in his heart, or maybe because he still loved her despite it all. In his later years he seemed to waver between trying to brighten her moods and ignoring them. But this is only what I remember now. Maybe there were more times when they were loving, joyful and at peace with each other. Together they traveled to the remotest places in the world, and there are photos showing my mother laughing and seemingly having a great time with my father. Given these moments, it can't have all been complicated or morose. But what do I know...?

Marlene had been watching him for a while, and when he finally came to her, she felt like saying: Don't you think you can impress me—but he did. Well built, energetic and slightly playful he had asked for a dance, *South of the Border*, dance and swing, and almost against an impulse to reject him—he could have asked her much earlier rather than first dancing with two other girls—she got up, a snappish smile on her lips, but yes, she wanted to dance! He wasn't a great dancer, teetering his shoulders excessively, but he charmed her and made her laugh. She didn't want to grant him that, no. But he kept moving and swirling her around, time and again, his hand on her back to hold her close. And she moved and warmed up and felt the heat under her sweater. Breathlessly she fell onto a chair. I'm Lukas, he introduced himself, and Marlene replied with: I'm Marie. Just a gag. He doesn't need to know who I am, she thought. He wants to have some fun tonight, and tomorrow he'll be miles away. Marie? Someone told me you are Marlene, Lukas said and looked straight into her eyes. What do people know, Marlene quipped, nobody knows anything about anybody anyway. Lukas seemed a bit taken aback. Is that what you think, he wanted to know? Marlene shrugged and lit a cigarette. But his directness touched her more than she liked to know. She'd always insisted on not needing anybody. And when Lukas extended his hand that night, she first had to reassure herself that she was not swayed by him. But she followed him home, to his home, not hers, because she wasn't ready to reveal her whereabouts. His room was small and clean, sparsely furnished, the shower across the hallway to be used by three other tenants. The war was over.

Here he'd run aground, now with her. That's how it may have started. In the morning they wake up together and lie, face to face, with open eyes just looking at each other. Marlene tries to understand why she doesn't get up and leave. It's Sunday, Enna is waiting for her at her foster mother's. Sundays they always go for a walk in the park. But Marlene stays put. Lukas runs his hand through her hair. What a night, he says. Next door someone has turned on the radio with some classical music. She is hungry, hasn't eaten for more than a day, just had a glass of wine last night, and now she would die for a slice of bread with butter and honey. And coffee. Let's go get some breakfast, Lukas says, as if he could read her mind. Quietly they walk through the deserted streets. Church bells are ringing. Marlene wonders what Lukas is thinking. Maybe he is already with his fiancée someplace else. But his arm around her shoulders stays warm and firm. He'll leave, at the latest when he learns that I have a child, she thinks, and her conviction hurts. Don't fancy yourself as his wife, she hears her mother say, and she defiantly responds, I don't want him anyway. But here she is, and Lukas invites her to a real breakfast: coffee with milk, two big rolls fresh from the oven, butter and homemade rhubarb jam. Marlene almost cries when the soft sweet warmth of her first bite fills her mouth with surging pleasure. Thank you, she whispers. Lukas smiles. I watched you last night, he then says. You were the only woman I felt attracted to. Blushing, Marlene lifts her big coffee cup to hide behind its ceramic. He just says so, she thinks, I don't trust him…What are you doing? she wants to know, and it sounds like she's challenging him.

It's not what you think, Lilli says and sits down next to me without even asking for permission. I hadn't noticed her entering the coffee shop and felt startled when suddenly a heavy purse landed on my table, almost knocking over my mug. Lilli! She looks at me with her big green eyes and says: I thought I'd find you here! Had she been looking for me? So what do you think I think, I pick up the gauntlet, curious about her ideas but also annoyed with her presence. Lilli lifts her chin. Peacock is not a bad person, she states. He is a brilliant researcher, and even though his area sort of overlaps with Sam's, he has a mind of his own. He loves to discuss his ideas with me, I am intrigued with his approach, and he listens to what I have to say. He finds my questions helpful. He makes me feel good. Sam never showed an interest in my thoughts. And barely did Lukas. I know you think that I was the difficult one and your father was a saint—always nice, understanding, accommodating, and what have you. But he too was difficult, he had a set of ideas, and I had to fit in. Lilli lights a cigarette, which surprises me because she stopped smoking decades ago when she was in her early forties. Oh, you're smoking…I say, and she replies, of course I do! The waitress comes and Lilli orders an espresso and a glass of water. Looking out of the window into her past she softly says: I had so many interests! I loved to read novels, philosophy, Freud, poetry…all that, but I couldn't talk about it with your father. He only read newspapers, political and sports magazines, once in a while a biography…He had no sense for my kind of ideas, she claims, shaking her head and waving her hand as if to show me that he knew nothing whatsoever about her. But that's not true, I think, he did read novels and short stories, he even wrote some. Meanwhile Lilli continues with her plea. The books I read intrigued me, she says, they gave me lots to think about, and I would have liked to share my thoughts with your father, but rarely did he say more than "hmmm…" or "yeah…" It made me feel so lonely…I was full of questions, and there was nobody…And now looking at me directly, she adds: The years when we both took time to talk after you came home from school were some of my best years. You too were into philosophy and literature, Kafka, Beckett, Sartre, Camus… We shared a lot, had great conversations. I felt inspired…I look at my mother's face, which is still beautiful, despite all its wrinkles. I remember our extended chats, I too enjoyed them, but I don't want to admit it, because it didn't last long. Soon I met my first boyfriend and continued my conversations with him. I let her down, I think, and feel bad.

Jules was an avid reader. Almost no text was beneath his notice. He'd studied the literary giants until they were friends, characters he felt at ease to love and criticize. He was curious about marginalized figures like Franz Jung, Mynona, Melchior Vischer, Ludmilla Petrushevskaya or Boris Vian, and explained where they fell short. Once he read us the first paragraph out of Urmuz' "Cotadi and Dragomir" and suggested that we write a piece in continuation of it, which we then compared with how Urmuz had continued. It was a most instructive exercise, and we had great fun with it. He introduced me to Albert Cohen and Clarice Lispektor. He was an unusual thinker, intriguing and challenging, an original voice with a venturous style. That night when he surprised me with his visit and talked about his epic, I thought of these background actors he used to dig out of the world's literary graveyards. Perhaps he was already one of them. In an effort to give me an idea of his work, he called it chunky, fragmented, loaded, subversive… and emphasized that this was how it was meant to be, it couldn't be polished, pleasing, or easy, he emphasized, since it was about everything that usually falls through the cracks as too painful, disturbing, too outlandish to be really looked at. However, his text was not cacophonous or extra-experimental, he reassured me. It was not his ambition to write something crazy just to stand out. On the contrary, he thought it was actually funny, exciting, revealing. Was he deluding himself?

The sun breaks through the clouds, a ray of light hits the diamond on Lilli's hand, and I have to close my eyes or else the reflecting beam would cut my cornea.—We had almost finished our Friday's mulligan, my father, Enna, and I, when Marlene came home, breathless and disheveled, wearing this big diamond on her finger, a new ring, and it wasn't my father's. All of a sudden this glittering stone flaunted on her hand like a punch in the face of decency. I think we all stared at it. Nobody said anything. My mother heaped stew on her plate. We had already finished with ours. The atmosphere was tense. Enna turned on the radio. And there came the news that JFK had been shot and died. We gasped. The shock absorbed all of our attention. For the rest of the day and the days to come we were glued to the TV to follow the events. Enna and I forgot about Marlene's diamond ring. Lukas probably not. And Marlene kept wearing it. Strangely enough, though, she sometimes left it sitting on the kitchen sink or the bathroom shelf, a much too careless treatment for such a precious gem, it seemed, until several weeks later she mentioned in passing that the diamond was a fake. Out of a sudden whim she had bought it at the supermarket. It looked real. I'm not sure that my father immediately knew that it was a fake. But at their next anniversary he gave her a diamond ring, the stone of which was much smaller but real. She wore it ever since. Looking at it now, I see her hand slightly quivering.

How was it when you first met father, I have the courage to ask my mother when she lifts her eyes from her espresso cup and looks at me. She smiles. Confusing, she then says, and after a while she offers: It was a difficult time. Lukas had found work in a construction company. Big parts of the city were bombed out and in ruins. There was a lot of work, removing all the debris. He'd learned to drive a wide-bucket excavator and worked five days a week, ten hours each. He made good money and saved most of it, because he wanted to restart his father's wallpaper factory. I worked as a secretary for a local politician from the conservative party, even though I was aligned with the progressives, but they couldn't afford a secretary. Work they had, but no pay…That's as much as she wants to say. I already knew that. Is it true?

But my father did work five days a week, and on the weekends he is free to see Marlene. She uses a white lie, telling Enna's foster mother that she has a lot of work and at this point can't come any longer on Sundays. Instead she would take Enna on Saturday mornings and add Tuesday nights for a brief visit to tuck her in. When Marlene explains these changes to Enna, the little girl looks away. Does she even listen? Marlene gets up and takes Enna's hand to go out with her for a walk, but Enna wrenches herself free, runs over to her bed, grabs her ragdoll, and holds her tight to her chest. There she stands, her legs stiff and thin and deeply plugged into the ground. Sure, your doll can come with us, Marlene says. Slowly Enna detaches herself from the wooden frame and tiptoes past Marlene through the door. We'll be back in two hours, Marlene says. The foster mother nods. On their way Marlene wishes she could just lightly chat with her daughter, but she has no idea what to say to this child. Later Marlene sits on a bench looking over to Enna, who is digging in the sandbox all by herself and as if lost in her little project. The wind is softly stroking Marlene's bare calves, a touch almost as arousing as Lukas's fingers when he's writing stories on her skin. Would Lukas like Enna? The child looks cute in her red pants and yellow sweater, her blond hair shining almost silver in the brightness of the morning sun, her long bangs emphasizing her big blue eyes, which occasionally wander over to Marlene, watchful as if to make sure that her mother is still with her. And she is. Seeing Enna, who has now turned her slim back towards her mother, Marlene again feels puzzled with having this child, who is as much hers as she is not, and whose attachment she so painfully craves but also resents. Once her new boss, Mr. Muller, happened to cross the park when Marlene was sitting on this bench, and Enna was digging in the sandbox. Well, well, idling away on a Sunday morning, he joked, and looking over to Enna apparently without thinking much he had added, Is she yours? No, she's my sister's, Marlene had claimed, without quite knowing why. She hadn't told anybody that she had a daughter. Of course, Mr. Muller confirmed, you aren't married yet. How nice for you to have a sister in town and a little niece. One day you too may have such a kid. It changes everything, I can tell you that! And tipping the brim of his hat he walked off.

I was searching for you to tell you that Cocky wants to marry me, Lilli says, and looks at me like she's ready for a fight. I'm baffled. Cocky? Yeah, Lilli concedes, Paul Peacock, I call him Cocky, it's just to tease him, and I don't like his first name, Paul. Again she waits for me to say something, but I feel so shocked, repulsed, offended, and disgusted that I can't think let alone utter a word. Lilli seems to sense the revolt in me. It's three years ago that your father passed away, she defends her announcement. You have your life with Sam. Enna too has her own things to do. Why should I sit alone and twiddle my thumbs until you shove me underground? She purses her lips as if to hide a giddy smile. It may be impossible for you to imagine, she continues, but with him it is as if I can realize something in me that I could never live. I'm not saying your father was a bad husband. We had good times. But there was something deep in me that he never reached. Cocky seems to get this about me. He's right there! I feel again like when I was young, 18 or 20 or so. It's totally amazing, she marvels, and her eyes seem to float in pure delight, now as if detached from all restraint, free and free again. I try to collect myself. Who am I fighting for? Is it my father, or is it Sam? I want to say: If you do that I will never see you again! But I can't get this out either. Instead I hear myself saying, well good luck then! Bitterness singes my heart, and not knowing where to go with this, I get up and head for the bathroom. I close the door, latch the lock, and sit on the toilet lid. I feel hot, my heart is pounding, I almost cry and my fists are clenched. This is not something she would do to me, no! She can't be serious! Sam would be upset, but I even more so. What would my father say? Maybe this is just another of Peacock's attacks on Sam—knowing that Marlene is Sam's mother-in-law, he wants to slime himself into our family and thereby silence Sam. Or is Lilli delusional? Is she making this up? Am I…? Eventually I leave the restroom, still without knowing what to say to Lilli. The old lovers look at me. Lilli is gone. My almond croissant has arrived.

I work to convince myself: This is not going to happen! Lilli will not wed Peacock! Unable to touch the pastry, I sit at my table and feel like I'm in a foreign country. This is not my culture, not my language, not my way of doing things. And all these people at the conference… Who are they? Where do they come from? What are they thinking? Why am I here? The waitress comes and asks if I want another cappuccino. When I decline she wonders why I haven't tried my almond croissant. I'm not hungry, I say. She suggests that I take it home. But where is home? When she brings the bill, she puts the croissant into a paper bag. I don't know why, but I resent this. Without further looking at her I pay the bill. Have a nice day, she says, takes her coat from a hook next to the door and leaves the coffee shop. She just leaves? The old lovers seem to have watched me, and noticing my confusion the man loudly tells me across the room: She always goes to therapy at this time, she'll be back in an hour. And the woman adds: In the meantime we have to fend for ourselves. She chuckles. Oh, I say, and Yes, and Thank you, I'm fine. And then the room turns silent again, except for the murmur of the old lovers' conversation.

After a three-hour ride on war-furrowed roads, battered and shaken they arrive at their new home. It's noontime on December 24th. Marlene with the newborn in her arm and Enna sitting on Lukas's knees, they are crammed in next to the driver on the front seat of the small truck, which carries all of their belongings. What to anticipate? A settlement of dark, old, hunched down houses, where workers of a formerly productive coal mine used to live, but after it got bombed and destroyed, killing most of the miners on shift that day, the remaining people, elderlies, women and children, had left, and refugees from the east had moved in, vaguely starting a new community, where hopes were dim, energies low, and anxious suspicions looming everywhere. Here Lukas has found a small apartment for the four of them. The landlady had been skeptical. Two kids, that's a lot of noise for two rooms, she'd weighed in. But this is what Lukas can afford. He gets out and together with the driver they open the hatch to the cargo area and start unloading the boxes and wrapped pieces of furniture. They pile everything on the walkway in front of the house. The neighbors stand behind the windows and watch. The driver is in a hurry, he wants to get home in time to light the Christmas tree for his children. Marlene carries the baby, thus can't give a hand. She is horrified. This is where they are supposed to live? Enna stands by herself near the truck's big wheel. It's freezing. Everything gets thinly sprinkled with icy snowflakes. Finally Lukas lets the last item plop next to the front door. He pays the driver, even gives him a small tip. Merry Christmas, he says, and the driver mumbles, same to you, before he mounts the driver's seat and drives off. Lukas looks over to Marlene. Here we are, he says and tries to smile. Marlene's eyes are in tears, and he notices it. Together they go up to their second-floor apartment. It is dark, empty, unheated and smells strange. Marlene takes a deep breath. Why don't you bring up the cradle first, she suggests. I've nursed Sine, so she'll sleep for a while, and I can help you carry up our stuff. Enna is given the task to watch over Sine. She sits down on the wooden floor next to her baby sister and wonders if her foster mother will come too, maybe a bit later. Instead box after box is pushed into the room, soon surrounding the kids and barring the view of the doorway out. When Lukas and Marlene finally grab the last suitcases to be carried up to their new home, the first- floor tenant opens her door and looks at this young couple, who already have two kids. Introducing herself as Ms. Meyer she states: There is a rule in this house; each month one of us tenants has to dig and empty out the cesspit, and as it happens it is your turn today. The pushcart is in the shed next to the back-door. You just wheel the shit to the town's collecting pit at the end of the road. And Merry Christmas, she wishes them before withdrawing herself behind her door. Lukas looks at Marlene, who struggles to absorb the insult. He would love to offer his family a nice Christmas evening. But this is what they have now. He is tired but determined to make it work.

Sitting at my table staring at nothing in particular, I may have looked bored, because the old people, each on their walker heading to the exit, stop next to me and ask if I would be so kind to watch out for the coffee shop till the waitress is back from her therapy session. Usually we do it, they explain, but since you are here and we would like to leave, we thought of asking you. I'm surprised but immediately intrigued. As a student I used to work in coffee shops, and I liked it. What am I supposed to do, I ask, and they say: Nothing much. Just in case someone comes in—which hardly ever happens at this time of the day—you explain to them that the waitress will be back soon. You may serve them some pastry, if you want, but it's not necessary. We've never done it. I nod to indicate my agreement. They wish me a good day, and maneuvering their support frames through the door, they leave the coffee shop. Only then I think that I could have asked them how they are living here, if they grew up and worked here, or what they know about this town. I regret having missed this opportunity, but now they are gone, and I feel too slow to run after them. Instead I get up and stroll through the room, not really interested though closely looking at everything as if in search of something I don't expect to find. What to do with myself? I proceed to move behind the counter, just to feel if this feels again like when I was 18 or 20, serving coffee, tea, and drinks, preparing snacks and chatting with the customers on the other side of the bar. The counter is dirty, stained with coffee and milk spots, smudges of marmalade, and bread crumbs, and seeing a rag hanging over the sink, I pick it up and wipe off the area around the coffee machine.

The door opens and Lilli and Peacock march in, all lovey-dovey, entwined around each other and seemingly in a great mood. With them a fierce wind gust blasts into the room, blowing Lilli's red coat wide open, in fact swelling it as if to cover, suffocate, and engulf the whole room, me included. Oh hello there, Lilli jubilates to me while assembling her drapery, who'd have thought that you'd find work so fast?

And turning to Peacock she adds, that's my little Sine, she was always a smart girl, neat and nerdy! Then she pulls up a stool and sits down at the bar right in front of me. Peacock, who wears a strange cap with a pattern that could easily be mistaken for a laurel wreath, establishes himself next to her. I know Sine, he says to Lilli, we've met at the hotel in some context, I can't quite remember what it was…probably on one of the coffee breaks. He rests his elbows on the counter and stares at me. What can I get you, I ask, totally perplexed about myself. Peacock draws a face as if abandoning himself to his whims. I'll have a vermouth, he says, and Lilli chimes in: Then I'll have one too. She takes Peacock's hand and beams at him. Seeing this I cringe and quickly turn around to the shelf behind the coffee machine, where I find a bottle of Cinzano Rosso. Peacock agrees to it, and I pour them two glasses. What am I doing?! Lilli raises her glass and Peacock follows suit. We're celebrating, Lilli announces. We've just signed a rental agreement for an apartment in the tower of the hotel. It's furnished and will be cleaned daily by the hotel staff, so we don't have to bother with any of the ordinary nuisances, we can just be creative, develop ideas, etc. While she is gushing her news, Peacock runs his hand up and down her back. And I'm just looking.

At this point the driver of the hotel car enters together with another fierce push of cold wind, sweeping Peacock's silly cap off his head and landing it on the stovepipe. Peacock rushes to get it back as the driver approaches Lilli, his eyes piercing hers. You owe me the money for your ride, he says. Lilli only shrugs. You didn't bring me where you were supposed to bring me, she claims, I don't owe you anything. I would have, had you not walked away, the driver counters and moves closer to Lilli. Hey, back off, Peacock shouts, jumping in between them. It's none of your business, the driver gives back and shoves him to the side. Where's my money, he asks and holds out his hand awaiting his fare. Ha-ha, Lilli laughs, you can't make me. You think I can't, the driver challenges, grabs her purse and opens it. Leave the lady alone or else…, Peacock yells and tries to wrest Lilli's purse from his hands. But the driver has already found Lilli's wallet, picks out a hundred-dollar bill and says: this is it with tip and interest. Thief, Lilli yells, give it back! The driver throws the purse into her lap. Peacock stands there, wide-eyed, slouchy, with his tail between his legs. Derisively the driver spits on the floor in his direction and leaves the coffee bar. Lilli starts crying. Peacock holds her with one arm and with the other he empties his Cinzano in one gulp and immediately orders another one. But I've had enough. Without looking at them any further I leave.

In the twilight hours we lean at the windowsill, grandma and I, our elbows comfortably bedded on a big pillow, looking out to the street while drifting through the falling night, and all is quiet. She and I and everything between us. Long ago the bats were flitting past the warehouse. Lilli wears her shoes in her hands. She tiptoes over the path to the barn. Hans awaits her at the door: Come here, Lilli, he whispers, what took you so long? She signals him to be quiet. Cautiously they enter the hall, stop to accommodate to the darkness inside, then proceed. Lilli and Hans, she 12 and he 14, holding hands. She goes first, he follows. Boxes of rock candy, ginger drops, cinnamon sticks, Egyptian licorice, Maté tea—my grandfather's merchandise piles up right and left on towering raw wooden shelves. The spicy odors make them sneeze and giggle. They have no plans, but their hearts are pounding.

There is this photo from my parents' first vacation by the sea… Marlene in her black and white striped coat and her long wide trousers next to Lukas in his parka, a woolen cap on his head, both facing the storm. And again Marlene's hair is flying in the wind, unruly, boisterous, she likes it and knows that it makes her look passionate (someone had mentioned it once, and she never forgot). And Lukas looks so happy! Maybe this is when he proposed to her. He says: Marlene, I've known you only for a few months, and there is a lot I don't know about you—but I feel like I want to get to know you for the rest of my life! Marlene is touched, he sees it and adds: Do you want to marry me? Now he's said it for the first and only time in his life. What about Enna, Marlene asks, and he responds, I'll adopt her, she's ours, she's mine too. His arm around her shoulder, he leads her to a coffee shop at the beach. It's late in the afternoon, and they are cold from their long stroll on the boardwalk. To warm up, Lukas orders hot wine punch, and as they are waiting for their drinks to toast their future, Lukas pulls a giftbox out of his pocket, an engagement present for Marlene. Curiously she opens it. A small golden watch! He looks at her, trying to figure out whether she likes it or not. My mother wore it, he says, now it's yours. Marlene puts it on. She smiles, radiates. This photo of their walk on the beach stands vis-à-vis my desk, and when I look up from my computer, I can see it. But did she say yes?

I'd already known Sam for a couple of years when I introduced him to my parents. It was on my father's birthday, and Enna had announced that she would come too, so we would all be together. Everybody was prepared to finally meet Sam. Still the moment itself felt awkward. Saying the obvious to my parents, *This is Sam*, implied as much. My parents may have thought: this stranger sleeps with our daughter. Quickly we moved on to having an aperitif and wishing my father a happy birthday. He liked the Glen Miller album we had brought him. Over lunch Sam tried to explain his research to my parents, and they did their best to understand. Maybe my mother was more enthused with learning something about brain science than my father, who after a while brought up how he'd rebuilt and expanded the wallpaper factory, mentioning that he had over a thousand employees. I noticed that he'd put the big binder with the sample collection on the coffee table. Enna made sure everybody was served well. She watched us carefully. After lunch my father invited Sam for a walk, while my mother took a rest. Enna and I went to clean the kitchen, just as we used to do when we were children. I still see my father and Sam walking through the garden gate and onto the field path towards the vineyards. My father slightly limping from a recent knee surgery. Sam a bit taller and his head respectfully bent towards my father, who points across the hills explaining the landscape. They walk together, and soon they are not talking anymore, just calmly moving ahead, side by side. Their steps softly creak on the sand. Summer flies buzz along. A woodpecker works a nearby pine tree. There is no need to chat. Both feel inexplicably close. They realize how amazing it is to have just met and be able to walk in silence. After a while my father says that his knee has started hurting and suggests they return. Sam agrees and offers support. My father says thank you and puts his hand on Sam's shoulder. Slowly they walk home, still enjoying the quietness of their first walk on this early summer day. When they reach the garden door, my father says: Take good care of her. And Sam says: Yes.

When I get back to the hotel, a big fire engine is just leaving. People from the conference, recognizable by the name tags on their lapels, are standing in groups chatting and squinting in the afternoon sun. Mechanics in blue overalls carry toolboxes, ladders and cable reels through the front door into the lobby. The elevator is out of service, and I have to climb the stairs up to our room. Sam seems to have been back for a while, because our bed is packed with his manuscripts, sections of the New York Times, emptied bags of salt pretzels and potato chips and him in the middle of it all. Where have you been, he asks me, and I say, in Watertown. Oh, had I known you were going there, I would have asked you to bring me a refill for my ballpoint pen, he says, and then tells me that his presentation and everything got delayed because there was a fire in the main conference room, apparently caused by a short-circuit; everybody had to be evacuated, and all meetings were moved to the next day. Are you disappointed? I want to know. He shakes his head. No, I'm fine with having a day of rest, I just missed you, he answers, and makes room for me on the bed. I sit next to him. This is a strange place, I say, and tell him about the family of the a-sleepers who built the hotel. Interesting, he says, that they had this prion disease… Jokingly he adds: I, on the other hand am just ready for a nap – want to join me? I feel tempted, but knowing that I haven't gotten far with grading my students' papers, I decide to work a bit right next to him. Okay, he says and closes his eyes. Soon he is breathing calmly. I like to watch him sleep. Then everything seems alright – but also precarious. How much time will we have?

Jules's note on the door, glued to the wood with an ordinary scotch band, unmistakably his handwriting: Don't come in, call 911. That's all! The door is closed. His note on the door. Don't come in. And Marian, returning home from her night-shift, is standing in front of this door, her hand at the latch, hesitating and afraid and knowing everything at once. Don't come in, he pleads. Don't go in, she whispers. Shock fills the hall with fierce pain. Her phone rings as if from elsewhere, too far away and out of reach. Call 911. The air conditioner clicks, starts up, cold winds blow down her neck – so cold. His icy fingers in his pockets, determined and frozen! No struggle, hands in pockets in bright daylight! Marian slowly sits down on the bench in front of his door. There is no noise, no breath, just icy air. Recall our plans, she begs, recall! Because she can't. On her own, in bright daylight, at six-thirty in the morning! Don't open the door. She can't! Her friends will come, will stand there, shocked, crushed, in disbelief! They will look at his note and this small but fathomless step, this final, desperate move, his mistake. How could he be so wrong! And she, glued to her bench, incapable of waking up! He's gone. She can't! – Later 911 came through the other door – they entered, went in, took him down, carried him out. They left with him. He went with them. He went there and left her here, where she can't stay, nor can she leave. But with a subtle sense of care they gently closed the door before they left. The door he'd asked her not to open. The door she would keep closed.

KIDS

Suddenly I hear a scratch at the door, like from a dog wanting in. Or maybe there is a mouse beneath the floorboards. Again I hear the scratch and also a soft thud. I open the door and see a little child, probably a girl, three or four years old, blonde curls, and big bright eyes looking at me. She's dressed in a red T-Shirt under loose-fitting denim overalls and holds onto a plastic bag, which is sitting next to her feet on the carpeted floor. Oh, hello, I say and step into the hallway to see if there is someone she belongs to, but there is nobody. You can't find your room? She shakes her head. I'm not sure what it means: did I pose the wrong question, or can't she find her room? What's your name? I inquire, thinking I'll have the concierge send her parents to pick her up. But again she shakes her head and keeps standing there, tender and stubborn, as if she were my daughter. Why don't you come in, I suggest, and even though she again shakes her head, she now slowly takes a few steps into my room, dragging the plastic bag behind her. When she is in, I close the door and kneel down next to her. May I see what you have in your bag? I ask, and to my surprise she gives me the bag's handles. I open and look into it – and there is Sam's monitor! Where did you get this? I ask her, but instead of answering me, she reaches into the bag, takes out the monitor, and throws it like a ball. The monitor utters a few beeps while rolling around, coming to a stop under the bed. The child, who had followed it with her eyes until it disappeared in the gap, now looks again at me and points with her finger in the direction of the monitor. I lie down on the carpet and peer under the bed. At first I only see black and fluff, but then I detect a thin ray of pulsating light, which tells me where the monitor is. I try to reach it, but my arm is too short and the space between bed and floor is too narrow.

I call Sam on his cell and get his answering machine. He's probably in one of his meetings. I leave him a message, saying that I have his monitor, just in case he is looking for it. When I turn around, the girl is sitting on our bed, her head leaning on my pillow, the empty plastic bag bulging between her legs. She looks cute, she moves me. I feel reluctant to call the concierge, but I do it anyway. A little kid, about four years old, came to my room, I say without mentioning that she brought Sam's monitor, could you perhaps figure out who her parents are and send them to my room to pick her up? There is a pause on the phone, and I think the concierge is studying the guest list, but then he says: This hotel doesn't admit children, we have no license for underage travelers; hence there is no child registered, and she shouldn't be in your room. She must have intruded illegally. Please remove her at once. I hang up. What a weird place this is! The girl looks at me, totally unafraid, and I don't know what to say. I sit down on our bed next to her and try to find a good way of asking her if she would tell me where she comes from or anything at all. But before I've made up my mind, she has fallen asleep, sunk down with her head on my thigh, her hand still holding the bag. Why did this child come to me? And how did she get the monitor and know where to bring it? Or did she just stumble in the right direction, propelled by this uncanny sense of certainty that little children have?

One day I took off on my tricycle, pedaled far away into a different country, took this straight road, which led from our house right into the open cornfields, pedaled carefully while looking around in pure amazement at the freedom I felt, the capacity to go and discover the world. On the right side of the street were the willow trees, a bench placed in between each of them. Nobody was sitting there on this special day. On the left side of the street a rivulet, I couldn't see it because it was lined with high reed, but I could hear it burble along. I knew I was not supposed to go near it, nor did I want to, because I was on my way into my life. Beyond the rivulet a lawn with wildflowers rose towards a wire-mesh fence, behind which I saw a row of brightly colored houses, bungalows in yellow, pink, turquoise, lime-green and white, the most jolly houses I'd ever seen. If I went there…Later I learned that this was a settlement of American soldiers, but it could just as well have been the land of fairies and magicians. Still sitting on my tricycle marveling at this miracle, my mother ripped me out of my dreams: Here you are, she exclaimed, I've been looking for you everywhere! Did you not hear me calling for you? Maybe I'd heard her. But a mother can call and not reach her child when she is elsewhere. Wouldn't she know?

Yes, she remembered and told me many times, and whenever she did, it was like now: Sitting in the sandbox building a castle, her feelings vague but simultaneously sure, so sure that something would happen, something new, Lenchen gently pads the walls with her shovel. A soft breeze is pushing petals through the air, lightening the dusk. Crows croak. Shouldn't it be dark by now? No. Today is the longest day of the year, her mother had casually mentioned in the morning. Immediately grasping the gravity of the moment, a moment foreboding, Lenchen had held her breath: the day of a lifetime, there it was! All could change, would change, because there was time, more time, better time. She would greet this day, she wouldn't miss it. Ever since this moment in the early morning she's felt elated, albeit strangely anxious, her heart beating faster, her cheeks burning hot, her eyes flickering and ready to tear up. Mother calls: dinner's ready! Lenchen shakes her head, eyes cast down, digging deeper into the sand. Her sister Odile scoffs, ah, goatish you again, and stupidly giggling she follows mother's call and disappears in the house. Lenchen stays behind. The world is hers. Someone seems to touch her shoulder from behind, but she's not allowed to turn around. The miracle would disappear. No voice heard. Her hands sieve the sand. She might find something special, an old coin, a golden key, a tiny bone...A door bangs shut. Her father's car roars in the garage; he's about to leave. Stay with me, she whispers. Don't delude yourself, her mother snarls. Mean she was, mean, mean, why was she so mean? A scrap of paper staggers through the air and settles near the castle. A secret message! You've been chosen, it says, or something, but for what, what's the secret? Time expands like a balloon — the time of the longest day. How long has she been here? A big drop splashes on her knee. Oh! Another hits her hand. And she hasn't quite yet celebrated! The courtyard turns darkish. Gusts of wind rip through the bushes, chase an empty cardboard box, howl through the gutters, make her skirt flutter. The castle's crown of twigs she'd so carefully plaited jumps up and flies off, off into the night. No! More drops hammer down, hit her face, lash the ground, turning everything dark and wet. Lene, come in, it's raining, her mother yells. What happened? What? Nothing! Nothing happened! Or she missed it, or she made a mistake. She ruined it...Or Odile did. Or her mother. Her father left, the garage door is open, his car is gone. Suddenly rain's pouring down, heavy rain. The castle's melting away. Lenchen jumps up, and with one last glance at the waning day, this longest day of her life, she runs through the courtyard and through the open door into the kitchen, where everybody is sitting around the dinner table having a good time.

Where are her parents? The girl still sleeps on my thigh. When Mikki was little, I enjoyed these moments when we were sitting together and chatted or played or she would parade her favorite teddy, Max, in front of me, explaining what mischief he was up to or what he had to complain about. She never played with dolls, but she had a big collection of bears, an extensive family with parents, grandparents, sons and daughters, uncles and aunts and cousins and even a nanny. They crowded her bed when she went to sleep, they were dressed and undressed, they went to school and she would teach them, they had to go to the doctor and got bandages or had their temperature taken. When we went on vacation, and Mikki could take only one of her bears with her, she always picked Max, because he was a scalawag and couldn't be left alone. And when she went to college and placed all her bears in a box to be stored in the attic, she exempted Max, sneaked him into her luggage – I happened to see it when I walked by her open door, but I didn't say a word. Max went to college.

No, the brute screams, his falsetto splitting the air like a flash of lightning, no, you listen! He licks his lips and picks his ear, drops of sweat bulging on his forehead, his silvery eyes almost falling out of their bloodshot sockets, the whole giant a trembling threat of plain folly. What has gotten into him, what? Enna slips under the table, goes into hiding, her lips quivering. He won't do anything to me, he won't be bad, she whispers. Marlene keeps lounging in her plush chair, watching the scene with remote delight. You can't make her, she lilts, and you don't tell her anything! Her hair, loosened from her bun, is twirling all over her face in the fan's fierce winds. The cat keeps meowing. From under the table Enna looks at the man's big feet in black boots right in front of her. What is he about to do? Enna hardly dares breathing. All day long Marlene's friend has been looking dangerously frail. Then came the phone call, and now he hits the table, hits it twice. I know what you need, he thunders. You need to come out. You need to listen. Marlene just laughs. Bragger, bragger, comes to swagger, she trolls, mocking the old giant. Enna thinks if she can fold herself four times while rolling into the small carpet under the table, he can't hurt her. Not good. A glass has fallen, pushed over by the brute's fist; red wine drips to the floor. Enna starts counting to ten, by which she will jump up and run out the door. Two—three... Suddenly the man stops moving. Four—five...Hey, darling, Marlene purrs, cool down, you're frightening the chicken. Shut up, he snarls, I know what she needs, and I'll give it to her, want it or not. Nine—ten...Enna whispers, still hesitating, but then, as if jolted by a sudden inner force, she jumps up, overthrowing the table, thus barring him from grabbing her, and reaches the door: almost ripping the handle off its stay, she flies out, out of her home and out of her nightmare, which trails her and lingers long, long before it eventually fades, this beastly thing, this useless threat that still, once in a while, can make her shudder.

The phone rings. The concierge tells me that he sent a woman from Social Services to pick up the kid. Before I can answer, he ends the call. I'm shocked! They will take her away, force her to say what she doesn't want to say, interrogate her at a police station, throw her into an orphanage...I have to protect her! I shake her. Startled, she awakens, looks at me puzzled and frightened. Someone is coming to fetch you, I say. Do you want me to hide you? She nods. I hurry her off the bed, open the closet and tell her to sit at the bottom between our shoes. I will close the door, I explain, and when they come in and you hear their voices, you have to be completely quiet, don't move. As soon as they are gone, I will open the closet and let you out. Dutifully she nods, pushes the empty plastic bag into her pants pocket, steps into the closet, and cowers in a corner, right next to my dirty hiking boots. I close the door and lock it, so that it won't swing open by chance. Then I sit on our bed and wait. I feel anxious.

Because death was present, always, lurking on the sidelines, sometimes waving his hand: uncanny; or grinning into the picture: awful. Death was a man, no doubt, a figure residing in the depth of our nights, a move inaudibly sneaking on lousy socks behind Marlene's busy apron. He usually wore a dark raincoat. His Borsalino overshadowed whatever facial features he carried, allowing him to remain unseen unless he bared his teeth in a mean grin. What was he so mean about? Or was he just sad? Why was he always there? He once had a lover to lose to their child. She chose his child over him. Oh dear! I wept when I thought of it. I wanted to look at him albeit in horror, but he disappeared whenever I tried. Fallen off his life's cliff when baby was born, he clung to Marlene to keep him from dying. Once I woke up startled – he was standing in front of my bed with his coat flanks wide open, fully naked. I screamed, hadn't I? I felt I had screamed, but nobody heard a thing. Nothing happened. Death was around but wouldn't be caught! Mother had her secrets. She slept with him in her bedroom. At night he came to her through the window, at night when she disrobed her morale, her duties, her responsibilities, at night, in the hour that was all hers, the hour before she fell asleep. Then she had this unbidden guest on her mind. Come in, come to me, you are no stranger, are you? She showed him what to do, he followed her hands, he struck her hard and stroked her with cold fingers, then wept a tear for a touch until she was completely soaked. Her lover was dead, and death was her lover. I almost knew it.

I hear a loud knock at my door, I'm all resolve. I open. Three people, a woman and two men, all in gray uniforms, red skull-caps on their heads, stare at me. We're here for the kid, the woman says, and wants to enter my room, but unmoved I stay in the doorway and fake surprise: Oh you didn't see her? She just left, went towards the stairs, she should have run right into your arms…The woman shakes her head and peers past me into my room. We took the elevator, she explains, we missed her. One of the men behind her speaks into his walkie-talkie: Tell the concierge to watch out for the kid when she comes down to the lobby! Can I come in to ask you some questions, just for the record? the woman suggests, and puts her foot on the doorsill. Reluctantly I step aside, and she moves forward while the two men remain outside. Surreptitiously she looks around. Can you describe her, the woman asks, and I say that she was cute, like little kids are. What was she wearing? Jeans and a red shirt. What is her name? I don't know. Did she say anything? No! The officer has been writing down my answers and not seeing anything indicative of a child, she quickly puts the filled out form on my desk, has me sign it, and gives me a copy titled *Official Complaint*. I hadn't complained, I say, I only communicated. The woman shrugs. That's just the form, she tells me, and leaving the room she adds: Call if the girl shows up again. I nod and close the door behind her, my heart fiercely pounding.

With a few steps I'm at the closet and unlock the door. The kid, cowering in the corner, smiles at me. You can come out, I say, they are gone. Again the phone rings, I go to answer, and it is Sam, who tells me that he is coming up, he has a longer lunch break and would like to spend it with me. How nice, I respond, and I want to add that there is a kid…but he's already hung up. When I turn around I can't see her, but I hear her heavily breathing and as if scratching under the bed. What are you doing, I call, bending down, and peering under the bed I see her wiggling her way towards the monitor. As soon as she reaches it, she gives it a push and it rolls out from under the bed. With a thud it hits the door and stops. When the girl reappears she is full of fluff. Well behaved, she stands in front of me as if waiting to be cleaned up, and I do as she expects. Thank you for getting the monitor, I say, where did you find it? She points to the bed and smiles.

And there is Sam! With one sturdy push he swings the door open and in he rolls a machine on a bulky wheelwork. It looks like a bargain from a junk-shop, the arrangement of rods rusty and bent, the apparatus weirdly mechanical with a handle to crank it up. Look what I found, Sam says and is all enthused, a film projector! It cost only 20 bucks! You bought it? I ask. Yes, he confirms. But how do you want to get it on the plane? We'll see, he responds. I just couldn't miss out on it. One can adjust the projector to 8 mm or 16 mm film – imagine, all the old films we haven't seen since our projector broke, we can watch them again. A while ago Sam had asked me to get our old family films digitalized, but I never got around to doing it. I apologize to him, but he won't have any of it. You don't have to do that any longer, he says, I can run them through this projector and thereby feed them into the monitor. That's much better! I am puzzled. How would that work, I ask, and actually what is this monitor – I've no idea what you are talking about! Sam gives me a brief hug. I'll explain later, he promises. Let's go get some lunch. He takes off his jacket, and throwing it on the bed he discovers the kid. What are *you* doing here, he asks her, and turning to me he appends that she is from the store where he bought the projector. How did she come here? he wonders. I'm surprised that he knows her. She brought your monitor, I explain. My monitor? Sam looks puzzled but then seems to remember. Oh yes, I did check my monitor at the store to see if it connects to the projector, and it does! But did I leave the monitor in the store…? Now it all seems to make sense. She must have watched me, Sam muses aloud, and she heard my room number when I put the charge on our bill. Okay,

I say, let's bring her back. Together we leave the room. I take Sam's arm, and the girl takes his hand. Like a young family we happily walk along the hallway to take the stairs down to the lobby.

But all of a sudden I get a terrible cramp in my right leg, something that has happened a few times recently, and I know it can last for a while as it comes and goes in waves, completely disabling me. It is so painful that I cry out. The girl flinches, as if I'd hurt her. I crouch down, whimpering, all consumed with this stinging pain. Sam looks startled. I tell him that I have a cramp and need to return to our room. He looks concerned but also irritated. Too bad, he says, and after a brief pause, he asks me if I want him to go back with me. No, no, I fend him off, I'll be fine, I'll follow you as soon as I can. Okay, he responds, I'll bring the girl back to the store and then wait for you at the milk bar. I'm fine with this. I only want them to leave me alone. Together they descend the stairs. The little girl holds on to Sam's hand.

And here comes Lenchen, already four years old and as smart as her sister Odile. She lifts up a paper carefully folded twice. I've written a letter, she proclaims, and now I have to mail it. Her mother looks at her, exhausted from working all day in the shop. She briefly smiles and massages her back. I've written this letter, Lenchen insists, waving the piece of paper in order to prove her skills. Yes, her mother says, looks like you made a nice drawing. No, I've written a letter, Lenchen angrily screams, and I need an envelope to send it! Her mother knits her brows. You don't scream at me, she warns her and challenges: so you've written a letter, then show me. No! It's not for you! It's private, Lenchen gives back. Odile scoffs: we all know that you are a big writer...Lenchen retreats to the bookshelf. You are mean, she says under her breath, you are so mean....Finally her father puts down his newspaper. Come, Lene, he says, let's get you an envelope and bring your letter to the post office! Lene looks at him with surprise. You can't go now, her mother demurs, dinner is about to be ready. Yes, we can, Marlene's father says and gets up, and in a flash Lene is next to him, and off they go to his study. He opens his desk drawer, pulls out an envelope and asks her: Shall I write down the address, or do you want to do it? Lene decides: you do it! And to who is it? To you, she declares, and beams at him. Oh, her father says, I look forward to receiving it. He writes down his address, lets her pick a stamp, a true stamp, and off they go to the post office. Lene walks at his side. The evening has fallen, and the streetlights are on. Never has she been out this late. Her neighbor's dog is barking, but she is not afraid. She is with her father. The baker rides by on his bicycle. The two of you are still out this late? he jokes. Yes, her father responds, we have to mail a letter. And on they go. A full moon lights their way. There is nothing that could stop them. When they reach the post office, her father lifts her up so that she can push her letter through the slit of the mailbox. Thank you for your letter, her father says, when I receive it I will send you my answer. How happy she is! Quietly they walk home.

When I get back to our room, the door is open but almost completely barred by a cleaning cart in front of it. Inside I hear some snicker. Entering I have to squeeze myself past the projector's support frame, which is draped with fresh towels and bed linens, now looking like a raised blind on a theatrical stage. Two cleaning ladies sit next to each other on our bed, their backs turned towards me, bent over something, snorting with laughter. Obviously they didn't notice me coming in, because they continue to giggle and splutter, one of them yelling: look at that, look, and the other shrieking with delight and pounding her hand on her thigh. What's going on? With a few steps I'm next to them and see that one has Sam's monitor in her lap, slowly turning it around while both goggle at it. It seems that there are images appearing on its surface, but I'm not sure. What are you doing! I yell at them. Shocked, both shrink back. In a blink I've snatched Sam's monitor from them. It is almost too hot to hold it, but I don't let it go. The cleaning women jump up, stammer some apologies, one quickly grabs our bedding to tear it off, throwing the used linens in a pile, the other starts running the vacuum cleaner over our carpet. Through the open bathroom door I see that they have thrown all my toiletries into the sink under the dripping faucet. I'm upset! A new wave of pain in my leg makes me drop down on the chair in front of the desk. You have no right to scrabble about our stuff, I snarl at the one with the vacuum cleaner when she brushes by. She behaves as if she hadn't heard me. The other, having finished freshening up our bed, now putters around the toilet whistling some stupid pop song. I can't wait for them to leave — just leave me alone! Finally they slip out of the room, closing the door behind them. I can still hear them puff and blow in the hallway.

Warm and faintly vibrating, the monitor is sitting in my hand, as my hand rests on the desk. I still don't know how it works, but the cleaning crew seemed to have figured it out. Or did they just stumble upon something that turned it on? How many nights Sam had spent working on it in our basement! After dinner he went down to his private lab, as he called it, to do — I don't know what, maybe to further develop something on the chip for better or faster processing of the data or to fiddle around with its algorithm or something. After dinner I wanted to be with him. But he had to work, he said. I wanted to continue our conversation, watch a movie with him, take a walk, go to bed, make love…But he was not available. Often he worked so late that I had already fallen asleep when he finally joined me in bed. Half waking up or still in my dream

I turned towards him, and he kissed me, tenderly and careful not to arouse me, but on some of these nights he did, and I wanted it and woke up to his strokes on my back, to his kisses on my face, to his hands on me, here and there and here again, stirred to know and excited to not quite know what was coming, slowly, silently, tentatively at first, and then stronger, faster, more determined, not yet, and yet and yet all in, still holding and then yes with both of us within each other and ourselves… oh Sam, how I miss you…and it won't end (will it?) – and the night melts into the morning, dispersing the glow, the warmth, and at last the smile, gently skimming the aches, smoothing the loss, and sweeping away what never can be solved. And so it goes. The monitor has stopped blinking.

But I don't want to stop, don't want to return, not yet, so I float around for a bit, briefly look at Sam's desk at home, see the framed picture of me, which he took on our first trip to Tuscany, how young I was, how relaxed. And then I move over to see Sam's monitor, this thing that I don't understand, and yet it is still sitting there, a terrible mystery or something to marvel at. But Sam didn't have to go out that night when I was too tired to go with him. It wasn't important! He shouldn't have, no, but on I move, and my father looks at me, affectionately but a bit concerned, and I don't want him to worry about me. How do you think about your life? I had asked him at his 85th birthday, and he had thought for a while and then simply said: It was good. How lovely that he could say this!

But in the beginning it hadn't been easy. The coal oven was small and had to continuously be refilled. The briquettes were stacked in a crawlspace beneath the staircase. The firewood needed to be chopped into extra small pieces to pass the mingy oven door. Lukas used old newspapers to light the fire. Often smoke filled the room before the flames flared up. The walls were stained, and it took a while before they could paint over them. They had no carpets on the floors, no pictures on the walls, no curtains for the windows. The furniture was cobbled together, whatever they'd found in second-hand stores or along the streets. Lukas had a hand for mending things and making them look nicer. For a while he worked in a lumber mill and got access to good pieces of wood, with which he built a closet for Marlene, a bed for Enna, a dinner and worktable for the kitchen/living room. Then it looked a bit more like home. When she was on her own, Marlene often cried. She wondered if this misery had trapped her for life. She looked at Enna, who was quietly sitting in a corner drawing a picture, and at Sine, who was sleeping in her crib, and she yearned to have back just one day of her time without children, when she could do her things without having to worry about anybody else. But she learned to greet her neighbors even if they looked at her funny when she brought Enna to the kindergarten; she swallowed her disgust when walking down the street past the hen houses and muckheaps to go to the only grocery store in this village, and she managed to shop and cook carefully, so that the family had one simple but healthy warm meal a day. Enna was shy. She tried to hide her head between her shoulders and averted her eyes when people looked at her. It took a long time before she joined the other children in the play yard. She didn't say much at home either, tried to behave well, tried not to annoy anybody, best not to be noticed at all. She watched her mother and father, somehow still strange people she had to adapt to and get along with. They were standing tall and talked about things she didn't understand. The winter was long, frost patterns glistened at the windows. But Enna loved little Sine and often spent hours playing right next to her crib, humming for herself and for the baby. When the children were sleeping, Lukas went to bed with Marlene. It's transitional, he would comfort her, soon we'll have saved enough, and then I'll restart the factory. Our life will change, you will see. And in the meantime I love you here, he said to her, and she smiled at him. Despite all the hardship they had to put up with, these may have been the most passionate years of their long marriage.

On Enna's eighth birthday someone happened to ring the doorbell. Enna went and opened it. A tall man in a rundown suit and a black hat stood there, surprisingly close. Enna blenched. The man gave her a friendly smile. He held a bag in his fist. Was he bringing a present? Was he coming to her birthday party? Neither he nor she said a word. A moment of mystery. As she later told me, it was as if she was doing something forbidden. She was spellbound. Then Marlene came rushing in from behind, jerked her back into the hallway, and closed the door up to a small crack. What do you want, Enna heard her hiss at this man. The answer was too hushed to be understood. Then the door closed bang shut. That's what Enna recalls from her eighth birthday. Later she wondered if this man was her father, if he had come to see her and give her a present. He was not allowed in. More likely he was just one of Marlene's suitors, one of those she'd dumped for lack of compatibility, as she put it. They kept calling or ringing the doorbell for weeks after she had discarded them. One of these men came back with a police officer, demanding that Marlene hand him over a sculpture he had given her as an engagement present before he realized that Marlene was married. It was a black marble bull with golden horns. Take it, Marlene snapped, I didn't like it anyway. The man looked deflated. The police officer gestured at him to take the bull and leave. And here, you can take this as well, another engagement present, Marlene yelled at him as they were walking downstairs. She threw a box of Camel cigarettes after them. It hit our neighbor, who was just coming up. How embarrassing!

When I arrive at the milk bar, Sam is texting on his phone. A big cheese platter, a bowl with butter and a breadbasket are sitting on the table next to a water pitcher, two plates, glasses, and silverware. Oh, you already ordered, I say. Yes, Sam responds, I hope it's alright with you. My lunch time is limited. Sorry for keeping you waiting, I concede, and tell him about the two cleaning ladies playing with his monitor, as if this was an excuse for my being late. He only shrugs. The warm bread melts the butter, the crust is crunchy, the cheese delicious! Sam is animated. A Californian tech company contacted him, he tells me, they are interested in his monitor! This could be a total game changer, he marvels, maybe I quit university, and we move to California. Would you want to do that? I wonder, and he says, Well it depends…But then I also would have to find a new job, I throw in. That shouldn't be difficult, he quickly asserts, there is a lot of fiction writing over there. Exactly, I say, the competition will be fierce…But Sam is already back at this new tech company, where he would have better conditions to do further research on his monitor, and given that he has a patent on it, it could also be interesting financially…On and on he goes, and I understand that he is excited, but I feel left aside. I know that Sam appreciates my work. In our earlier years he sometimes bemoaned my lack of an academic career, as if I had just taken an easy way out. But that's not true. For a while I had worked in the literature department, I had given seminars and spent a lot of time, actually too much time, in faculty meetings. I had tried to awaken some enthusiasm for literature in young students, but so many were just figuring out what was the necessary requirement for graduation. I felt discouraged. Then I signed up for a summer program in creative writing, and I felt inspired! These students were more curious, engaged, daring, they were dreaming of becoming successful writers. Only a few would make it, but nevertheless they tried.

That night when Jules came to our house, I did realize how upset he was. I know how hard it is to receive the editors' letters of refusal (if any at all). Every writer experiences this, and before I gave up, I did too. Most writers think the publisher just didn't bother to get immersed in the text sample, didn't read carefully enough, had a bad day, missed the hidden quality, etc. Or did they pick a misleading sample, should they have sent in different pages? Not so for Jules. That night he said, these publishers had a good point, he now thought his text was flawed – he'd thought it would hold, he'd hoped it might, but he was wrong. It was a mistake, he declared. I sensed that he waited for me, his teacher, to validate his epic (of which I hadn't seen a shred), to give him a convincing argument for why it was salvageable, a word which would rescue his ambitious project. I did try to say something that would prop him up. I suggested that it was much too early for any final judgement on his text, that he should keep working on it, that four publishers don't make the literary world. He just shook his head. He emphasized that he valued these publishers, their program, and if they declined to publish his text – or to discuss it, work with him on it – then it meant it was hopeless, not worth the trouble. It's null, nothing, he concluded and added: I feel terrible! Shaking his head he had averted his eyes and stared at the carpet between his feet. It pained me to see him so hurt. What could I have said that would have made a difference? I did reassure him that it was only now, after just having received the rejections from these publishers, that he felt so hopeless. I did explain that a publisher's decision reflects many things, not only literary criteria but also financial risk assessments, difficulties in program and marketing strategies, etc. I did suggest that for a while he put his text away, focus on other projects and then reassess it anew in three or six months. While I was saying this, maybe even urging him not to throw away what he had invested so much in for so long, I noticed that he shut down. It even seemed to me as if he threw me a hostile glance. He stayed silent for only a few moments. Then he said: I can't do that! And left.

Sam is gone. I want him here, but he is gone. He has signed the bill. All is paid. There is still bread and cheese, but they look wilted, and the butter has dissolved into a puddle of golden slurry. When I raise my eyes, I see Marlene and the little girl sitting in a corner of the milk bar with two big sundaes in front of them. The girl dangles her legs under the table, rhythmically banging one foot on the chair leg. Whenever she wants to pick up the spoon next to her ice cream bowl, Marlene's hand darts over and slaps it back to the table. They don't speak a word, just stare at each other as if in a struggle of wills. I want to rush over to interfere, want to shirtfront Marlene: leave this girl alone, let her enjoy her ice cream, but I feel strangely paralyzed, my arms and legs are heavy as lead, and my chest is so tight that I can hardly breathe. I feel bad about not helping the little girl, but I'm also curious how this power struggle will end. Now the waitress comes to my table and starts to clear away the dishes, and with a clumsy move she knocks over the water pitcher, which crashes down, and with a big bang breaks apart, splashing water and chunks of shards over the floor. I'm shocked, I see Marlene looking over, everybody is staring at the commotion. That's when the girl picks up her sundae and runs out of the milk bar.

Marlene twitches with her lips as if chewing words in her mouth. She often does this when she's annoyed. I walk over and challenge her: What was that all about? None of your business, she mutters. No, tell me, I insist. She looks up to me, and to my surprise, I see her eyes in tears. We had an agreement, she says. I ordered the bigger sundae for her, conditioned on her promising me to wait five minutes before eating it. She's only a kid, I demur. Marlene shakes her head. She promised, she insists, tears running down her cheeks. I'm baffled and sit down opposite her on the chair where the child sat just a moment ago, it is still warm. Why is this such a big deal, I ask her, softened and sorry for her being so upset. I made this mistake, my mother mumbles. I couldn't wait and was punished for it. I brought it onto myself. She looks at the door through which the girl ran out. What did you bring onto yourself? I ask her. Nothing, nothing, she whispers and shakes her head. Silently we sit and wait. The ice cream ball in her bowl is slowly sinking into a pond of white foam out of which it blossoms like a pink water lily. Go, my mother says, maybe you'll find the girl. She took the spoon. It belongs to the milk bar. Return it, if you can. My mother leans back and takes her hand off the table just when I wanted to touch it. She waves me off. Go, she repeats, and I get up and leave, step into the muted light of the courtyard, where all is quiet and lost in reverie. The little girl is sitting on the back of the cow licking her ice cream. She smiles and waves to me with her silver spoon.

CHARCOAL

Unexpectedly Sam opens the door and enters our room. I was just about to grade another paper. For the longest time I had been looking out of the window, fascinated with the heavy storm that is bending the tree in front of it, pushing its crown almost to the ground, and throwing its leaves all over the parking lot. Gusts of rain are lashing the barren land. Some mingy plants got ripped out of our balcony's flower boxes and flew away with the crows. No chance to get out of this place today. But Sam's conference takes place in the hotel's basement, which should be untroubled by any weather. So why is he not with his colleagues? He looks pale, agitated, desperate, up in arms. What is it? I ask him, feeling anxious. What are you doing here? Softly Sam closes the door as if not to awaken a sleeping child. They canceled my presentation, he then says in a flat, dry voice, with each word as if crushed between his thoughts. Slowly he puts down his briefcase, then keeps standing there, looking lost or unsure what to do, a tall thin frame of reference for too much to hold or let go. I get up from my chair to hug him, but with a small gesture of his hands he tells me to not, please not approach him, not now, and I stop. We're both standing three steps apart, waiting.

Officially it is because the fire has destroyed one conference room, Sam finally says. My lecture was planned in a different room not affected by the fire. However, yesterday they reshuffled the allocations and placed me where they now tell me I can't present. Meanwhile Peacock has claimed the room where I was supposed to give my talk. I had already installed my equipment. All who registered for my presentation will go there – now just to hear Peacock. What does that mean? I have to admit, I start thinking, he may be better than I thought. Maybe I was wrong to disregard his research and just focus on my monitor…Sam, I interrupt him, that's not true! You told me many times that Peacock is a schmuck. He's a mean, envious guy, he always competed with you, he would have knifed you down had he not found your research too valuable to miss out on availing himself of its results. Sam shakes his head. That's how it seemed to me. But why would they give him the big lecture hall, which they first assigned to me, and displace me to a much smaller room, which as it now turns out is completely carbonized? They basically kicked me out! Doesn't this tell me that they consider my work worthless? I've seen Sam discouraged once in a while, but never was he so despondent as he seems now. What can I say to lift him up…? It's not the quality of your work, I say.

You have a long list of publications and awards, Peacock's can't compare, not even remotely. He's just better connected than you, and his family foundation has given considerable grants to your institute, so what do you expect? Sam gives me a faint smile and finally sits down on our bed. Maybe I should quit, he says, just quit!

It is with some trepidation that Lukas unlocks the main door to the factory, which hasn't been opened in at least three or four years. Sensing his heart beating fast, he had crossed the courtyard, which is completely empty on this early Sunday morning. He had briefly stopped at the big chestnut tree and touched its trunk to feel the rough bark with his hands. The shadowy place under the tree has always been one of his favorite spots. When he was little he used to lean his back on this trunk and lightly rub his hands on the bark, and while enjoying the soft titillation on his bare skin, he followed the workers going in or coming out of the production hall, where the print machines were singing and humming, and the pallet trucks were circulating back and forth. Twelve noon, and his father appears at the smaller side entrance next to his office, and seeing Lukas squatting at the chestnut tree, he strolls over and asks: Want to join me for lunch at the canteen? Lukas jumps up, happy and eager to have lunch with his father amongst all the factory workers and employees. One day you'll be the director of this factory, his father had once said, and ever since Lukas has felt some ownership and a proud responsibility for all that went on at this place. He never got tired of watching how his father talked with his people, how he scrutinized the tone of the print color spreading on the paper, how he finetuned the pressure of the engraved copper cylinders, how he discussed the speed of the print machines with the mechanics, and how he evaluated the quality of the final product. Lukas was impressed. This whole process seemed so incredibly complex. Would he ever be able to do it as well as his father? He still isn't sure as he now unlocks the door and steps over the threshold into the quiet entry hall that has been waiting for him in all these years and still doesn't seem to give him much of a welcome. Streaks of sunlight drill their spare light through the dust-clogged windows, leaving most of the room in the dark. But Lukas doesn't need to see much to find his way around. It had been his intention to inspect the state of the building and the machines to assess how to structure the necessary repairs – if there was still anything usable at all. Yet he suddenly feels that this Sunday visit is not about that – rather it is about trying to find out how he feels in these halls…Is this the place where he wants to spend the rest of his life? Or had he just assimilated his father's wish that he would take over the factory? His father passed away. Whatever Lukas would do, no longer could he disappoint or please him. And with this in mind he realizes that his long-standing determination to honor his father's work has lost its ground. Now it is his task, his alone, to decide what to do with his life and with this factory. The suddenness of this insight almost throws him off kilter.

When I enter the elevator to get down to the basement, I see two of Sam's colleagues, who some years ago had once stayed overnight in our house. Both have since turned gray and a bit chubby. I smile at them and ready myself for a brief chitchat, but they only glance at me, seemingly uncomfortable, and mumble something that sounds like "sorry, sorry" or "condolences" – but that can't be: on what would they condole with me or be sorry for? Puzzled, I look away as if I don't know them. Silently we continue the ride, studying different corners of the elevator. When it finally stops with a jar, they politely step aside, even emphasize their courtesy by excessively pressing themselves against the elevator's wooden panels, as if I needed more than the whole width of the opening door to get out. With a vague nod I indicate my appreciation and step into the hallway, briefly stop at the display panel to see if I have to turn right or left, and then follow the signs to Marcus Aurelius. Sam's colleagues follow me at some distance. I hear their muffled conversation and their steps on the floor, and I wonder if they are eyeballing me from behind. Finally they seem to take a turn, the sound of their steps trails off. I continue along the hallway reading the names of the conference rooms: Augustulus, Tiberius,

Caligula, Claudius, Nero, Titus, Hadrian, and finally there it is: Marcus Aurelius, the big lecture hall that had been assigned to Sam's presentation before he got displaced.

The ceiling lamps throw their glistening light on endless rows of empty chairs that are standing, orderly packed like soldiers mustered to cheer their Führer – why would I think that! Shaking my head I approach the podium. Sam's bulky support frame with the attached projector towers over the speaker's desk, and it is only now that I notice the little girl, hanging with the hollows of her knees on an upper bar of the pipe buggy, lightly swinging back and forth. Her face is red and her eyes look as if ready to pop out. Come down, I immediately say, anxious that she may get hurt during her exercise. In response she grabs a lower bar with her hands and deftly rolls her small body in a somersault down to the floor. Sheepishly she looks at me. What are you doing here? I ask her. She only shrugs. This is a place for grown-ups, I say, trying to explain the inappropriateness of her presence here. But the girl clasps Sam's scaffolding with her hand as if to claim that this is her place! Now I understand, she used to play and exercise on this rack before Sam bought it. I see, I concede, and in return the girl digs two golden wrapped candies out of her pants pocket and offers me one. I'm touched. I thank her and sit down on the floor next to her. She too squats and carefully unwraps her candy. Sam bought this piece of equipment because he needs it for his work, I clarify. But since he won't be presenting here, we could bring it back to our room, or maybe he doesn't need it anymore, and you can have it back…(I know this is only my hope to not have this monster travel home with us.) The girl doubtfully looks at me while playing with a red plastic lighter, flicking it on and off, on and off. Are you allowed to have that? I ask her. Instead of a response, she suddenly jumps up, runs across the stage, and disappears behind the big curtain that lines the back of the tribune. Where is she going, I wonder before another question jolts me: did she cause the fire that destroyed Sam's conference room?

Suddenly the lights go off, all is dark. Hello? I softly call even though I know there is nobody, and I realize that I said it to no one other than myself, I do it again: Hello – hello? A strange sadness fills me up to my throat. I want to try it again, hello, but now my lips barely move, my voice is gone, I only exhale. It's okay. I can stay here on my own, I'm not afraid of the dark, I will just wait till they turn on the lights for the next presentation. My arms feel heavy, my head throbs. This isn't right. I lie down on the bare wooden floor that smells of detergent or wax. Feeling the cool planks under my hands gives me a sense of stability. Sam, come here, find me here, don't let me down! You can call me anytime, Enna says. But I don't want Enna. What could I have said, should I have done differently? Sam smiles. No, he doesn't smile, he looks pained, and it pains me so much to see him like this that I hear myself whimper. Be quiet, it's okay…But it's not. And I walk through the fields of my father's land, walk with the winds and the racing clouds, because I want to be there in time and not too late…

I had taken my car when my father called me to pick him up. He'd spent four months at a remote place in a tiny hut three hours from home. When I arrive, he's standing in the doorframe, his small luggage next to his feet, and before I can even get out of the car, he locks the front door, approaches the passenger side, opens the door and gets in. Thank you for coming out, he says, I'm ready to go. I am puzzled. Can't I see where you spent all this time? I ask. Not now, he replies, next time. Next time? Yeah, he says, I bought this hut. It's a great place to be when you want to clear your mind. I feel disappointed, even a bit miffed. As we slowly wind our way on the narrow dirt road to the next village, he asks me how things are going in my life, and how Enna is doing, and if Marlene is okay. I think he doesn't want to talk about himself. But I ask him anyway: What have you been doing all this time? Well… he says and launches into a long pause. Is he about to tell me that he will divorce Marlene, and if so, should I be the first to know? But after a while, to my surprise he says: You know, I always dreamt of being a writer. And in these months here

– my sabbatical, if you will – I did a fair amount of writing. I enjoyed it. But I figured out that I'm not a writer. I think I've come to grips with this discovery. Maybe it'll make my work in the factory easier, less wistful, less torn between what I have to and what I want to do. Or maybe I just lost a dream.

But how could he live without a dream? How can I? Do I? And what ever became of Mikki's love for stories? Are we a line of writers at a loss? Many years ago I committed myself to writing for half a year. In a small study I worked every morning on a novel about a man who was trying to write a novel. After 128 pages I hit a dead end. I failed even before my protagonist could fail. I didn't know why. Now I think, maybe I was writing about my father, a man who had given up on his dream. Yet a few years before he passed away, he'd asked me if I would help him write his memoir. He would start by telling me about his childhood, he said, for instance with his first memory, when he as a three-year-old ran towards his mother, but before he could reach her he stumbled and fell down. Shocked and with his knees grazed and bloody, he got up and said: *no hurt!* Did his mother come, hug, and comfort him? That wasn't part of his memory. The scene he recalled ended with *no hurt!* He braved his defeat, swallowed his pride, and stood on his own. Throughout his life he would remember: *No hurt!* At that point he stopped.

It's only natural to recoil from pain, isn't it? Maybe, Sam said, but you can't flee forever. And yet on this stormy day, I saw him walk across this barren land with no umbrella over his head, no raincoat over his shoulders, and no shoes on his feet. Squalls pushing him hard led him astray. Standing on our balcony, desperate and freezing, I called him, yelled and franticly waved. To no avail. Out of reach of my feeble voice he trudged over rock and marsh, through heather and fern, down and on, in circles, only in circles—but then he came back. He went to the bathroom, took a shower, crawled into bed, and slept for an hour. Looking at him I tried to tell myself that we would overcome…

We would grow old together. Tenderly holding hands, a bit wobbly on our feet – Sam, a decade older than I, every so often losing his balance, swaying but holding onto my arm – we would walk together in the dusk of our days, a four-footed manifest of our long life, joint in the belief that something good would still come out of our endeavors after all. At times we had talked about our various disappointments and where to take them in order to not being taken by them. More often we'd left it alone to simmer or sink into each of us at our own pace. The flame once burning hot would finally have settled in a warmth-sustaining glow, the embers wouldn't cool down too soon. We are temperamentally different. Sam will always hold onto the wound in his core and battle the crux of defeat; I instead over time slowly withdrew from my initial goals, still continuing my quest, now solely for the sake of its own value. I smile. Sam looks at me. He finds it sad that I won't aim anymore for public recognition. Here, I disagree. I feel equanimous. Still enjoying what I am doing, I steadily continue, whereas he is shaken by bursts of hope and bouts of misery. Either way, I think, our steadiness will suffice because together we walk that line.

Only sparsely illuminated by the red EXIT sign above its entrance, the Titus room lies as black as the coal cellar of my childhood. Everything is charred to the bone! The chairs are stacked in bulky clusters, their contorted legs entangled and glued together with what looks like the melted plastic of the seats' cushions. The burned carpet has crumbled off the concrete floor and is lumped in heaps between puddles of fire water and quench foam. The place reeks of soot and pungent chemicals. Had I ever thought I could fix this for Sam's presentation – this is impossible! Anyway, Titus would have accommodated not more than forty or fifty people, while Marcus Aurelius could certainly hold several hundred. How offensive for Sam to have been relegated to this place! It now seems like a stroke of luck that he didn't have to present here. I'm just about to leave when I hear a soft cough from the back of the room. I take a few steps in and try to pierce the darkness with my eyes, but before I can detect anything,

I hear Sam calling me. Sine, come here, he whispers. I'm shocked. Sam, I exclaim, what are you doing here? Shush, he says, nobody is supposed to be here. The arson is still being investigated, the place is considered hazardous. Let's be quiet, not to raise the janitor's suspicion. Slowly I feel my way to the back of the room where Sam is sitting on the floor. Sit down, he orders, and I sit next to him.

This cubbyhole is where they placed my presentation, Sam states. I may be on the brink of one of the most important developments in the field of neurotechnologies – and they exile me here. I don't get it! He shakes his head. Even though his inner revolt is palpable, he appears to be clear and composed. So I dare to ask him: what is it, actually, that you are working on, what is this monitor doing? Well, Sam says, and seems to search for a simple way to put it, you could call it a *mind reader*. I look at him trying to figure out if he wants to take me for a ride. You can't be serious, I counter, that's fantasy! No, Sam says, it can be done. Already now neuro-technology can read and visualize what a person sees or even only wants to look at. This technology enables quadriplegics to lift a limb or to move a cursor on the computer screen merely by thinking of it. Imagine how essential it would be to have the technology for not only reading but also writing to the brain, for instance when you want to communicate with patients suffering from the locked-in syndrome. There is already non-invasive brain-reading technology – like the use of infrared light or ultrasonic waves – which successfully transcribes what occurs during all sorts of mental processes. It is relatively simple and straightforward to experiment with the visual, speech, and motor cortex or with thought processes that are conscious. But why shouldn't it work as well with unconscious processes, with memories and dreams, and even with thoughts that we have picked up from others without being consciously aware of them – like unconscious communications or thought transferences, things people usually call telepathy? That's what my monitor is about. My algorithms not only integrate the results of heterogeneous research data – which alone wasn't an easy feat – but go beyond that and reach data deep in the unconscious, recreate what we have dreamt of, forgotten, or were never aware of. I understand that this sounds crazy, but I think it's possible. Sam rolls his monitor from one hand to the other, back and forth, back and forth. I sense he is waiting for me to say something. I feel numbed and uneasy. It's huge, I eventually acknowledge, what a journey! He nods and says: now I have a plan!

No, Sam had no plan and nowhere to go. Disheartened and spent, he withdrew into a shell of silence. I saw him sitting with his hands over his head, cautiously groping about as if in search of an idea. At night he blew smoke at his laptop. In the morning I found him asleep in his office chair. My touch would startle him. What? What! Impatiently he yelled at me and then apologized. I pretended not to notice that he wasn't working. Or was he? He used up stacks of print paper and ordered more. I wanted to help. He wouldn't let me. The months went by. Sometimes my thoughts flew with the sun to the sea and the beach and the soft hills of Tuscany, but my heart anxiously stuck at home with my man unmoored, waiting for a move, a resolve, a breakthrough. And then one morning when I came into the kitchen, Sam was sitting at the table, a cup of coffee in front of him, and his face as clear as ever. I found the algorithm, he said, I solved the problem. And I was so exhausted, I could only cry.

Here is my plan, Sam says, and extends his open hands as if serving it to me on a silver platter. I'll attend Peacock's lecture, and at the end I'll ask him questions he won't be able to answer. I know where the challenging points of my research are, he doesn't. I'm certain that he hasn't even noticed that there remain serious weaknesses in my conception, on which he's based his claim. He'll be perplexed. That'll reveal who he is! Sam's plan makes me uncomfortable. You want to pay deference to him in order to expose his limits? What good would it do to you? I ask, trying to hide my doubts, but worries make my voice quiver. Sam droops. I don't know, he admits, maybe it's silly. Silently we sit in the dark. The sharp stench of burnt materials gives me a headache. I should have rooted him on. He wanted to claim what was his. Hurt but still alive he'd screened his options with none of them great, and now I've squashed the only one that seemed viable to him. Let's leave tomorrow, I suggest and take his hand. He withdraws it. Or at least let's go to our room, I suggest. Yeah, he says, why don't you go ahead, I'll follow in a bit. I hesitate, don't want to leave him at this stony-broke place? But he gently nudges me on. Go, he says, I'll just finish my train of thought here. Then I'll come up. So I get up and walk towards the door, and when I turn around to briefly wave my hand at Sam, I see next to him the little girl, flicking her pocket lighter on and off, on and off.

In a dark, broad-striped suit, a pink-on-gray dotted tie over his white shirt, and a black crocodile briefcase with a golden clasp in his hand, the banker enters Lukas's office, comes to a halt at the door, looks around the room, and only then seems to notice my father, who had risen from behind his desk to formally greet his guest with due respect. The banker says hello and sits down without having been invited to do so. Both men silently face each other. No water, coffee, or whisky is offered. Lukas doesn't want to. He feels shaken down by his lender. He doesn't know if this will be a new opening of their dispute or the end of their collaboration. The banker opens his briefcase and pulls out a stack of forms. In principle it's easy, he declares. You sign these papers, and we leave you alone for now. Lukas only briefly looks at the papers and asks: Is this what you sent me last week? The banker smiles and nods. Lukas struggles to keep his emotions in check. His hands tremble. So you want to exchange a default of just eighty thousand for a fifty-one percent ownership of my company? The banker doesn't move nor does he respond. Or, more likely, he comes up with a flurry of seemingly tempting but nonsensical arguments for why this is an excellent opportunity to put the company on sound footing, etc. Lukas doesn't waver. I call this attempted extortion, he retorts. If you don't come up with a more reasonable offer, I will inform the authorities and the press. The banker slips his stack of papers back into his briefcase, which he carefully closes at the golden clasp. As you wish, he says and smiles again—but more likely he never stopped showing his sleazy smile. He gets up, ambles to the door and leaves the office. On the chair's cushion where he'd just been seated, two damp impressions mark the shape of his thighs.

When I get back to our room I'm surprised to find Lilli sitting at the desk reading my students' papers. What are you doing, I ask her, and how did you get in? Oh, she says, the door was open, the girls from housekeeping were just cleaning your room. They're actually quite nice. I chatted with them. I want them to like me. We'll need their support, once Cocky and I have moved into the tower. I've been waiting for you. Do you want to come up with me and have a look at our suite to give me your ideas about decorating it? Completely oblivious to my annoyance with her for being here and snooping through my stuff, she beams at me like a little kid, and I can't help but reward her with a smile back. I love her when she is as happy as she seems now, and even though it bothers me that she is so frank about her new love-nest, I'm also curious to see it. I say okay. Enthused, Lilli jumps up and marches straight to the door. Don't forget your keys, she instructs me, as if I were a kid.

The elevator takes us only to the 15th floor, then we have to walk another flight of stairs up, 37 steep steps I count. That'll keep you fit, I say to Lilli, who is wheezing and panting in front of me. Don't say that, she moans, these steps were almost a deal breaker. But then she proudly opens the door to her new home. Look at that! A spacious octagonal room opens with windows all around and so much light that I can't stop myself from saying: Here you can really be on cloud nine. Lilli doesn't respond. Maybe she didn't notice. She walks, almost dances into the room, with every step clanging on the wooden floor and her hands waving here and there in pure delight. Finally she stops at a coffee table, and noticing that I just keep standing at the door, she waves me in. Only now do I see Peacock sitting on a sofa opposite the hotel's night porter, both playing chess. Peacock, squinty and lurking like a cat ready to pounce, watches as the night porter seems frozen on the spot with his hand hovering over the chessboard as if in search of a way to wiggle himself out of a dangerous trap. Both men don't seem to notice that we've entered. It is as if we aren't there…or they aren't here? Lilli pulls at my sleeve. It's a wonderful room, isn't it? It's what I wanted all my life! But where will I hang my art? There are almost no walls…

My mother loved art. She used to hang pictures on our walls, keep them for a few months, and then exchange them with others. Some were her own paintings, most of them done with charcoal; others she'd found at flea markets or in galleries; she also made friends with a few artists, who lent her their pictures. She didn't mind returning them after a while. But there was one small picture she always kept: it was Enna's and showed my father, mother, her and me lined up like organ-pipes riding on a horse. Enna was only eight years old when she drew it, and it was amazingly detailed and artistic. Mother hung it next to her desk, and it still was there when I left home. Where might it be now? Would she drive a nail into heaven to hang it there? Peacock, looking up at my mother, says, I don't need pictures, I just need to look at you: nothing could be more gorgeous! My mother smiles.

For as long as Marlene can think back, she's been searching for something yet never could quite grasp what it could be.

Her quest was a chameleon. When she was young it was for a grand future showing itself in changing scenarios. Later it could be for a free afternoon with no set time to come home, no need to take care of Enna, Sine or Lukas. At other times it seemed to be about a sparkling life of purpose and recognition or creativity and discovery. And when nothing came to mind that would anchor her restless heart, she would yearn for something about the old days when the sky had no limits, and she was young and beautiful and slaphappy, her unruly self, deliciously foolish! Those days…Bertram had led her on, hadn't he? Marlene squeezes the dust cloth in her hand. Lukas reads the newspaper. What does he know – he has no idea! Her hand automatically wipes the sideboard, back and forth, back and forth. Bertram, so handsome, and from a wealthy family! One day he said, I enlisted in the army, I hope they'll send me to Paris, to all those beautiful girls. He winked at her. Don't you dare, she snapped back, only jokingly! But the needle of jealousy had pierced her – still does. You have no idea what I – I might be doing here while you are gone, she challenged him. Bertram laughed. Go have fun, he lightly suggested, derisively adding: but you won't, you'll sit here, waiting for me and my letters, crying your eyes out! Not for you, she countered, pretending pride. I am beautiful, she thought, what do I care if he's philandering in Paris! But she felt so bad, so ugly, so unfairly put on the spot. Lukas folds the newspaper shut. Stop that dusting, come here, sit with me, he says tenderly, smiling at her. Just let me finish first, she grumbles. Bertram left. He looked dashing in his tight gray uniform, a sharp-edged cap restraining his blond shock of hair, a bit lofty maybe, but adorable! On that day, his last, she'd given him a small token wrapped in shiny paper. A picture he'd taken: she standing upright in her bathrobe, her hair flying in the wind, a good picture it was, and she'd put it into a tight leather frame. Bertram hadn't opened his present. He'd looked surprised, or was it embarrassed? Thanks, he'd just said, I'll look at it later, and added, I may not be able to take it with me – restrictions, you know? But thanks anyway! And fleetingly he'd kissed her, a kiss askew, half on her lips, half on her cheek; it left a wet mark, a cold spot she hadn't dared to wipe off. His last kiss. He left, was sent to the Eastern Front, and two weeks later he was dead. So there! Lukas looks at her. Yesterday on my way home I saw a beautiful dress in Madam's showcase, he says, I thought you'd look gorgeous in it! Shall we go and see if you'd like it? Tomorrow? Marlene tears up but quickly catches herself. Still sulking a bit, she says, let's see what tomorrow looks like. Despite craving it, she doesn't like it when Lukas is spoiling her. She takes the dust cloth to the kitchen closet. When she turns around, Lukas is standing right behind her. He takes her in his arms and kisses her neck, gently rubbing her back and moving his hand under her sweater.

All these stories, it's hard to grade them. I fulfill my duties by commenting on things like the overall structure, choice of metaphors, persuasiveness, etc. Does it help? Jules always got the best grades. Once he challenged me about it; he submitted a ridiculously sloppy paper, a mere provocation. I handed it back to him with no grade, suggesting it was a mistake. He smiled and left it at that. Igor was standing nearby watching our short exchange. No grade, he mused aloud, is this bad, or is this an invitation to redo it? He fiercely competed with Jules. Probably he knew that Jules was the better writer. But with three early publications by the time he came to my course, Igor behaved as if he was the more promising one. He made snarky comments when Jules spoke, questioned him openly, claimed prior rights to a thought Jules contributed, which could amount to almost an accusation of plagiarism. In these moments Jules was gracious, acknowledged Igor's contributions even if they were on shaky grounds. Igor was good but not much above average. To me he appeared cranky, resentful, cocky. But Jules liked him. They often hung out together, and once they jointly wrote a play. They never showed it to me, and I don't know what came out of it. It's delicate to give feedback. I want my students to know what I think without discouraging them. Is their writing as good as they want it to be? Or are they calculating their effects on the reader, distracted by current trends, aiming at a particular publisher (which never works as intended)? It took me years before I was able to give critical feedback in a constructive way. I think now I can do it.

I haven't seen Enna in a while. Maybe we can meet at the bar and have a Campari. I call her room. A male voice coughs into the receiver and then says, Hello? I'm totally surprised. Oh, isn't this – I want to – Enna? There is no such person, the voice says, seemingly annoyed. But isn't this room 923? I insist, and impatiently he growls, yes it is, and hangs up before I can utter an apology. Did I mis-remember Enna's room number? Did Enna change her room? Did she leave without letting me know? That can't be! I call the reception desk and ask about her. The person who talks with me is reluctant to provide information, but when I explain that I am inquiring about my sister, the receptionist says she sees a letter in my box waiting for me and asks if she should send it up to my room. I decline, saying that I'll pick it up. I take the stairs down, just for a little bit of exercise – not sure if I'll take them back up later on. Why would Enna leave early and without talking to me? Had she fallen sick? Without wanting to trouble me, she may have thought it best to return home and see her primary care physician. She looked tired lately, sluggish, not her usual self. I should have asked her. Maybe she thought I was too preoccupied with my own things. Had I offended her – by neglect or by pushing too hard for what I wanted?

The receptionist looks at me funny, as if she knew something and wouldn't say it. With a smirk she hands me a blank hotel envelope and then turns back to her computer. I go to the bar and order a Campari – maybe Sam will join me later. I'm anxious to read Enna's note, but afraid to open the envelope. I put it on the counter and watch the barman prepare my drink and pour peanuts in a bowl. I'm the only person sitting at the bar. At the end of the day this place will be crowded with all the congress participants. The barman places my glass and the peanuts in front of me and says: Awful weather today, isn't it! I take a sip of my Campari and wait till he goes back to cleaning a stack of dirty glasses in the sink. Then I open the envelope and pull out a notice from Randy's Road-runner Rentals informing me that since I haven't returned the tandem after seven days, they have started to charge my credit card on a weekly basis until I return it. The tandem! I had completely forgotten about it! And where actually is it? I'd left it in front of the hotel, but I haven't seen it lately. And is it already seven days ago that I rented it out? And where is Enna?

I decide to deal with the Randy business right away. I don't want them to charge me for something that I don't need or even think of. Come with me, Enna, I plead, help me bring back this heavy tandem, it's not made for one person only. I leave the hotel and cross the forecourt to get to the shed, where, as I had noticed, they park the limousines overnight. At the front door I see the chauffeur, slumped down on a chair, his chin sunk to his chest, asleep. Next to him on a chest of drawers is a big birdcage with a white cockatoo sitting on a piece of a branch. What is this precious bird doing at this shabby shack? Shouldn't it be in the hotel lobby? The cockatoo looks at me as I'm standing there looking at it. Maybe it was left here by its owner, one of those wealthy permanent guests, who may have died without having deposited any information about his relatives' whereabouts, and now they were stuck with the bird…The cockatoo suddenly caws *Goodbye!* Now the chauffeur wakes up, scowls at me and growls: what do you want! I explain that I am looking for the tandem. Immediately he jumps up, as if I had given him great news, and gestures me to follow him to the back of the barrack, where he points to a makeshift tent pinned to the wall. There it is, he says, take this down! And he adds: You owe me the parking fee of 10 dollars a day, makes 70 dollars. I resent his charge, and I'm not sure what to do with this tent, but before I can even say something, the chauffeur tears the rag off the wall and unveils the tandem leaning against what seems like an elaborate doll house showing little pieces of furniture, pots, pans, and pillows, as well as a number of teddy bears, ducklings, Mickey Mouse figurines, and wind–up play cars neatly organized on three flimsy shelves, the highest of which reaches the tandem's saddles. On the floor, the little girl sits with her legs crossed, a baby doll in her lap. She looks at me with big eyes.

I don't want to take the tandem out of this construction. But the chauffeur brutally rips it off the wall. Everything in the dollhouse crashes and tumbles. The little girl sends off a piercing shriek, leaps up and darts off with her speedy little feet as if flying away. She is gone, and I'm shocked. Take it, the chauffeur threatens me, I'll put the charge on your bill. Struggling to push the tandem out of the garage I notice that it has a flat tire. When I ask the chauffeur if he has an air pump, he just waves me through the door. *Goodbye*, the cockatoo snorts.

Maybe the tire wasn't flat after all, because I can ride the tandem quite easily. In fact, the road towards Watertown seems slightly aslope, and the bicycle rolls almost by itself. The wind is chilly, I should have prepared myself for the worst, but I'm not going to return now that I've already come so far. And then I hear Enna whisper in my ear, as if she had somehow managed to jump onto the saddle behind me, I don't know how, and I won't question it. I'm so glad you are here, I say back over my shoulder, I was worried you had left me. And we speed through the open fields that stretch to the horizon right into the deep hanging clouds. I think I should plan how to return from Watertown. Maybe Sam could take a limousine and pick me up. But where is Sam? I haven't seen him all day. I'll definitely have to call him when I'm at Randy's. I hope he'll have time for me now. And then at some point I spot my father sitting on a milestone at the side of the road, and I mention this to Enna, but she doesn't understand where to look. When I pass, my father smiles and waves to me, and then I know he has my back all the way down to Watertown.

ENIGMA

—— · ——

When will we go home? I ask Sam, who is sitting opposite me at our desk, brooding over a pad full of small numbers, words and sketches scribbled down within the last hour. Hmm, he says, and doesn't even look up. Randy's charged me for a second week, I argue, I'm sorry, I totally forgot about the tandem and somehow lost track of time. But didn't you say the conference would last only five days? Now Sam looks up and says: I know what you mean, to me it also feels like we've been here forever. And yes, I agreed to leave early, but now I think I want to stay till the end. His response takes my breath away. So when will it be over? I whisper. On Saturday, Sam mumbles, again hunkering over his pad. On Saturday…I marvel, but I don't know what day today is, and I'm too embarrassed to ask him. Clearly, he doesn't want to be bothered right now. I better be quiet and grade another paper.

Yet instead I look at the monitor that is sitting on the table between us. It is softly humming. *A mind reader!* What a wild idea Sam is chasing. I feel only half convinced of what he had explained to me. Maybe it's totally beyond feasibility, and that's why the organizers kicked him off the program. Now I feel bad about doubting him and siding with the Peacocks of his field. Sam was always off mainstream, he'd told me. When he was little, he rarely was out and about with friends. He rather hung around the living room where his mother worked on the typewriter or was on the phone with her authors. She translated fiction from German, French and Italian into English. She was very gifted with languages. Her mother was French, her father Italian, she'd grown up in Germany and moved with her family to the United States at the age of ten. Sam wondered why she only spoke English with him. But she relished her work as a translator. She could get lost in it for hours, her cheeks red, her hair undone and all her pencils chewed up at the ends. When she had finished a first draft, she would have long phone conversations with the authors about the use of certain words, the sound and rhythm of a phrase, or the subtle connotations of an idiom. Sam loved to hear his mother speak in these foreign languages. Quietly he would sit in the hallway next to the open door, trying to follow the fragments of their exchanges without really understanding them. He told me that he filled in the blanks, gathered their meaning, even pictured his mother's interlocutors, and often, he asserted, he came pretty close. He blushed over his claim. He told me that once in a sudden surge of anger, he'd shot a book he was supposed to read for school at his mother. It hit her in the head. She gasped and reflexively threw up her hands, thereby losing control of her mug, and the hot coffee spilled onto the table drowning the manuscript she was working on. Panicked, she jumped up trying to save what was still dry. She was so preoccupied with her rescue operation that she didn't notice the blood running from a laceration on her left temple down her cheek. But Sam saw it. Aghast and frightened, he found himself locked in a paralyzing tremor from which he eventually could wrench a thin piercing shriek. Then he fainted.

Sam lifts his head, looks at me and says: What are you thinking about? Shouldn't you grade your students' papers? I nod and try to give him a smile, but I feel numb and puzzled and strangely disoriented. Sam puts his pencil down. I think I know what I'll do, he says, and looks at me with an air of resigned determination. I'll give my lecture right here in our hotel room. I'll send people a link to remotely join me for a life-demonstration of the monitor. And that'll be simultaneously my pitch for the California tech company. Hmm, I say, and look around trying to picture how we could arrange things in this room to make it look like a professional setting. What do you think? Sam urges me, and I feel he needs my support, but I'm not sure about his plan. People shouldn't see our bed, I caution, it would be awkward. That's secondary, Sam replies, the bigger problem is how to pick a random person to demonstrate the working of the monitor. If you or I made ourselves available for that, people would think of it as a setup. It would be much more convincing if I could pick someone ad hoc. His idea upsets me. What do you mean, I challenge him, are you thinking of reading my or your or anybody's mind in front of an audience? Sam shrugs. Yeah, that may be necessary, he ponders. But you can't do this, I assert, thoughts are private! If people's thoughts were revealed and exposed, they could feel publicly humiliated or betrayed, be threatened or charged of all sorts of things, who knows? I would never accept being your guinea pig in such an experiment, maybe not even just for you alone. Sam looks at me and nods. I understand, he says, I feel the same, and I have struggled with this problem for quite a while. My research could yield huge benefits in the medical field, but it could also be misused say by state agencies, the police, or even commercially…I haven't figured out yet how to prevent that.

And then Sam thinks of my father, somehow I know this, or I want Sam to think of him, because I believe my father came to grips with the setbacks he experienced. He could be angry, but never gave up. Quietly and often over a long period of time, he considered his options and eventually decided how to proceed. That's my father. See, he now says to Sam, and points to the new print machine that is running at high speed shooting out a band of white wallpaper with a delicate light-gray design. I've just started a new wallpaper series, which I call the Enigma Collection. He hands Sam a prototype. How do you like it? Sam casts a brief glance at it. Looks intriguing, he responds, and wonders what this is about. Lukas steps closer to Sam to let a pallet transporter pass. There are many different ways of publishing, he says. Take this sample sheet: just a nice design, isn't it? But if you study it closely you discover small letters; more precisely: what looks like a random squiggle is micro-text, little stories, each no longer than a paragraph, observations of everyday life, random musings, dreams, ideas…I've written them by hand, and now they are printed, published, if you will, they are *the writing on the wall* he quips, and peers over to Sam expecting his response. Sam is astounded. He scrutinizes the paper in his hands, but the letters are too small to be read. I reduced the size electronically, Lukas explains, without a magnifying glass it's hard albeit not impossible to read this. What an idea, Sam says, and looks at Lukas, who impishly smiles. But people will crop the wallpaper according to their needs and room sizes, so the texts will be all garbled, he demurs. That doesn't matter, Lukas responds, the enigma exists whether it's detected or not. The buyers may see just a decorative design and never gather that they have surrounded themselves with my stories. Still it could do them some good. Maybe one night the eyes of a sleepless person will wander along these lines on the wallpaper and will be affected by one of my stories to fall asleep with. What an idea, Sam repeats, and tries to imagine such a moment. Now what about you, Lukas asks, pulling at Sam's sleeve, would you give me some of your scribbles and sketches as a wallpaper design for my Enigma Collection? I could print them mirror-inverted, which would make them even more mysterious. To me your equations and drawings and your handwriting look like an intriguing pattern! Maybe in blue? Sam is taken aback! What an idea, he reiterates, you want people to plaster their walls with my ideas? Yes, Lukas confirms, they won't know what they have, but nevertheless it may inspire them. Sam is completely flummoxed. I'll think about it, he promises. My father nods. Both smile at each other like impish conspirators.

The streetlights pierce through the shutters, spread over the doorframe, bounce from wall to wall. Stars rain from above and sprinkle the ground whenever a car drives by. Sam's curly hair brushes the twigs and tendrils on the wall, a forest with shrubs and weeds. Big snakes sneak towards his oh-so-tiny body. His mother says, you are a man, and he looks at his hand and can't understand. The grandfather clock in the hallway rings three. The house door opens and softly closes. The corridor's light flashes in through the slit under the door. Moving shadows mingle with hushed voices. Mother's coming home. She's not alone. Sam hears a strange voice, a man's harrumph prompting mother's suppressed laughter. Sam feels hot, furious and lonely. He turns towards his shrubs, crawls into his forest, seeks refuge in the jungle's caverns. But the woods ache, the climbers rustle and whisper, the night birds shriek and chirp *tee-hee*…! Sam pulls the pillow over his ears, and yet…What…! Oh! Come on! Shoes drop to the floor. The bedsprings gasp. Watch it! Sam starts humming: birdy-birdy goes to school, makes me look just like a fool, birdy-birdy lalala…A woman moans, a man groans. Birdy-birdy…A police car races through the night, lashing the room with blue strokes. A truck has killed a girl. The girl lies on the street. Her name is unknown.

As far as I know, Jules had a girlfriend, Marian. He once mentioned her in passing, emphasizing that she was a pediatrician on a tenure track and worked a lot, which gave him space for writing, often deep into the night. Had they lived together? Had she read his texts? Had she kept them? Had she known how despondent he was after he had received the last rejection, the one from his own publisher? Had she been at work when he vanished? Or would she still have been back in time to make him stay and live on? In the early morning hours when she enters the apartment after a long night shift, all is dark and quiet. Rather than heading straight into the bedroom and slipping under the comforter next to Jules, she goes into the kitchen to fix herself a hot chocolate. She's had a stressful night; one of her patients had suddenly and for no discernible reason spiked a high fever, had difficulties with breathing and almost went into cardiac arrest – she had worked with her team for hours and managed to save the kid. All night there wasn't a moment to eat or drink or even sit down. Now she settles at the kitchen table feeling her limbs heavy as lead. She sips at her hot chocolate. Having been able to contain her angst of losing this child and make the right decisions feels reassuring. She is humbled by the force of nature she'd barely been able to readjust that night, and she knows that there will be other incidents when she will not succeed. But having given her little patient the chance of living his long life makes her smile. Will he retain some memory from his early brush with death? Will his parents overcome their worries and relax again into treating him like a healthy kid? What will become of him? Over such musings she falls asleep, her head sunken down on her tired arm, her hand still holding the empty cup.

Sam collects his papers, stuffs everything in his briefcase, and heads to the door. See you later, he says, and steps into the hallway, but then he briefly turns around and asks: Shall we have dinner tonight, just you and me, somewhere far from this conference circus? His suggestion immediately gives me wings. Yes, I respond, that's a lovely idea! Sam smiles. Why don't you find out if there is a good restaurant in Watertown and make a reservation for 8 PM? Shall do, I say, and off he goes. How nice to have a date with Sam! I lean back in my chair feeling happy and light. He never forgets about me. As much as he may be involved in his research, he keeps me in mind and turns to me before the end of the day. Maybe I can surprise him… I could rearrange our room for his video conference! Yes, I could set it all up as if he were speaking in a big auditorium. I could push the bed into this corner… and drag the wardrobe over to the window, which would free one side of the room; I would take the pictures off that wall and pull the table right in front of it; I would have to cover the table with our bedsheet, because its squiggly Louis XIV style doesn't fit to a neuroscience presentation, definitively not; the white sheet would completely cover the table and make it look like a normal podium, yes; however, I would need another sheet to cover this flowery wallpaper (awful!) – guess I could pilfer a fresh sheet from one of the housekeeping trolleys parked in the hallways, yes, and I would pin the sheet to the wall (maybe I could find a hammer and some nails in the hotel garage?), and if Sam then positions his laptop at a good angle, so that it would just show him and part of the white wall behind him, and if he would use a split screen for his projections and PowerPoint presentations or whatever, it could really work. All enthused I jump up.

However, the bed is heavy or stubborn, I can't move it. I need help! I call Marlene. Immediately she picks up. Mother, I need your help, I blurt out, and she seems pleased to hear that and says, of course, I'll come down to you in a second! And in fact, a few moments later and without bothering to first knock at my door, she enters and right behind her the little girl marches in, the empty plastic bag in one hand, the spoon from the milk bar in the other. What do *you* want, I ask the kid, and feel irritated because my project doesn't suit a small child – or does it, rather…? Let her be, Marlene says, she's with me. It irks me that my mother claims to be with the little girl who I thought belonged to me, but I can't deal with this now that I want to transform our bedroom into a conference hall before Sam comes back. Still I can't stop myself from putting forth that the girl has the spoon from her sundae. I know, my mother says in a slightly condescending tone, I think she can have it. And looking around she asks me: what do you need my help with?

For the next two hours we work on the transformation of the hotel room. As it turns out, the little girl is of great help, because after my mother and I had tried hard yet in vain to push the bed from its prominent to a more marginal place, the little girl crawls under it and discovers that its legs are locked to the floor. She also finds a screwdriver in the lumber-room on our hotel floor and manages to take out twelve big screws together with their fixtures. While she is working down there, Marlene goes and snatches two fresh bed sheets from the storeroom, and I take down the golden framed reproduction of Jacques-Louis David's coronation of Napoleon with Joséphine kneeling in front of him. We nail the bed sheet to the wall, taut and neat, it looks great! When the girl finally reappears from under the bed, she again has fluff all over her hair and clothes (they never clean under the bed!), but she beams with pride and shows us a silver pen, which she found in the dark. Ah, Marlene comments, that's the kind of thing I thought I would give Peacock as a present after his lecture tomorrow. I wonder if she is thinking of taking the pen from the little girl and quickly assure her that since she found it she can keep it – just to make clear that it won't end up in Peacock's pocket. Marlene briefly looks at me but doesn't say a word. Exhausted, we sit down on the bed and look at the podium, where Sam will give his online presentation.

Picnic near the Black Forest. They put bread, cheese and cold meat on paper plates over a blanket. Enna gets apple juice, mother has white wine. Happy vacation, Marlene says, and they touch glasses. I am in the hospital with an ear infection. Father is in Chicago on a business trip. Just the two of them remain. Silently they eat. The sun is warm. Now we can talk, Enna thinks, but as much as she wants to engage her mother in a conversation, nothing comes to mind. At some point she feels like saying, Rosane's father got a new car, but that seems just stupid. Marlene has turned her face to the sun. What is she thinking? She looks like an Egyptian

Pharaoh, beautiful and unreadable. After a while mother turns to her and asks, Are you glad that school is over? Enna nods, hiding that it brings tears to her eyes for no reason. Three yellowjackets come humming over the turkey breast, and for a while they both wave their napkins to fight them off. Finally Marlene suggests putting the meat and cheese back into the plastic containers. The suntan lotion smells like sweet oranges. Marlene announces that she wants to take a short nap and lies back. Enna puts her book on her lap, but doesn't feel like reading. The sun burns hot on her face. The principal had said: You cheated on your test. He didn't expect her to answer. Enna had felt herself blushing. He had held her paper in front of her eyes as if to stick it in her face. She stood stiff and still next to her desk as he had ordered her to do. The principal smelled of garlic. Her classmates whispered and giggled behind her. I've noticed that about you, he continued, you are a fraud! His voice threatened to crack. This can't possibly be your essay. You plagiarized! And then he read it aloud: An important person in my life – he is tall and dark, far and unknown. He taught me to dream. I dreamt of him being there next to me where I struggle to pass what's in my way. He's there, not here. Were I to forget him, I'd be doomed. So I think of his hands, which carry the stick. I picture his feet, which won't come my way. His voice is hoarse from holding his calm. Once, only once, did he scream, once when I cried. It made me stop right away. He won't forget – forget about me…The principal put the paper down on Enna's desk. Then he hit her, just once, briefly but sharply hit her cheek. Then he left the classroom. Mother is elsewhere. Enna looks across the lawn right into the softly swinging shadows along the edges of the Black Forest.

Good for you, Marlene says, as if concluding a long train of thought, you're supporting Sam with his presentation. He may even get a bigger audience online than Cocky will have in Marcus Aurelius. She crosses her legs and fidgets with her short pencil skirt. Still, it's not fair, I counter, Sam was supposed to get the big lecture hall, not Peacock! It wasn't his decision, my mother defends her new lover, for unknown reasons the congress administration rearranged everything. Marlene looks at me as if to win me over, but I won't budge. Guess Peacock worked it out that way, I snap at her, and regret having asked her for help. But mother puts her hand on my arm, slightly squeezing it. Let it be, she softly says. These things happen. What's important is what you do next. Sam came up with a great solution, and you are helping him realize it. That's nice! I look at my mother and feel a bit mollified. Sam fights for his ideas, she continues, and he should. I wish you had tried harder to stick to yours as well, she then adds. This startles me. What do you mean, I charge, and feel ready for a fight. Well, my mother drawls, slightly swaying her head as if to indicate the doubtfulness of what she's about to say, of course it's okay and respectable to teach students writing fiction. But what happened with your own writing? Where did that go? You used to write so well. Why did you give it up? Should I have done more to encourage you? Did I do something wrong? Marlene looks as if she were ready to take any blame, but I am so surprised by her validation of my early writing ambitions that I don't know what to say. You see, my mother continues, I too had my dreams. I loved to paint. I wanted to learn the basic techniques from a painter. I told you about it. But I wasn't courageous enough. When Enna came, my life got more complicated. And then you came. I don't even know if I wanted children, actually I think I didn't, but you both came along, and I had to take care of you, and Lukas demanded attention, and life went on, time went by, you grew up and left, and there I was sitting by myself in our quiet living room wondering: *what did I do with my life?* What happened to my dreams? Did I have the talent to be a painter? Did I squander it? Could I still try? So many questions, but before I ever could answer, your father came home from the factory, we had a glass of wine together, a nice evening, and everything went on… just everyday life. Recently I've started to read biographies and memoirs of artists, which is interesting! Many of them weren't good companions; if they married, sooner or later they got divorced. If they were good, they were in love with their art. It made them successful. Did it make them happy? Maybe they weren't interested in being happy. In fact, many of them led a torturous life. So there! And yet… My mother takes a deep-drawn sigh. In the dim light coming from the window, she looks at all these options gone by that from the distance of old age now resurface, and I feel the throbbing pain of those lost opportunities, hers and mine.

Ha-ha, Lenchen sings and jumps from one leg to the other, ha-ha-ha, and hops from stepping stone to stepping stone, the wide skirt of her new red dress lifted up with her delicate fists. Ha-ha, another short octave higher, and the sun is shining, and the wind is blowing over the flat land, where once upon a time… Her cheeks are glowing. She has a secret plan. Nobody knows, and that's the best. Ha-ha! It's her sister's birthday, not hers. A special birthday: Odile's 10th! All the fuss they'd made last night to get Odile's cake ready. Ha! The house was decorated with little bunches of daisies and buttercups, which Odile had gathered in the morning. In the hallway they'd put up a table for the presents Odile's friends would bring. She invited 15 classmates, 15! Her mother had rolled her eyes. Where will I be sitting? Lenchen had asked after circling the dining room table, which was already set for the occasion. You're not invited, Odile had said, this is only for older children. What??? Her mother had intervened: Remember, Odile wasn't part of your birthday party either, she said. But Odile didn't participate because she didn't want to, not because I didn't invite her! Lenchen was struck! Grumpily and in search of she didn't know what she'd roamed through the house for a while, and when she came past Odile's door, she thought she might as well enter. Her sister's room was all cleaned up. Was it always that tidy, or just today to show off to her friends? On the bed Odile's new dress is spread out, white with blue stripes and little pink roses in between. That's what she would wear for her party. Lenchen felt like cutting a little hole in it. But there were no scissors around. Oh well! Then she saw Odile's silver necklace with the small heart-pendant that her father had gotten her for Christmas. It just lay there on her night table. Would she wear it with her new dress? No, she wouldn't! Lenchen quickly slipped it into her pocket. Ha-ha. And out she went, and flew over the garden fence, and sailed across the lake with its swans and ducks, farther and farther, and somewhere along her way Odile's silver heart must have slipped out of her pocket and dropped deep, deep into the woods or waters or who knows where…Lenchen stands still. Nobody around. The winds are howling. She starts digging in the soft ground, hacking with her heel and grubbing with her hands a hole, a grave of sorts…Then she opens the clasp of her silver necklace with the heart pendant, the one she got from her father at Christmas, takes it off her neck and, after giving it a last glance, drops it into the hole. She throws dirt on it, fills the pit with soil, then pounds the patch with her feet, ha, and stomps the spot until it's all hard and firm. So! The winds have stopped howling. All is quiet now. Lenchen wipes her earthy fingers on her crumpled skirt and walks home.

I sit down behind Sam's conference table, open my laptop and click on *Start Zoom*. A woman shows up looking youngish despite her white hair, which falls down on her shoulders in soft, uneven waves. Her black sweater emphasizes her light-skinned face, which looks translucent, almost otherworldly. A small string of pearls shimmers around her neck. She gazes at me, her blue eyes inquisitive, as if she just met me. I smile and she too smiles. Will we get along? Hello, she says, and looks from one side of her imaginary auditorium to the other, thank you for joining! In the next hour I'm going to present to you the recent advances in my neuroscientific research, aimed at developing noninvasive brain-reading and -imaging technology. To be precise, the technology is noninvasive, but the reading itself *is* invasive, albeit currently more explor-atory than revelatory! My question is: what do we sense and perceive on an unconscious level while we talk with a person? Do we receive and also store data active in this person's mind even if unrelated to the ongoing conversation? Do such hypo-thetical thought clouds – as I would call them – cover only the object's thoughts, stories, dreams, etc., or do they also reflect and combine with the subject's own conscious and unconscious contents presently activated? And do we carry such data – let's say trillions of gigabytes of information – through life? And if so, what for? I believe there is nothing unserviceable in nature. Thus we may come to conclude that this may be the secret of human creativity and ingenuity… My screen turns black, I forgot to plug in the power-cord. Anyway, I've seen that it works, it looks professional enough, Sam can do it. Sorry, I say to my audience, I didn't mean to go on and on. Marlene gives me an admiring glance. Interesting, she says, you know a lot! She gets up and walks to the door. I have to go now, she declares, send me the link to Sam's presentation, I want to attend his lecture. The little girl follows her, the silver pen in her fist.

Dinner is at seven. It's always been that way. One week Enna sets the table, the next week it's my job. Since mother started working as a real estate agent, she has little time to prepare the food, but she always whips up something tasty. Father reads the newspaper. And then we all sit down and serve ourselves. You can have as much as you want, my father reminds me, but you have to finish what you take. Reluctantly I balance a scoop of fried rice towards my plate and – too bad! – sprinkle some grains on the table. Enna picks them up for me. She doesn't like rice and has taken only a tiny bit to honor – as required – what is dished up. My father clears his throat. We have some complicated news for you, he says, looking at Enna and me. You may have another sibling, and I will relocate somewhere else. We will still see each other regularly, but not live under one roof. Your mother and I will separate. Silence. Nobody moves. The shock has frozen us on the spot. Mother says: We'll see…But father cuts her off: That's what's going to happen! Enna slumps down in her chair, tears rolling down her cheeks. Seeing this, I pull myself together. You make another child and then you move out? I look straight into my father's eyes, challenging him to rescind his announcement. My father looks straight back at me and just says: *I did not make another child!* – My goodness! Mother gets up and goes into the kitchen. Through the closed door we hear her sobbing.

The Kawa is known for its Japanese cook, who for unknown reasons got stranded in Watertown of all places, yet quickly built the reputation of running a must-try gourmet place. Only by a stroke of luck had the hotel concierge been able to make a reservation for Sam and me: Just when I had asked for a recommendation, the chairman of Pinpoint Pharmaceuticals, who is attending the conference and had booked at the Kawa months ago, had to cancel his reservation because he'd come down with the flu. I decided we'd go on his behalf. Around 7:30 PM, Sam and I left the lobby. Silently we were sitting in the back of the limousine riding to Watertown. Sam held my hand. His head leaning against the neck-rest, he seemed to relax with his eyes closed. The driver put on a

CD with Beethoven's violin concerto. Immersed in Ann-Sophie Mutter's entrancing playing, I wished this ride would go on forever. But now I'm glad we are here. The restaurant's interior looks plain but elegant, its décor sparse and sophisticated. Dimmed halogen lamps mark small circles of light on square tables with black plates on red tablecloths. The menu is printed in Japanese. Patiently the waiter explains and describes the composition of every dish to us — but in the end he suggests the chef's selection, and we agree. What a place, I say when he leaves, and Sam nods. He seems a bit absent minded, perhaps still thinking of the conference presentations he'd heard. So I ask him how his day went, and he says it was okay. To lift him up, I tell him that I prepared our room for his online conference, proudly describing all the mischievous maneuvers that went into achieving a satisfactory result. I expect him to be pleased, but Sam hangs his head over the first plate of our seven-course dinner, a beautifully crafted object in white, yellow and black, and says: Look at that, I've no idea what this is! Let's enjoy these precious arrangements and not talk about work right now. He is right, but not to show any interest in what I did for him or at least thank me for my efforts startles me. It's so unlike him. Also, his voice sounds like it's loaded with bad news. I feel my heart pounding. I'm anxious but know nothing to be afraid of. Plate after plate arrives, each one carrying only a spoonful of something, and for a while we engage in a guessing game about the food's ingredients, but only few sparks of joy flash up and quickly go out. It's a shame we can't enjoy this meal. Several times I ask Sam what's going on, what troubles him, but he only shakes his head. Finally, as we are waiting for the dessert, Sam sits up straight, looks at me, and tells me that in the afternoon the Californian tech company had called again, urging him to present at their headquarters in San Francisco on Friday. There is a lot at stake, Sam says, I'm sorry to not have discussed this with you first, but they needed my answer right away. I agreed to their request. I have to be at the airport tomorrow morning at 6 AM. They have arranged for a driver to pick me up here in half an hour and bring me to the plane. I'm speechless. I think I have heard this before. This can't be! Finally I splutter: You're going without me? Just leaving me – leaving me here? Sam lowers his eyes. It's only for a couple of days, he tries to assuage me. I can see that he is guilt-ridden, but also desperate and not ready to discuss any of this. Instead he turns the tables on me saying that he's been thinking it could be a chance for me as well, I could relaunch my own career as a writer, yes, quitting my teaching job – he would make a lot more money in tech than in academia, so we wouldn't need my income – I could try out what I always wanted to do but may have lacked the stamina…What? I challenge him, I like my teaching job, I decided to do that! Well okay, Sam gives in, but you've done this for years now, you know you can do it, and I noticed that your passion for teaching has declined.

I'm just saying: sometimes a disruption of old comfortable habits is necessary to create something new, and San Francisco could be just the right challenge for both of us – maybe we can break free…

I almost left, the driver of the hotel car grumbles when I approach, is your guy not coming? And when I shake my head he simply orders: Hop in! Off he goes. I'm in a hurry, he explains. The gardener just called, the queen of the night has opened. Have you ever seen a night-blooming cereus? They unseal their beauty at dusk, gleam for just a few hours and wilt at dawn. It's awesome, magical, I saw it once, I can't describe it, you have to see it! And raving about the hotel owner's passion for tropical plants curated in the greenhouse behind the garage, the chauffeur races with almost light-speed velocity towards this natural wonder, as he gushes, this brief twinkle in the night that outshines everything else in the universe, and what have you! I feel numb, my head is spinning, I had too much wine. But I've abandoned myself to his raving lunacy, and when we finally enter the hothouse, I do feel like waking up on a different continent! Soft twilight soothes my troubled view, tropical air wraps its moist wings around my worried heart, I hear cicadas chirr and little fountains burble, see insects and butterflies crisscross the hall – and where else would we want to be, where, if not here? Completely under a spell I follow this excited bear of a man as he gingerly tiptoes on the small path cut into this primeval jungle. Now the chauffeur abruptly stops next to a little congregation. I see the tree man with the binoculars whispering to the night porter, who stands there rather disheveled with his uniform not fully buttoned up and his suspenders hanging down to his unlaced shoes; a clerk from the reception desk has thrown his arm around one of the maids, slowly swinging her back and forth like in a dance; the hostess of the milk bar is twirling a loosened strand of her hair while sucking coke from a straw in a bottle; at some distance I notice an older man with a moustache, who I recognize from a painting in the lobby as the hotel owner. Everybody is staring in one direction. I follow their gaze, and then I too am awestruck: there she is, the queen of the night, bright white, a spark in the dark, delicate, innocent, and ignorant of the brevity of its existence…!

Did this really happen? Is this how it was? I couldn't tell, but I doubted it. Maybe it was all a dream, a strange dream. When I woke up the next morning, everything looked as it always did. No conference table arrangement, the bed in the middle of our room, the closet at its place – weird! Maybe housekeeping rearranged everything while we were at the Kawa. I took a shower and dressed. The monitor was sitting on the windowsill. Had Sam gone to San Francisco, wouldn't he have taken his monitor with him? I had a headache, I felt sad, I needed coffee, first and foremost coffee. Walking through the corridor I saw most of the room doors open, big service carts lined up, many of them loaded with piles of used bed sheets – people seemed to have checked out. Was the conference over? Was it already Sunday? Uneasily I lumbered along. When I finally entered the breakfast area in the lobby, the tables were all cleared away. Nobody behind the bar. The waiter was standing at the window, looking up to the curtain rail where the cockatoo sat scratching its head. Come here, the waiter called trying to bait the bird with an apple slice in his raised hand, come to me, come, come…! The cockatoo looked down and away, down and away, and eventually croaked *Goodbye!*

Did he leave, or had she sent him away? The last I saw of my father was his raincoat waving or flapping through the door, then billowing in the sudden draft from the open window when the sleeve swung into the stairwell, and for a moment it looked as if the coat's loose belt was going to get hooked on the hinge with a chance of holding him back, but alas, it only slapped the metal, briefly and with a bang, when the buckle touched the screw, and then his foot, his left foot, the last on our home's ground, flew out and away, his raincoat deflated, as if punctured by this last remark that made him run, and he was gone. Cowering on the sofa with my tearing eyes peering over to the hallway where our mother was now leaning against the coatrack, her face pushed into the crowd of winter fabrics, her meager hands clawing the wooden frame in an absolutely necessary effort to keep herself up, up, I realized that he had left me too, and all of me wanted to run after him, follow the echo of his steps on the stairs, these dark thuds, which paved his way into the unknown. Where was he going? How was he doing? Would he come back? Would he visit? It had been raining for days, and kept raining and raining, and huge puddles or rather torrential streams, separating the walkway from the street, were spilling out of the sewers, which rather than swallowing the floods were discharging the overflow of all that had already come down. My father briefly shivered and paused, maybe pondering the momentous step he was about to take, maybe thinking of me? No way to stem the tide that was tearing apart our family. I saw him turning up his collar and huddling his chin into his woolen scarf while walking – yes! – walking towards the lights of Broadway.

TODD

The hotel is now almost completely deserted. They have reduced their staff: only one clerk at the reception desk, whose assignment includes concierge jobs; only one waiter in the dining area, who also serves as a barman; only one driver available for rides into Watertown. This one is very friendly with me. Yesterday I asked him if he knew a place to buy rollerblades, and he took me right there and back in less than an hour. Ever since, I've been enjoying riding through the long hotel corridors on my rollerblades. Thanks to the carpeted floors they move smoothly and almost soundlessly. It's like gliding along the waves of history because the castle's galleries are decorated with the pictures of famous guests, many of whom have signed their photos with a personal note of appreciation. Arthur Rubinstein: *Being here feels like a throwback to my earliest childhood.* Frederico Fellini: *Dietro ogni porta una commedia tragica!!!*[1] Samuel Becket: *Not my place!* Renzo Piano: *Here the light seems to come sideways.* Pope John XXIII: *Consult not your fears but your hopes and your dreams.* Woody Allen: *I came with my mother to show her*

---

1 *Behind every door a tragic comedy!*

a moose; I also invited the Berkowitzes. Coco Chanel: *Des lieux comme celui-ci révèlent la nécessité de la beauté...*[2] Henry Miller: *Why am I here? If only Brenda had come along!* It's interesting to read all these dedications and see the photos, most of them official portraits, but some were taken right here, for instance Prince Charles sitting in bed with a breakfast tray over his knees; Bill Gates in rubber boots and a raincoat at the hotel entrance, obviously coming from a hike; Michelle Obama on a bike perhaps doing a soul-cycle (I didn't know that the hotel has a fitness room). Studying these pictures distracts me from worrying about Sam. Sometimes I enter an unoccupied room (they leave the doors open, maybe to bring the air into circulation), I look around and always end up standing for a while at the window, keeping an eye out for something new, a discovery, something to be explored – but in the end I'm just hoping to see a black limousine bringing Sam back to me. All cardinal points offer the same view: low stacked rocks on gray ground, once in a while some shrubs or small evergreens, here and there a spot of red heather. Only once it seemed to me there was a silver lining on the horizon, maybe from a lake, or maybe just a mirage glittering amongst the deep hanging clouds.

Since there are no more guests hanging out in the hotel lobby, and they have turned the heat down (probably to

---

2 *Places like this reveal the necessity of beauty...*

save on costs), which makes the place uncomfortably cool, I now have breakfast in my room. I sit in bed, room service places a tray over my knees, just as they did for his highness, Prince Charles, and for a while I enjoy the luxury of toast with orange marmalade and cappuccino. A long day ahead. Will I hear from Sam? By now he should have arrived in San Francisco. Listening to some music I pick up the newspaper, which they deliver every morning to my door. On the front page an article about a parcel bomb sent to the Pentagon, which had raised suspicion and was removed before it could go off. A photo shows an officer standing next to a package. Good that they found it in time – whereas I didn't, I could have, I should have, I didn't…One Sunday morning, I had decided to finally clear out the entry hall, where over time lots of stuff had accumulated, piles of my journals, tool and supply boxes, bundles of my old clothes ready to go to charity, cartons with Mikki's toys and school books, stuff she didn't want anymore. At the time I had lots to deal with, and these things never bothered me much, but eventually I wanted to sort it all out. I was determined to not look at each and every piece, and yet for a while I got lost sifting through some magazines, almost feeling like back then when I was still very interested in fashion and got excited about new styles. Amongst all of this, right next to the front door, I noticed a case, which I assumed contained more of Sam's worn out shoes, but when I opened it, I found a stack of paper, a manuscript, Jules's magnum opus, all 1,328 pages! I was stunned! How did it end up here? It hadn't arrived by mail. The case was neither sealed nor labeled. The only way to explain it was that Jules must have brought it the night he came to our house. He must have left it there. I don't think he forgot about it. Had he wanted it back, he would have come to retrieve it. He hadn't. Immediately I knew that he had left it on purpose, he wanted me to read it! He may have felt shy to ask. He simply left it there. It was up to me. And I hadn't noticed. This unimposing case had been sitting there for certainly more than a year! Waiting for me to be discovered.

Marlene was standing at the stove turning the wooden spoon round and round while looking at the bubbling brew of plum butter that had been cooking on a slow burner for already more than two hours with many more to come. Today I'll cook the plums, she'd announced at eight, repeating it at ten, and again at eleven, and finally once more at one-thirty when she started to core the prunes she'd bought the previous day at the farmer's market. Her face was red and stained, gleaming with her effort's sweat and dripping from the steaming pap, her lips were melted in an enduring smile, so sure of the good stuff she was cooking. Enna didn't feel like spending much time in the kitchen, and yet she kept sitting there as if glued to the spot, dreaming along with the soft beat of the wooden spoon. Big chunks of Marlene's hair had slipped out of the two golden barrettes she always plugged to the right and left of her temples, and as she was stirring the marmalade her curls dangled with each of her moves over her shoulders and breasts—these breasts that arched fuller than usual over her brazen belly some eight months-plus pregnant. How strange, Enna thought, despite being worn by her odd gravidity, mother looks lovely, still lovely.

My cell rings, it's Sam! Hi, he says, and I get so excited, as if this were our first date. He tells me all about his flight on the company's private jet, how elegant and comfortable it was, that he slept a few hours stretched out as if in a bed. He says that they put him up in a lovely hotel close to their headquarters, and that his presentation will be tomorrow. You didn't take your monitor along, I say. He laughs. These people only need me to explain the math, the principle, the design, if you will. And then he asks me where I am, and I say, I'm in bed. Oh, good, he says, can you go over to my desk and look into the green folder next to my computer…He obviously thinks I am at home, so I explain: I'm in the hotel! Oh, he says, and it sounds as if he's totally surprised. You didn't return home? No, I respond and defend my being here by adding, I thought you would come back and we'd return together? Ah…, Sam responds, and then he hastily adds, let's talk about it. I'll call you back.

Enna told me that when she saw the baby, she immediately noticed a strange bulge on his forehead, not too big, but clearly noticeable. What's that? she asked, but Marlene seemed too exhausted to hear her; it's a boy, she whispered. It could be a normal deformity from labor, Enna thought. The midwife packed her utensils into her big black case. Just call if something comes up, she casually dropped the instruction she was supposed to leave behind. The sweet smell of scorched plumb butter waved through the bedroom. On her mother's shoulder the baby lay all bundled up in a white towel, exhausted from his way into the world and his first cry at all and everything. Both rested with their eyes closed. Enna walked over to the kitchen where mother's water had broken right next to the stove. Suppressing her disgust she swabbed the puddle down the floor, then moved the pot off the stove. I'll name him Todd, what do you think? Her mother called from the bedroom. Sure, Enna answered, Todd it is! – Todd is odd, she immediately thought, and looked over to the empty crib next to her mother's bed.

I don't know if the small gesture of his hand was meant to be an invitation or a warning, but without hesitation I find myself climbing the tree in front of the hotel, where this strange man with the binoculars has been sitting every day as if glued to his branch. My feet hardly get a hold at the trunk, its bark is scratching my hands, and hundreds of flies are buzzing around me, but I'm not giving in, and eventually I pull myself up and come to sit right next to this stranger. He looks at me, suspicious but also curious. I feel a little uncomfortable because he isn't saying anything, just licking his lips with his large tongue. Long, filthy strands of hair flow from his head into his feral beard, and were he not scrutinizing me with intelligent eyes, I'd even doubt his humanity. Hi, I say. He doesn't respond. Again he puts his binoculars in front of his eyes and looks over to the hotel and into our room, which is just in front of us. The curtains are open. To grab his attention, I pull a tuna wrap out of my pocket, twitch at his sleeve, and when he turns to me I offer him half of it. The tree man accepts and bites into it. Silently chewing we sit next to each other on his branch. I'm Sine, I say when I have swallowed my first bite, and wait for him to give me his name, but he only nods indicating that he heard me. This morning I was thinking of Todd, I continue, he was my brother, but I hardly knew him. I was already at boarding school when he was born. He disappeared just after he'd turned six. The police searched but never found him. The tree man, noticing that I'm not eating, gently takes my half of the wrap out of my hand and finishes it off.

Odd he was. In the years to come, Todd's forehead bulge grew bigger. Mother covered it with woolen bonnets in all colors. Enna knitted one for each of his birthdays. He also grew a few other bulges: one on his left shoulder, one on his right elbow, and several along his spine. His feet were a bit twisted, so he had difficulties with walking. The doctors were interested. It must be genetic, they stated. Someone suggested that it could be a variant of neurofibromatosis. Also, Todd grew curly hair not only on his head, but everywhere except his face. He hated to be shaved. Finally mother let him be. A hairy monster, smart and funny – terrible to look at. Enna loved her little brother, the person he was, strange and wild, helpless and with a limited capacity to speak, due to an abnormality of his vocal apparatus, they said. Still Enna always knew what he wanted to say.

There is a ring, the tree man pulls his cell out of his pocket and says: Hello? I hear someone speaking into the phone but can't understand what's being said. The tree man says: Oh…, and without further ado he jumps off his branch to the ground. Now the hotel's back door flings open, the kitchen staff come pouring out, the doormen and the driver join, and all are running behind the tree man to the vegetable garden. A police car slowly rolls over the gravel. All are now behind the hedges and out of sight. What's going on? Then I see Sam. It's strange, he looks much younger, very attractive! How could he be back so soon? He comes from the garage and walks over towards the lobby. The little girl is merrily jumping next to him. Sam, I call, when he is close enough to hear me. He stops, apparently surprised, looks around and then discovers me in the tree. What are you doing up there? He asks. I shrug because I don't quite know myself. He smiles and waves his hand. You are funny, he says, won't you come down? But I don't know how to get down from this tree. It seems too high to jump, and I'm afraid I'd slip if I tried to crawl down. I'm too embarrassed to admit it. I just shake my head, as if I want to keep sitting on this branch. Sam moves on. Did he? Would he?

Sam, if only you had stayed here! And if only you had told me much earlier that I should clean out the stuff in the hallway. Maybe I would have discovered Jules's package while there was still time. But that's not fair. Sam did ask me to tidy up this mess, actually repeatedly he'd told me how much it annoyed him that I let everything sit there. But time went on. And then I found Jules's manuscript! It was a tsunami approaching! I quickly closed the box and moved it to the side. Jules wanted me to read it. He wanted me to say something about it. To rescue him…Over a thousand pages, my goodness! I thought, maybe during our next vacation, or when I would have a good stretch of free time. I should've at least read the first few pages right away… But I couldn't bring myself to even look at it.

Todd crawls on the floor, his face red from trying so hard to drag his limp feet over the rough carpet. Come to me, Enna says and opens her arms. Waaaa, Todd wails and looks desperate. Come on, you can do it, she lures him. And he tries. Spittle drops from the corner of his mouth. Uugga, he says. Are you hungry? Enna asks, and shows him the cookie. Uugga, Todd says again, and then he falls to the side, falls to the end of his tether, shivering and sweating and convulsing, and Enna throws herself above him trying to hold him down, clinging to him as if he were a rock just about to split off the cliff and drop deep into the sea. Todd, she pants, stop it, Todd! The smell exuding from his bulges is overwhelming, Enna fears that she will faint before she has calmed him down. Todd! – Later they will sit next to each other in the warm afternoon sun sharing the cookie.

Marlene is in her office. The secretary is out for lunch. The air conditioning hums. On the coffee table sits a white plastic container with caesar salad. Disgusted, Marlene turns her head away. Todd would have it for dinner. Todd! Destiny had thrown a wedge into her life. She should've aborted him. But she thought she could do this – one more time. And then Todd! She'd hoped to sell a pricey mansion to this gorgeous man who'd become her lover. She'd loved to show him the houses that her agency commissioned, fancy villas nicely staged. Opening the front doors was exciting, and closing them from inside even more so. When she showed him the master bedroom on the top floor, he'd run his hand over her back. An hour later he joked: let me try out the shower; it'll help me decide if I like it. It was already clear that he didn't. Marlene was sitting at the edge of the seller's bed hearing the water splashing over her client's body. A strong body, hairy, masculine – a strong potential, a vague promise. Later she had to go back to clean up. Next time he wanted to try out the kitchen counter. It nearly broke her neck. Obviously this house was too small. She took it off her list. He was charming, fifteen years younger than she but a foot taller and so vigorous! To their third showing he brought a bottle of champagne. They emptied it all. He was from Texas, made lots of money in oil, recently divorced, he said. They had fun. When she told him she was pregnant, he seemed delighted. She suggested abortion. Oh no, he said, I have no children, this will be my first, my only heir. She'd never thought of such a thing, had she? Whenever he flew in from Texas for another showing, he would first press his ear to her belly. It seemed to arouse him. When she was six months pregnant, he decided to go for the big mansion, situated in a huge park, beautifully tended. Would he move to the East Coast? Unfortunately, I can't do this, he said with real regret, it seemed. But he planned to open a branch of his business here. So I need a nice home, he explained, and you will set it up for me, won't you? Sure, she said, and imagined how they would live an elegant life in this elegant mansion. A short dream! He never followed up on anything he'd told her. A week before the closing date he canceled the deal. She called him; at first she wondered what happened, then she blamed him for deceiving and deserting her, and finally she reminded him of his responsibility for the child she was carrying. He got very angry and threatened her: If you ever bring up my name in this context, I will sue you for damages; you took indecent advantage of your client, you may have threatened me with a knife, who knows, now you're blackmailing and stalking me...Don't you ever call me again! Marlene was shocked. She hung up. It was the last she'd heard from him. Maybe this isn't how it was. Just because once in a while Marlene babbled something about a Texan...She'd been secretive all her life. This was no exception. And what do I know what she did with her clients? I never saw her cry. The phone rings, and her secretary tells her that her son is sick, she must stay home for the rest of the day. Okay. Again Marlene is on her own. She always was. She leans back in her chair. The door opens, and in comes a new client.

In the late afternoon I decide that it's time for a little exercise. I put on my rollerblades to explore the second floor. Most of the hotel's facilities are here. In the big ballroom all the chairs are on the tables, the dance floor is littered with filled trash bags, as if the cleaning crew had prematurely deserted the place, and on the grandstand nothing other than a drum set, dismantled. The business center is dark except for the computers' small lights twinkling like lonely stars. In the gym neon lamps glare at a jungle of iron bars, wheels, and weights; a thin stench of sweat turns me off. I quickly move on. In the corner a closed gift shop displays stacks of sweatshirts with the hotel logo, a showcase with fake diamond jewelry as well as a collection of hairspray, toothpaste, and deodorant next to pills for headaches, constipation, diarrhea, and more, and in the background I see a small book display with a plaque announcing mystery stories, memoirs, and cook books – who would buy a cook book in a hotel? What a somber place this is! I turn around to visit the other end of the gallery, hoping to see some more celebrity photos, and immediately notice light coming out of a guest room! Quietly I approach, stop and listen. Two men are talking. Nothing is as infuriating as man's ingratitude, one says. Tell me about it, the other responds. If I weren't sick and stuck with the flu, I would show them, the first continues. Sure you would, the other affirms and adds: you're the founder and CEO of Pinpoint, they can't remove you, can they? Threatening me with criminal charges, the first sneers. Egregious, the other agrees. Then there is silence, and I wonder if I should quickly glide by the open door or return, when I hear the other say: You can stay here as long as you want, unofficially, I mean, not in the books; I could give you the room at a good rate…And before I can hear a response to this proposal, I sneeze, I can't suppress it in time, it just happens. The hotel owner steps out of the guest room and sees me standing there. Good evening, madam, he says, and makes a small bow, can I help you with something? He twirls his moustache and stares at me with a hint of hostility. I blush and don't know what to say. Don't be shy, he nudges me, I can do anything! I'm just waiting for my husband, I splutter. Well, he's not in this room, the owner declares, and starts laughing out so loud that I flinch. Check it out, he adds, gesturing inside. I take flight into the open elevator and ride to the eighth floor. Up there I still hear the owner's laughter roaring through the stairway.

When I was home during one of my school vacations, I got a pet mouse as a present for Todd. It was a tiny white one with pink paws, pink ears and white whiskers around its little nose. An albino! He loved it! During the daytime it usually slept in a cotton ball in a cage in Todd's bed next to his pillow. When Todd lightly tapped at the silver bars, it came out, squinted at Todd and yawned. He called it Moony. Diligently he removed its droppings and cleaned its cage, daily he replaced the water and food, and when all was done he tenderly stroked the silky fur of the sleeping animal with his forefinger. Moony was his, all his. I'm sure he talked with Moony just by looking at him and thinking it all. It's important to have a confidant, and there must have been things he wouldn't even tell Enna, like the sexual stuff. At night Moony got lively; it ran around in its cage, fervently exercised the small wheel next to its feeding trough, and when the sawdust sprinkled Todd's face, tickling and waking him up, he enjoyed watching his little friend running for his life. It was a short life. One day when Todd tapped the bars, Moony wouldn't come out. He thought it was fast asleep. But at night Moony wouldn't come out either. It had disappeared into the white cotton ball that wrapped its cold body and shielded its open eyes from seeing the end of its world. Todd was devastated. He cried. With Enna's help he tinkered a little casket, using samples of white wallpaper from Lukas's collection. Then they went to an undisclosed location to bury Moony. He never told me where.

Do I still have Jules's manuscript? Where did I put it? I know that I brought it to my study. I really want to read it. But I can't picture it anywhere. I wish I were home. I would search for it right now! A few days after I had found it, I wrote a note to Jules, apologizing for not having been in contact earlier, explaining that I was swamped with work, promising that I would soon get to reading his work. What a pledge! As soon as I had sent the letter, I thought I should have been more circumspect. 1,328 pages! I waited to see how he would respond. Other things came up. Life interfered. I had almost forgotten about it, when four weeks later my letter was returned with the stamp *Addressee Unknown*. Obviously Jules had moved. I felt a bit relieved. I couldn't reach him. I wouldn't have to hurry with fulfilling my promise. I hadn't even made this promise. Sam tried to support me. It's an unreasonable demand on you to read over a thousand pages, he said, and he isn't even your student anymore. True, I wasn't obliged to read it, but I felt I should. I know how terrible it feels to say something and get nothing but silence, as if you hadn't been heard, as if you hadn't said a thing, as if you didn't even exist. Still I couldn't shake my reluctance to take the manuscript out of the box. Yes, I could have, should have given it at least a weekend's time and read into it, think about it, and let him know. Something…!

Marlene interrupts my thoughts. After a brief knock, she marches in. Quickly scrutinizing me as if to figure out what kind of mood I'm in, she launches herself next to me on the bed, where I had spread my students' folders to finally read the rest of them, but now she is sitting there with her heavy legs heedlessly crinkling the papers. Watch it, I say, and pull one story out from under her behind, but ignoring my remark she places a box with chocolate truffles between us and opens it. Are you lying here all day long, she asks, more curious than critical, but it makes me feel like a kid, glad that she is here and annoyed that she can ask me such a question. No, I was out, I defend myself. Don't worry, she reassures me, the weather is nasty, who wouldn't want to stay in bed. Mollified I take one of her chocolates. Cocky is depressed, Marlene tells me. His presentation wasn't as successful as he expected. And now since the conference is over, and nobody in his field is taking an interest in him, he wants to chuck it all! Marlene scrutinizes the chocolate truffles in the box and continues: Yesterday he confided in me that he actually wanted to be a chef. He was smart enough to do science, and his parents pushed and promoted him to his current position – but all he wanted was to be a chef! That was his dream! He loves to cook, he reads each and every cooking magazine. He has a whole library with cookbooks at home. I don't know what it is about cooking, but that's his thing! Marlene shakes her head and picks a truffle with silver sprinkles on it. Well – I hear myself saying, it's never too late to change one's career! Marlene looks at me funny. Imagine, after so many years at the university, she weighs in, but it's not good when he is so depressed, and if this is what will make him happy…I told him to ask the hotel owner if they need a cook for the next season, and he may do that. Good idea, I say, and think of calling Sam and telling him that he may get rid of Peacock. I can't work when he is so depressed, Marlene continues. But look what I did yesterday! She pulls out her phone and shows me a picture, geometrical shapes in strong colors, red, yellow and green. I'm impressed, and I tell her: Quite a painting, interesting! You like it? She asks, obviously pleased with my judgement, and I affirm, yes, I do, I really do! Now Marlene gets all enthused. Come up and have a look at it, the photo just gives you a glimpse. The picture is much better than that, and it's big, three by five feet! You have to see it! But that's the last thing I want to do right now. I can't, I decline, I still have so many papers to grade. Tomorrow I'll come up, I promise! What about eleven, Marlene asks. I nod and give her a little smile.

Todd has grown more anxious. Each day is a huge challenge for him. When Marlene wants to take him to the doctor or grocery shopping, he insists on being told exactly the way they'll be going, or else he won't come along. He pants and sweats. Sometimes he cries or furiously lashes out at my mother, who just wants to get him into his anorak. Because he is so reluctant to go forward, he often stumbles and falls. The kids on the playground make fun of him; they copy his moves and fall dying of laughter. They call him *scaredy-cat*. They shove him around and run away. Marlene tried to teach him how to fight back or avoid these clashes. But somehow he can't do it. Someone needs to be with him all the time to intervene, protect him, pick him up. He doesn't like it. I can go out on my own, he claims when Enna offers to take him to the park. Instead he stays home and plays space shuttle. Weeks ahead of his first day at kindergarten, Todd got more anxious and testy. He couldn't sleep. Enna thought he might be dreading the barrage of ridicule he would be exposed to. She offered to go with him. That morning when she entered his room to pick him up, Todd was dressed all in black, even his satchel was black, and he wore his black astronaut helmet with the two metal antennae sticking up into the air. That's how he wants to go? Enna asked our mother. Marlene shrugged. He was adamant, she said. Todd nodded. So they went. They were late. The students were already in the classroom when they opened the door. Everybody looked at them. For a moment Todd seemed frozen to the spot. But then he let go of Enna's hand, stepped forward, and with his voice loud and clear he declared: I'm Todd-Tech from Mars! The children were stunned. They stared at him in awe. The teacher smiled. Then everybody laughed and clapped. Todd-Tech had conquered his place on earth – if only for a short time.

I know I should get up, shower, get out of this room, go to the bar, and have a snack and a drink and see people, at least the few still roaming around this weird place. But I'd much rather stay in bed. I don't feel well. My legs are heavy, my back hurts, I have a headache. Maybe I'm coming down with a cold. When I'm sick, Sam always takes good care of me. He cooks chicken soup with rice for me, brings tea to my bed, suggests some light and fun movies to stream on my computer. But now he's not here! What time is it in San Francisco? I call his number. It rings and rings – eventually he picks up. Did I wake you? I ask, and he says, yeah, I just had a lovely dream that I wanted to go on. Oh, I'm sorry, I say. Don't worry, he responds, maybe it was your call that brought it up. Because in my dream I had been waiting in line to be admitted to something, perhaps a presentation, and each time the door opened for the next person, a bell rang; finally it was my turn, and when I entered the conference room, I saw that my father presided over the meeting. I was so surprised! He smiled at me and invited me to sit next to him at the podium, but the bell rang again – and I woke up. What a lovely dream, I say. Sam agrees and continues: Yesterday, when I arrived here, I briefly had the distinct feeling that he was here! How strange, he passed away decades ago, and I haven't thought of him lately; but yesterday he felt so present – as if he could just come up to me and say *Hi!* There is a pause, and I notice that I smile. Your father would have loved to attend your presentation of the monitor, I suggest. Yeah, Sam says, in my dream I would have presented it to him.

At night Todd grows wings. His bulges open and spray silver powder all over him. His shell crumbles, he feels free and soft, he can breathe and move. Only his right foot keeps hurting, so he cuts it off. Moony is sitting on the windowsill scratching his ear. Enna gets up from her chair and opens the window. All three are flying out. They are sailing above the hills on their way to Tantaree, where Tata is waiting for Todd. She's wearing a silver dress, she too looks silvery, and so is her voice when she says *hello, Silvery!* Enna takes Todd's hand and leads him to Tata's divan. Moony sits next to Tata. Enna pulls the curtains, darkening the room. Only silver lightens the mystery. Tata takes Todd's penis and carefully strokes it, and it grows big and strong—then it too turns silvery. Moony sneezes. Todd smiles. *I'll marry you*, he says to Tata. Enna nods. More of Todd's bulges open, spraying silver powder all around. It's hard to see anything, even for Todd. He feels manly and happy. Moony is sneezing some more. Then they walk through a long corridor; it grows longer the longer they walk, and Todd feels a bit tired. I just have to sit down, he thinks, and then the corridor will end. That's what he does. That's what happens. Todd and Tata look out into the garden that is full of orange and lemon trees. The branches are swaying in the wind, throwing oranges and lemons into the grass, here and there, plop, plop, they fall and roll like balls downhill right into the juice factory. Lukas opens the door and lets them in. He is the factory master. Enna hands Todd a bottle of fresh pressed orange juice. Todd looks at Tata. *I love you*, he says. They both drink orange juice from the same glass.

Night has fallen and millions of stars conglomerate in misty clouds deep into the black universe. Standing on my little balcony, my eyes stray along the Milky Way, indefinite and leisurely and yet as if in search...Do they know where Todd got off to? – all these years back, so long ago…? Is it real? Did I only make it up? But if so, why? Until now I have avoided thinking about one thing: What if Sam decides to take the job offer in California? What if he returns telling me that this would be the right move for him? And what if what he tells me doesn't sound worth leaving all we have built up to resettle in a place where I don't know anybody and have no idea how to reestablish myself professionally? Of course I could work at making connections. But do I want to change this late in my life? I could consider early retirement. But what would I do then? It's true, briefly I'd felt intrigued when Sam suggested I could resume writing. But wouldn't that be pathetic? At my age such an effort would be doomed to failure. Would that matter? Couldn't I simply write for the love of it? Do I need recognition, success in finding a publisher, selling books and having all the world read them? How dependent is Sam on getting the recognition he feels he deserves? How supportive of his decision should I be? Could I deny him if only the hope of a breakthrough somewhere else, just for the sake of keeping my cozy place, unchallenged and predictable? – High up in the sky a plane soundlessly crosses the night.

Todd's babysitter is running non-stop, like a headless chicken, looking here, touching there, pausing briefly, again racing back and forth, searching, fleeing – the brute force of evil close at her heels. Her eyes wide open, an abyss to engulf Todd's mother, who keeps hurling horror over horror at her, relentlessly, desperately and oh so determined that the babysitter ends up almost doubting her own truth. Only briefly she'd fallen asleep on the sunny bench, and when she opened her eyes and peered over to the playground, Todd was gone! The prosecutor looks at her sternly, points his finger, lowers his head in consternation. Who could even think such a thing? Bewildered to her bones and alienated from herself, the babysitter feels like cutting off her own hands, these hands pinned to the crime of having handed over to some desperado a helpless child entrusted to her care. How in the world could she…, his mother's attorney whines, squirming with pain and ostentatious disbelief. The prison door shuts as close as a noose around the babysitter's neck. The prisoner is racing back and forth, four and a half steps wall to wall, the half step jolting her each time. Todd's mother keeps shaking her head, the lawyer stands pale and petrified. The babysitter is led out of the courtroom, shackled and shocked. Time and again she runs to the street: Todd! Help! The kid is gone…! Dead! What happened? The officer yells at her: What happened! She's forced to sit down. What happened? The coroner is waiting. The mortician places his business card on the table. The mother is sobbing. The babysitter wants to get up to get some water, but the policeman holds her down. You stay put! Thirst swells her tongue. And again the door shuts with a bang. Getting life! Life behind bars! Todd crawls to her, cries, whispers: You didn't do it, you didn't, I'm sorry…The prisoner looks at the kid, devastated. Her cell looks northwards. There is no sun in the north. She won't see the sun anymore. Just light and night. But she needs the sun! And she's racing again, back and forth, and the further she runs, the smoother she feels, increasingly tired, exhausted – shush those roaring thoughts, shush – and then there is no noise anymore, all grows silent. For how long? Just now, relief for now. She wanders off, slips into her red shoes, oh, the ones she got in San Francisco, yes, first strolls through Madison Garden, and then with Todd holding her hand she travels to an undisclosed location. Finally she can ask him: Why did you leave? Where did you go? What happened to you? The child can't talk. They sit on a bench in plain sunshine, eat raisin bread and drink the open air, there forever, vanished together.

You don't know…? My student looked at me as if wanting to recoil from what I had brought up, when I had asked her if she knew Jules's new address. It was weeks after my letter to him was returned to me. Being of two minds about what to do with it, I had put it in the box on his manuscript and left it at that. Then at a social gathering I happened to overhear my student talking with a colleague about her friend Marian, mentioning that she'd been Jules's partner. Thus when she came to my office to hand me her paper, it crossed my mind that I could ask her. She had already extended her hand, which held the paper, and I had seized it, but when I asked her, she pulled back, as if she had changed her mind, and in a reflexive countermove I'd held on to it, which was weird, because briefly we both were tearing at it before she let go. No, I don't, I responded and felt uncomfortable. There was a silence, which took the air out of the moment, and right then I think I knew, it hit me with acute clarity, because I saw the student struggling for words, but suddenly her cell rang, she looked at it and back to me and flatly said: He killed himself. Then she turned around and left.

TRANSITION

When I look up, the monitor stares at me. I stare back. It blinks. What is it? An incalculable device or an obedient tool? I notice that the electrical cord has been pulled out of the plug. Probably housekeeping needed the jack for the vacuum cleaner. I wonder what would happen if the monitor ran out of energy. Would its innards die? All storage lost? What's its memory anyway? Maybe Sam left it here to have it tell me something he wants to know and can't retrieve? Tell me, I whisper, and feel a bit silly. The monitor keeps blinking, a calmly pulsating light flashing into space. It shows that it's alive in its own way. Sam's creature! When he gets an idea in his head, he's relentless. Curiosity is his nature. He loves to experiment, gets all excited about it. In his early twenties he had set up a lab in his father's garage. There he spent most of his free time with a friend, tinkering with stuff, joyfully and earnestly probing…And then one day, Sam tried something and left the shop just after having started an experiment. Only briefly did he go over to his parents' house to fetch a soda, and the thing he had put on a slow burner blew up, exploded while his pal was sorting instruments on a sideboard. Fortunately, he wasn't hurt – except for the piercing of his eardrums, which permanently decreased his hearing. But he quit that afternoon. Nevermore did he want to do these experiments. Sam profusely apologized to him but couldn't save their friendship. To this day he can't understand; he concedes that he shouldn't have left the Bunsen burner on, and yes, it was shocking, but it was an accident, he reiterates and claims that had it happened to him, he wouldn't have given up on his friend. It gnaws at him, I can tell. But he still loves to experiment.

Now that I've thought of it, it's hard to let go. It's pointless. Yet I obsess with what I could and should have done differently. Sam told me to not impugn myself. I tried to push it aside. And yet ever so often I replay the scene: The doorbell rings. It's 10:30 at night. Sam is watching basketball. Nobody comes that late and unannounced. Better I don't open – and what if I hadn't? But of course I do. And there is Jules. He carries a box, yes, I would see it right away. We go to my study, and I sit down behind my desk, because there is only one other chair in my study, which would be for Jules. But Jules doesn't sit down. He drops the box with his manuscript on my bookshelf and paces back and forth. He's upset. I understand. His work has been rejected. That hurts. When I'd tried my usual things – normalize, relativize, reassure – nothing had worked.

Now instead I sharply say: Sit down! And Jules sits down. My tone reaches him. Let me look at your manuscript, I order. Jules sneers. Don't bother, he says. No, show me, I insist, you brought it here, you wanted me to look at it! Jules shakes his head. His hand waves me off. No, no, he splutters, you would look at the first page, maybe also the second – what would that tell you about the whole text? And with biting calm he states: The thing is flawed. I failed. It doesn't work! I thought it was a great idea. But it was a mistake! His verdict is final. He is the definite authority on that matter. And now I realize what I didn't at the time: Jules declared his own intellectual bankruptcy. He sided with the publishers' rejections and completely devalued his writing. He wasn't angry at them, didn't feel misunderstood or unappreciated – no, he was angry at himself, he'd sealed his fate! I should have challenged him, yes, calling him too susceptible, urging him to do more work on it, blaming him for not standing up for his convictions, everything I could have come up with to make him reinvest in his work, reconnect with his dream, save it – save him. Yes, I should have yelled at him, shaken him, scolded him…He, who always was decent, prudent, considerate, he, who always spoke softly – and now raged inside. Or did he? It all went so fast. He got up and left.

I go to see my analyst. I say: I told you what happened, all these facts, but facts won't change. What else is there? What do I imagine? For instance: You! I don't want you to be a fact. I want to look at you and find you looking with me at the things I can't look at by myself. Tell me what you see. Tell me!—My analyst sways his heavy head. But you are here, and I am here, he claims.—I know, I say, but that's not what this is about. I am stuck. I've lost my zest! I've given up!—My analyst looks at me, his hand playing with his iPhone. You are depressed, he claims.—I don't think so, I protest. No! It's something else. I have all these thoughts and I want to play with them with you.—My analyst purses his lips. To play requires acknowledging the basic facts!—The basic facts? What is he suggesting? I'm not at war with basic facts. I feel discouraged, bored. Then I kick myself and try again: Can't you just listen to what I come up with, picture it, and tell me what you see?—My analyst doesn't respond. His head is sunken down, his chin rests on his chest. His shirt is white. He's sleeping! Through his loosened fingers his iPhone has slipped down into his chair's cushions. An iPhone, the newest edition! His linen pants are bulky, nicely rumpled, and right down at the bottom, where his white sneakers blink twice, they snuggle casually around his big feet, touching the woolen carpet at his heels. He's sailed off. I'm stunned: He fell asleep on me! I'm wide awake. Quietly I lift myself out of my chair across from his, my eyes firmly fixated on the sleeping colossus. I've made up my mind. I tiptoe around the coffee table. I've always wanted to do this! I feel a spark of joy tickling inside. I hold my breath. My hand on the doorknob slowly moves. No sound to be heard. I'll make it, I think. I inch it open, still looking at him, slowly steadily…But then, just as my foot crosses the doorstep into the hallway, my analyst's dog, a Newfoundlander that had patiently waited for the end of this session, jumps up, barking and wagging its tale, this friendly creature, all excited, runs past me through the open door, barking, to reach his master, his master in his chair. Now he'll realize that I wanted to sneak out, I think, startled, embarrassed, still hesitant. The dog barks, pushes his snout into his master's lap, barks and pushes, barks. His master doesn't move. He doesn't wake up.

My cell rings. It's Enna. I'm so relieved to hear her voice. How are you? I ask, and she says: fine — and how are you? What can I say? I don't know, I reluctantly offer, and then I ask her: Do you remember Jules? — Jules, what Jules? She asks back. — My student…I start to clarify, but she interrupts me, Oh, the one who killed himself? She just says it. I feel like hanging up on her. Sine, she asks, are you still there? I take a deep breath. Yes, I'm still here, I whisper, and don't know what else I could say. Are you still thinking of him? She more states this than asks. I just nod. I hear her breathe. We both keep silent. Then I say as if to myself: imagine what he might have accomplished, imagine, his talent…Maybe, Enna responds and then adds, or maybe not. Oh, I'm sure he would have, I emphasize, he was extraordinary, his writing was amazing, I've never had a student with such promise… Maybe he couldn't fulfill this promise, Enna gives back, maybe at this point he decided to kill himself. But this was a mistake, I assert. It was his choice, she insists, you have to accept that. But he was in a state of desperation, I plead, he wasn't his rational self, I should have noticed…It's so long ago, Enna says, let it go… We both fall silent again, but then I have an idea: I told you that he brought me his manuscript. What if I edited it and try to publish it, even if necessary with some self-publishing company? What do you think? Enna seems taken aback. Sine, she finally says, we've talked about this at great length, remember? You doubted that you had the right to publish his work. You wondered whether his name would be tarnished if it wasn't a Kafka-Brod case…Yes, that's what I wondered, I admit, but now I think: I could judge the quality. I could read it and see if it is worth editing, or even if it could be published unedited as a kind of literary stone pit with lots of uncut gems in it, rough diamonds, you know…? Enna doesn't say anything, so I continue: I could at least try, have a look when I come home. And as I'm saying it, this suddenly turns into an interesting project, something I'd really feel like doing. Enna interrupts my thoughts: You still blame yourself. You want to apologize, do reparations, is that it? Maybe that's part of it, I concede, but I do have some time till the start of the next semester, I could make it my project, even take a sabbatical to do it, because it surely would be a lot of work, more than thirteen hundred pages… And I think, maybe that's the perfect plan, to take a sabbatical, go with Sam to California, he tries out his new company, and I edit Jules's manuscript while exploring other options over there… Well, Enna slowly says: didn't you tell me that you got the manuscript shredded? – Shredded! – I forgot, I brought it to a shredder, and now I see it vanish, hear the screeching noise as the machine crushes it, and the ground breaks, I'm falling, try to grab for something but only catch some airy paper shavings… Yet again there is Enna's voice saying: Let it go, Sine, let go.

I have to get out. I feel imprisoned, and there is no need to confine myself in this room. But the weather is awful, deep hanging clouds have engulfed the hotel, heavy rain whips the windows, squalls rattle the shutters – here I am. I could ask if the roof restaurant still serves the last few hotel guests. Or maybe the gift shop is open, and I'll have a chat with the salesperson. At least I could get a cappuccino at the bar. I shower and get dressed and already feel better. Slowly I walk along the hallway. A young woman is loading a cleaning cart with piles of fresh bed linens. I ask her to clean 859, my room: 859, I repeat to make sure she got it. She nods and disappears in a service station. I take the stairs to the second floor and stroll past the business center, which is empty. How can this hotel survive, died down as it is? When I enter the gift shop, a bell rings, and the hotel owner, who had been leaning his elbows on the sales counter reading a magazine, straightens up. Good morning, madam, he greets me. Can I help you with something? No, thank you, I say and smile a bit, I just want to look around, I'm not searching for anything in particular. I feel uncomfortable, because he scrutinizes me, as if checking me out. There is no one else around. The hotel owner clears his throat and offers: The salesgirl called in sick! Oh, I respond, and think he wants to explain why he's behind the cash register. I stroll past a clothes rack with fancy blouses, jerseys, and rain coats, all the time feeling the hotel owner's eyes following me. This may be just my imagination. You should look at those sweatshirts, the hotel owner now blares over to me, they are half-price if you buy three. How annoying he is! I don't need sweatshirts, and I'd rather be left alone while looking around. Now I feel irritated, and without really meaning to, I say: There's not much going on here – I wonder how your hotel can survive with so few guests. The hotel owner looks baffled. We both stare at each other from opposite sides of the gift shop. Then he seems to recollect himself and says: Right, I too wonder! Do you want to buy a suite? You can even have a whole floor! He must be kidding. No thanks, I say, and laugh as if he'd made a joke. But he doesn't give up. Your mother feels fine up there in her tower, he claims. This puzzles me. How does he know that

Marlene is my mother, I wonder. That's okay, I say, and look at the sweatshirts thinking I may get away with buying one of these. But now the hotel owner stands right next to me, his face so close to mine that I can see the corrosion of his white skin, broken like crumpled paper. His gray pupils drift in the yellow lake of his eyeballs, which are slowly oozing rills of tears at their red-rimmed borders. Twirling at his moustache, he says: I noticed you at my greenhouse. You didn't seem to be impressed by my queen of the night. Are you not touched by flora's beauty? His question surprises me. Yes, it was amazing…I stutter. The hotel owner now briefly touches my arm. Don't worry, he says, it just crossed my mind. You are right, he continues, how can anyone survive here? It was a dumb idea to buy this castle, even though it was cheap as dirt. That should have been a warning! And softening his voice as if to make sure that nobody else could listen in, he murmurs: My uncle was an eccentric, he poured all he had into this place, thought he'd make it a real big deal. And then one day he took a walk out there and fell into a peat hole. The moor is treacherous, it's hard to see where you shouldn't put a foot. He struggled all night not to drown and was found and rescued the next day. But the cold moor gave him pneumonia, of which he died a week later. I was his next of kin. I should have declined the inheritance. I didn't, and here I am, trying to figure out, what to do! Any idea? Even though challenging me with his question, the hotel owner now looks a bit shrunken. I feel sorry for him. What can I say? I know I will soon leave this place and never come back, for sure. But before I can even come up with a response, the curtain in front of the changing cubicle opens, and a young woman appears, dressed in a silk blouse with its price tag hanging down from her neckline. The hotel owner seems startled. I thought you were sick, aren't you…? he babbles. I take my chance and quickly slip out of the giftshop.

Maybe he is having an affair with her, I think and walk to the end of this floor and then up the stairs, as I used to do when we still lived on the fifth floor, and when I open the door, my father is sitting in the living room at the window reading the newspaper. This is his favorite place. He looks relaxed. I'm so glad he came back! Does he still bear a grudge against Marlene? Will her tragic caper always smolder in him, a subtle resentment and suspicion, ready to break open? Or did he get over it, completely? The weekend has started. Mother clatters in the kitchen. Soon she'll call me to set the table. I sit down on the sofa and just want to be here. My father looks up from his newspaper and says Hi, how was school? Okay, I respond, and remember how quickly I felt challenged in those years. I always suspected that any answer to such a question would invite his recommendation to do my homework, whereas I would want to ask for permission to go out with my friends or to the movies, get an early allowance or the like. But now

I want to just sit with him. I wonder what will become of me, I say, as this has just crossed my mind. He smiles. What would you like to become? He asks back. I don't know, I say and after a while I try, maybe a lawyer, or an architect, or a writer, or I study literature, psychology, go to medical school, I don't know…He smiles. Great options, he says, good that you still have some time to make up your mind. How did *you* figure out what *you* wanted to do? I ask him. He takes off his reading glasses. I don't think I had much of a choice, he responds. Actually, this isn't true, he immediately corrects himself, we always have a choice, even when we feel pressured in one way or another. Are you happy with what you decided? I ask. He thinks a bit and then says, yes, I am. I too had other ideas, just like you now. But rebuilding the factory was a good challenge. I'm proud I succeeded. And to keep it up remains a valid task. Not always easy, he adds, but I like it. My father folds the newspaper and puts it on the carpet next to his seat, because now he is having a conversation with me – I wish we'd had this conversation – and I continue: It was your father's factory. What if it hadn't existed? Would you have built a factory to produce wallpaper? Probably not, my father concedes. We all are born into certain circumstances. That's where we start. But don't you worry, he adds, you won't have to take over the factory. I'll sell it when I'm ready to retire. Doesn't it bother you to think that it will belong to someone else someday? I ask. No, he replies, I think that's the course of history. We hand things over when our time is up. I used to wonder how my life would have been, had I done something different. Yeah, I interrupt him, you wanted to be a writer! He smiles and nods. True, he admits, that was one of my dreams. But would I have been good enough to make it? Could I have supported my family? Frankly, I doubt it. So I prefer to think of what was good about my decision: There are people who have decorated their homes with my wallpaper and live surrounded by my design. In this small way I have contributed to their wellbeing. And then my father adds: Also, I could travel the world getting inspired for new designs, each year someplace else. That's a privilege! I always wanted to travel, and I've already seen a lot, I wouldn't want to have missed that. At this point my mother would come in with the salad bowl for dinner. Where will you travel next? I ask my father, and he looks at Marlene and says, maybe I take your mother to Japan. I can see she is surprised.

I hear a noise like some knocking at the door, and the person who opens is naked but not ashamed. I have an appointment at six, I say, and the person disappears, dissolves into dark air. I find myself in a waiting room with lots of people sitting on old sofas and armchairs, reading on their electronic devices or staring into space. Are you all waiting for the doctor? I ask, and this sentence echoes back and forth. Or did I ask repeatedly? I can't remember. Nobody looks up, nobody seems to hear me. Anxiously I walk towards a footrest, crouch down, and start waiting like everybody else. Next to the door a faucet drips water into a small sink. I adjust my breathing to the drum of its beat: in – out – in – out…A sign above the sink indicates that we're supposed to wash our hands right after entering. I realize that I haven't done this and debate with myself if I should get up and still do it. I can't make up my mind. Then a curtain lifts at the back of the room, and the little girl – *my little girl!* – shows up, makes a bow as if to an audience, but nobody looks at her. Unperturbed, she starts producing summersaults in a wide circle, thereby working her way closer to us. I worry that she'll get too close to the end of the stage, will fall down and break her neck. Then a young man walks onto the stage. He is tall and slim, he looks a bit like Jules, but it can't be him. Still I jump up and call: Jules, hi, hello! Frantically I wave, but the man doesn't react, he doesn't seem to hear me, and only now I realize that there is a big glass wall between the stage and the waiting area. I'm relieved. The girl can't fall down. And there is no way that he can hear me cry.

Was this some kind of premonition? When I enter the milk bar I see the innkeeper sitting at a table with lots of empty bottles in front of her. She is eating pizza. Seeing me she says: We are closed! I enter anyway and ask if I can keep her company for a bit. Okay, she says, and continues chewing. Sitting opposite her with all these bottles in between us, I can only see her head and the upper rim of her shoulders. What's the plan with these bottles? I ask. The innkeeper averts her gaze and shrugs. Maddy refuses to be milked, she then explains, she lows and kicks when I approach. And the girl is gone, I can't find her. She always had a good hand with Maddy. I have no one to help! Seeing the innkeeper so resigned nudges me to lift her up. I could help you find the girl, I offer. The innkeeper looks at me. You would? Yes, I confirm, and want to know: Where did you see her last? Where does she usually go? Where does she actually live? The innkeeper swallows her morsel and leans back. She's always around here, she then says. I thought she belonged to the couple who runs the pawn shop. But when I went over to ask them, they said she wasn't theirs. For a while I thought she was with the hotel owner, but I've never seen them together. She often plays in the garage; the chauffeur suspects that some guests left her behind, and that this is the reason why they established a no-child policy here; but nobody cares about that either. You see, there is not much to go for. The innkeeper now looks distressed. You like her, I softly suggest, and she nods. I like her too, I agree, let's just go everywhere and look around. Maybe we get lucky…

And we go, cross the big hall by giving Maddy a wide berth, walk through the lobby where the night clerk is lighting the chandeliers, one after the other, descend to the lower floor, where the conference rooms are lined up, dark, empty, and useless, proceed through the long hallway guided only by the red Exit signs, and end up at some utility cellar. I'm reluctant to enter, but the innkeeper pushes the door wide open and calls: Sweetie, are you there? Silently we are standing in the doorway harkening into the dark. A cool draft gives me goosebumps. Let's go, I whisper. The innkeeper doesn't move. As if under a spell she stares ahead. I follow her gaze, and suddenly I see the little girl sitting on the top shelf of a storage rack, stiff and cute like a doll.

We have to get her down, the innkeeper says. Somehow this annoys me. She climbed up on her own, I assert, she will get down when she's ready. The innkeeper shakes her head. No, she counters, it's easy to ascend, but hard to descend; that's when the risk of falling is greatest. And without waiting for me to agree, she grabs some plastic boxes nearby and starts mounting them at the bottom of the storage rack, on top of which the girl is sitting. Clouds of dust are swirling up, and something seems to be flitting through the air – I worry that there are bats – but it is only the flickering shine of a light bulb from the ceiling. I hear the timer tick; soon it'll be dark again. The innkeeper works. Why don't you give me a hand, she pants, and I'm just watching. The pile of boxes grows. Now she could invite the girl to come down on her own. Instead the innkeeper clambers up, with the boxes precariously slipping and wiggling under her feet. Watch it, I shout. But she doesn't stop: with one hand she clings to an iron post of the storage rack while stretching the other towards the next shelf. Meanwhile the girl has pulled up her legs. Curiously she watches the scene. And I'm standing there looking at the innkeeper's apron dress, which keeps shifting upwards with each of her moves, now barely covering her behind and exposing her big naked legs with their flabby flesh that slumps down into her black lace-up shoes – old, dimpled flesh, like my mother…Help me, the innkeeper now calls back over her shoulder, hold the boxes, steady them, so that I can take another one, I'm almost there. Reluctantly I follow her order. But just when the innkeeper mounts the next box, the little girl gets on her feet, jumps all the way down to the cellar floor, and runs out the door.

Why didn't you catch her, the innkeeper yells at me when she is back down again. You wanted to help me, and you just let her run away? She's upset. She grabs my arm. Her chin quivers as if she can barely keep herself from bursting into tears, and her eyes desperately cling to mine. Why, she demands – and then she lets go of my sleeve. She looks deflated. How can I explain? I was so surprised, I offer. It went so fast, I try. I didn't want to force her, I lamely add. The innkeeper waves me off with her hand and turns away. Exhausted, she sits down on a heap of empty jute bags. You don't understand, she says, and I feel ashamed. She's right, I let her down. And I wish I could say something that would lift her up, but all I can do is sit down next to her and wait for her to recover. The light's timer ticks – till it doesn't any longer, and we sit in the dark. Wouldn't it be nice if right now the little girl came back with her pocket lighter and offered the innkeeper a cup of fresh cow milk, still warm and foamy, fresh from Maddy's udder? The innkeeper sighs. It's okay, she says, let's go.

Back in my room I find a message from Sam on the hotel phone. Why hadn't he tried my cell? And where is it anyway? It pains me to have missed his call. Hi, he says, where are you? I've tried to reach you several times…I hope you are doing okay. There is a pause, and I think, this is strange, I'm here all the time. Where is my cell? Then Sam says: I just wanted to give you a brief update. This startup – it's a weird group of young people. I don't know if this is the right place for me. Anyway, they made me two offers: One is to sell them my patent for the monitor and basically be out, leave every further development and the way they would market it up to them. Essentially, it would be a complete abandonment of my device for a lump sum. Or, second option, I join their startup as a partner, which would require me to put the commercial-ization rights of the monitor plus a considerable amount of money into the company; I would be on the board of direc-tors, would be the lead developer of this product, but still my vote would be just one out of five. There is another pause, and then Sam says: I don't think that either option works for me. I would have loved to talk with you about it. But maybe it's good that you'll have some time to think about it first on your own. – Oh, and there is some more news, he then adds: I just learned that Peacock – of all people! – will receive the 75th Lasser Research Award honoring his monkey brain studies, for which he appropriated a number of my methods and findings. You see…? What can I say! We'll talk later. Right now I'm tired and want to sleep. I'll turn off my phone, so don't try me. I'll call you tomorrow. Love you.

Oh Sam! How I wish to be next to you now. I'd just take your hand in mine while we both fall asleep, embark on a long journey along our momentary moods, linger where we'd feel like staying, detached from all obligations, ambitions and goals, just live our life. We could do this. Be on an island. Sit at a riverbank. Cross the Sahara, rest for a while behind the walls of a Kasbah, and drink fresh peppermint tea. Would we invite Mikki and Hank to join us? No. They are young, they are at a different place in their life, they are striving, as they should. But shouldn't we as well? I know Sam isn't ready to give up. I couldn't even say that I am. We're not the youngest anymore, but we aren't the oldest either. Still, my arm's skin is a bit loose, and I have these lines on my upper lip, nothing is quite as it used to be. It bothers me. Yet Sam loves me, he really does.

Time goes by. One morning, getting up from his desk to meet the sales manager, Lukas briefly staggers. Oops! It surprises him. He quickly steadies himself. This can happen. The day was long, he was distracted by a phone call, he'd just overcome the flu. But it keeps happening. In particular when making quick movements. There are days when he feels a bit wobbly. Not every day, but now and then…He notices that he feels reluctant to go over to the production facility midmorning, even when he is curious to see a new print. I can swing by at lunch, he thinks, deciding for one instead of two trips over. At his regular health check-up, Lukas mentions it; his doctor runs some tests, doesn't find anything concerning and eventually sums it up: You're growing older; just be more careful, all is fine. Good, I'm healthy, Lukas thinks. He also is a bit more tired than he used to be. I am old enough to take a nap after lunch, he decides. Marlene agrees. Even though she still feels quite energetic, she likes these midday naps, where she dozes and imagines all sorts of things, most often art projects that never get realized. It's just nice to have these dreams. Lukas's thoughts are different. He wonders when he should retire. How will he manage the sale of the factory? Will he get enough money to provide a good life for Marlene and him and, in case of any unforeseen need, a safety net for Enna and Sine? These considerations walk with him, and it's true, he doesn't feel so steady on his feet anymore. Also, occasionally he notices that he doesn't focus. Is he just not as interested as he used to be in all the details of the things at stake? He went through them so many times! And then, once in a while, a word doesn't come to mind, nothing fancy, just an ordinary word that was there a moment ago, and then it's gone. It bothers him. He doesn't feel quite sharp. It's embarrassing, or sad, or both. This all develops over many months. He forgets something. He loses something. He pushes something over. Do others notice it as much as he does? It's on his mind. He doesn't want to unnecessarily worry Marlene, but doesn't want to deny it either. I'm growing old, he eventually says. You are just overwrought, she allays his fears at first, and Lukas likes to hear this. But he is an honest man. I'm not so quick anymore, he mentions. Let others run, Marlene suggests. Nevertheless she gets a bit impatient when he forgets something. This can happen, she thinks. But it happens too often. Pay attention, she demands when she wants Lukas to do something. It hurts to hear that. Why don't you do it yourself? he snaps back. But he isn't really angry with her. He is discouraged, a bit worried and tired. He gets hearing aids. This helps, and for a while he again keeps his head up and smiles. Still he cannot deceive himself about his increasing frailty. One evening when he is sitting on the terrace in the evening sun, he says to me: In a couple of years or so I will retire; I'm thinking of selling the factory. Think about it. Is there anything you want in this respect? – What did he mean? I've never figured it out and still wonder…In my leisurely hours, like now, sitting on my bed with the last papers to grade next to me, I think: Maybe there was a bit of hope in my father's heart that I would take over the factory. That Sam and I would run it together? Or Enna and I? Anything to not have to completely give it away, not to let go…?

Something held me up. I'm late, and on top of all I'm not appropriately dressed, because the bulb in front of my closet was broken, and mistakenly I had picked the wrong jacket when I decided for a suit. I look awful, a literal misfit. On my way through the campus I run into the Dean who seems startled. My dear colleague…he grunts and smirks. I only give him a rushed *Good morning.* When I enter my class, the students are already seated. Some chat, most stare at their smart phones, texting or scrolling. Some look up and giggle when they see me. I'm standing at my desk, supposed to start my class, but I feel such a strong resistance and an over-whelming sadness, which I fear could burst into the open at any moment, that I struggle to keep my composure. Will I really stay for the hour or leave right away? Should I cancel the class, even announce the end of my seminar? Could I simply walk out? Curiously, the students are watching me. My stomach grumbles, last night's pepper sauce didn't agree with me. The assignment for today was *Transition.* Maybe that hadn't been a good idea! I wanted them to reflect on the area where reality – or what we often take for reality – moves into fiction, our personal take on everything. Just try a short piece, I'd suggested, and think about it! It was meant to address a new aspect of fiction writing. By now they have learned the basics: to avoid word repetitions, to listen for the tone and rhythm of a phrase, to consider the range of a metaphor and how it relates to the text as a whole. I wanted them to explore their own inclinations as writers. My students know that I have a fancy for weird authors, peculiar texts, odd characters, surprising moves, and open endings. But I've emphasized that this is just my personal predilection, and they certainly can focus on more traditional or totally experimental styles. As I'm standing at my desk and looking at my students, all my interest in this assignment and where it might have taken them is gone. Hi everybody, I eventually can bring myself to voice, and then to my own surprise I hear myself saying: This is my last seminar. I've decided to retire. Some students chuckle.

I put the paper down. The hotel is deadly silent. Am I the only person in this castle? The wind whistles through the door canyons, the timbers creak and crackle, the long case clock in the hallway just beat the eleventh hour. I'm not afraid. I'm not tired. I have an idea. I put on my running clothes, buckle on my rollerblades, grab my key and open the door. Immediately the light in the corridor goes on. Off I go. Soundlessly I glide past the guest rooms to my right and left till I get to the elevators. I decide to go down to the lobby. Maybe I can still get a drink at the bar. The elevator arrives, the door opens, I enter and press the button to the ground floor. The lift cage rumbles down. Then it stops. The door opens, a woman enters, mumbles good evening, the door closes, the lift cage sinks further. Then it stops again. All lights go off. A blackout! What now? In search of an emergency key, I feel for the panel, sense and push a number of buttons, press them one after the other, and finally one produces a dial tone. I ring and ring. Eventually I hear a voice from the loudspeaker saying: What's the matter, are you having a problem? Yes, I yell, the elevator is stuck! – Oh, the person on the other end responds, sorry, that happens once in a while. I will come get you. A click in the loudspeaker, then silence. How long will we have to wait to be rescued? We – that's right! The other woman hasn't made a move or said a word, but I hear her breathing. Are you okay? I ask into the pitch-black void. Yes, she says, and I hear the swishing noise of her clothes. I'm Sine, I offer, hoping to strike a conversation. I'm Marian, she gives back. Then we are both silent, but my heart is hammering in my chest, and I wonder if she can hear it as loud as I do. Marian, I finally try, what happened to Jules? There is silence again, but then she says: he is gone. I know, I press ahead, how did it happen, what did he do? I can't talk about it, she says. It was such a mistake, I blurt out, his and mine, I so much regret, I failed him! That's what *I* blame myself, Marian gives back, but he failed me too! Then we both stay silent again, because what else is there to say! I've been there many times, go round and round in circles, but the fact never changes, there is nothing I can do, nothing can be done. We're sitting in the dark. How long will it take before we can continue our ride? If only I had taken my cell, I could use its flashlight to see Marian. I would see her face reflecting Jules's – his bright spirit, his strength, his defeat, his renunciation – all these traces carved on her love, her loss, her agony – hers and his. And my eyes fill up with tears, thick and plump tears, which cling to my lashes, sit there and won't drop. However, now the elevator starts rocking and swinging, we still have no light in the cabin, but at least we are slowly trundling down. Finally the cage stops with a jar, the light flickers on, the door opens, a shadow glides past me, and when I get out, I find myself in front of the night clerk. He gives me a cranky look. What are you doing here in the middle of the night, he asks, and looking down to my rollerblades he shakes his head and grumbles: unbelievable!

I enter the lobby. The bar is closed. Nobody there. Only the Chairman of Pinpoint Pharmaceuticals is slumped in a wing chair near the fireplace, asleep; his one hand sits on his thigh holding an empty wine glass, the other rests on his belly. Slowly I roll past a pile of bundled magazines, filled plastic bags and boxes, and exit through the revolving door into the fresh air! The forecourt is illuminated by two vintage streetlamps. The garage door is closed. It's cold. I look up and see a big white moon blasting from the black sky. A tawny owl is calling nearby. Suddenly the night clerk stands next to me lighting a cigarette. Can't sleep? He casually asks. I'm not tired, I respond, and look at his pasty face with its deep wrinkles, the beard stubble around his pale lips and his eyes – friendly eyes looking at me. Do you mind me asking you something? he says while buttoning his coat up to his chin. No, I give back, perhaps too quickly, so I add: maybe, I don't know yet…The night clerk nods. Why do you always come here? He then asks almost as if in passing. I'm totally perplexed and feel defensive. What do you mean? I ask back. Well, he says, this is no place for a lady like you. He makes me feel uncomfortable. It's because of the conference, I say. The night clerk smirks. What conference, he says, there is no conference, is there? This is annoying. I know, I say, the conference is over. But there was a conference! Again he nods his head and softly says: Yes, there was a conference. That's what brings you here? Why did he ask me this? My heart aches so much that I can barely hold up. Maybe I will have a heart attack and be dead in a minute. Anxiously I grab the night clerk's sleeve to steady myself. He thoughtfully looks at me and then says, I want you to know something: soon the hotel will close. I mean, it'll be closed for good! There won't be any more conferences here, no rooms to rent. They'll demolish the building. It'll be finished, done, gone – you understand?

And since I only stare at him, because what he's saying makes no sense to me, he insists: You can't come back here next year, you just can't! Now he looks almost pained as he searches my eyes for a sign of recognition, and since I still don't know what to think or say and don't want to confirm what I've heard, shaking his head he turns around and shuffles back into the lobby. Soon the soft sound of the revolving door stops. I stand rooted to the ground in front of the hotel and look at the plain landscape that is illuminated by the rising moon. In the far distance I see what looks like two people in tight embrace – or is it rather one? – walking away. A lone voice is wailing.

WINDMILLS

The waiter, who has just brought my usual cappuccino and croissant breakfast, is about to leave without saying a word – not *good morning*, not *enjoy your breakfast*, not *is there anything else I can get you*, not even *beautiful weather today* – not one of these easy formulas, with which to lightly connect in a civilized world, so I rudely grab his arm, hold him back, and ask in the middle of his fossil face if it is true that the hotel will be torn down. He looks at me startled, annoyed, his eyes turning dark. Who told you such a thing, he mutters brushing my hand off his sleeve, but he keeps standing there as if waiting to find out what else I might know. I feel protective of the night clerk. Oh, I say, it's the talk of Watertown…He cuts me off: Of course they would make a big deal of it. If they decide to build a windfarm on this land they will get a lot of new jobs for their community – anyway, it's just talk, a fantasy, nothing else. He walks away not noticing the table napkin, which has slipped off his forearm, flapped to the floor, and now lies there, a casualty of his grumpy departure. A windfarm! What a great idea! Nothing grows on this depleted land, so why not replant it with a bunch of windmills – hundreds of these slim, white technical wonders reaching high into the sky to silently turn their blades in the endless currents of life…Enough, back down to earth!

A loud honking rips me out of my thoughts. The man from the reception desk looks up, the hotel owner peeks through the velvet curtains that hide his office, and now both start scurrying through the lobby and out the revolving door. A huge truck has backed up towards the entrance. I hear voices shouting, the chauffeur is exiting the garage and waves with both arms to indicate something. The cockatoo comes flying from the shed's roof and settles nearby on a rain barrel. What's going on? Finding myself sitting at the perfect observation post, I decide to stay and watch. The men are talking. Once in a while the truck driver's colleague is pointing towards the empty loading space, then looking at the revolving door of the hotel, shaking his head. The hotel owner is repeatedly shrugging his shoulders; he has pulled a paper out of his jacket's breast pocket and waves it in front of the truck driver's eyes. Then the chauffeur seems to have an idea, because he points to the big window next to the revolving door, just where I'm sitting. Everybody is looking over. I tentatively smile, but nobody seems to notice. Now the chauffeur reaches into his pocket and produces a folding ruler; he approaches the window and starts measuring its height and width. When our eyes meet, I smile again, and he nods in recognition.

You've picked a great spot! I hear my mother's voice, and turning around, I see Lilli. She wears bright red leggings, a wide yellow sweatshirt covering her thighs almost to her knees, and a flowery silk scarf around her neck; her hair is held back in a bushy ponytail, her eyes wear heavy mascara, her lips are as red as her leggings. I'm totally baffled! My goodness, I can't stop blurting out, what's up with you? Lilli smiles. I just did my workout, she claims. No, you didn't, I give back. You are right, she agrees, I was trying different outfits when I heard the truck arriving. I wanted to see…But where did you even get these leggings, this sweatshirt, I've never seen you wear these, I insist. I bought them online, my mother explains, they arrived last night by express mail. But why did you order them, I mean — isn't that a bit flashy considering your age? My mother looks at me, insecure, saddened, or ironic, then lowers her gaze towards her outfit. You think so? She murmurs. Now I feel bad and sorry for her. Well, of course you can wear these things, if you like them, at home, or when you paint…I suggest, but perhaps not in the lobby? Actually, Lilli says and straightens up, I've bought these for my vernissage, which I titled *Yellow/Red*, and that's why I got these…Your vernissage? I wonder. Yes, she confirms, and then tells me that on Friday she'll have the opening of her art show in the lobby of the hotel! That's why the truck came, she explains, they want to empty the area in front of the elevators. About a hundred people are expected to show up, almost half of them journalists…I feel totally snubbed. You planned all this without at least consulting me? My mother smirks. I've done a lot of things in my life without consulting you! Although lightly shaking her head, she holds my gaze, firm and a bit amused, as if enjoying my discombobulation. I feel shocked, alarmed, and yet so admiring of her audaciousness! She did it, I think, she finally reached her goal, she got her own art show! My mother plucks some imaginary crumbs from my shoulder. You know, she says, now that your father is gone – he would never have approved – and now that Cocky has decided to realize his life's dream and become a chef, and now that the hotel owner supports my project, I feel I can do it. I hope you'll be proud of me, even get a kick out of it! You could give a speech at the reception. Will you do it?

I see my mother living near the sea, in a house at the beach, all the windows open, a fresh breeze moving through! Canaries cruise the hallway, sit on picture frames, lampposts, or the big wooden mantelpiece in the living room, peer and chirp, fly in and out. She stands at her easel in front of the window and looks at the high-tide waves rolling in and breaking just in front of her eyes with sun-filled foam-drops sparkling in the air. It's mesmerizing. Thoughts and images floating by, lingering, disappearing, and eventually prodding a gesture of her hand that is holding the brush. This is how she paints. She stands, a blank canvas in front of her, she harkens and waits. She waits for a spark to grow inside until it hurts, burns, gives her a bit of a searing scare — and finally catching the drift and fanning it, there would be a whoosh, and all would come soaring out, a storm, soft and strong — and she would be flying without fear. It's miraculous. It's mysterious. She has no idea what will emerge. I only made it up, but I can see myself sitting at her feet, and my presence would be nothing other than an occasional move, just adding to the draft she's gliding in. And so goes the day.

Again and again Marlene wondered whether this would be all she would make out of her life: just family? In those long silent hours when Lukas worked in the factory, Enna was at school, and Sine was sleeping in her crib, in those endless stretches of time when the smoke of her cigarette would curl over her coffee cup as if veiling her dreams, she tried to imagine that someday there would be something else, something? Every so often she puzzled over her lack of courage to at least make use of the watercolors she'd secretly bought and hidden in the closet behind the bedsheets. She could start, she thought, and didn't move, even though hours would pass before anybody came and claimed her attention. It could mean a lot! For instance, she could take this nail she'd picked up on her last walk through the fields; it had caught her eye with a sudden spark of crimson gleam; she could glue it on the canvass, she thought, or pierce it through the dense material so that only its head, crusted with rust – this natural expression of time passing, she mused – would stick out right in the middle of the blank screen, and then surround it with – what? – yellow or red? – or black? – colors flowing from the outer rim towards the center, blending there in a puddle before seeping through the fabric's pores and leaving behind nothing but a dingy spot. Life. We appear and slip away, she pondered, we fumble without reaching the hand we're groping for. And then she wrote on a piece of paper: Strange signs cross our efforts, but the yearning persists; will I ever lift the veil…? Finally, as if awaking from these obscure reflections, she would give a nod to herself, reassured that there was a place in her mind that was all hers, and nobody would ever guess that it even existed.

Sam calls. I missed my flight, he says, I couldn't find my car. I know I parked it close to my hotel, but now it's nowhere. I walked and walked, looked everywhere…I have to return it! He falls silent, because this is where he is now, at the end of his wits. You missed your flight for a rental car? I say, and feel how much it upsets me. Maybe it's stolen, he tries with little conviction, I have to take care of this, go to the police…I pull myself together. I understand. Okay, I say, that's a good idea: report the car as stolen, and get onto the next available flight. Shall do, he says, and adds, I'm sorry. We hang up. But then I think, he didn't rent a car! He was picked up by the people from this company. Could he have forgotten? Or why would he have rented a car? I call back, but now his line is busy. Again and again I try, but can't get through. Maybe now he is talking with the police…

Lukas closes his eyes. He feels tired. Lately he could lie down for a nap as early as midmorning. Instead, Lukas asks his secretary to bring him an espresso. But when she enters with the scent of freshly ground coffee beans around her, Lukas has already fallen asleep in his chair, his chin on his chest, his hands in his lap. Quietly she puts the little cup on his desk and tiptoes out. He may as well take a little rest, he is not the youngest anymore. But when Lukas awakens from a short dream that slips away as soon as he opens his eyes, he's ashamed of himself. Lately many things that he used to find no trouble with, feel exhausting. Or boring. Lukas sits up and sips the cold espresso. He grabs the phone receiver to finally make this call – who did he want to call this morning? It seemed urgent when he remembered, and now he can't remember what it was. But since he already has the telephone receiver in his hand, he dials the food vendor's number and orders an extra delivery of fresh berries to upgrade the desserts in the cafeteria. Then he looks out of the window over the factory's courtyard, and for a while he watches the leaves of the chestnut tree move in the summer breeze. I'm growing old, he thinks. How many summers will I have left? I must sell the factory, find a new owner, someone who takes good care of my employees. How fast these years went by, and yet it seems a long time since I started to rebuild it all. A long life, so many collections of wallpaper – father would have been proud to see his factory blossom – or at least make it – well enough. Would it really matter to him if he could see what his son achieved? Yes, he had hinted at it, but in the end, how much did he care? Maybe it was I who wanted to do something for him, if only belatedly, something he'd be pleased with. Or was it just the best opportunity for me at the time? Maybe both. What else would I have done? And once I started, I made it mine. But now it seems again like I did it for him. And when I think that there may be only a few years left to my life, maybe three, five, eight…everything short of ten years sounds so awfully short. If I knew I'd have ten or more years, I would relax. But I don't know. And the years are rushing by, faster and faster, while I take longer and longer every day to do even the ordinary things…And then my father looks down at his hand, this strong knobby hand with its warped fingers, its wrinkled loose skin, and its protruding veins, this hand that has gripped, tackled, and held whatever came along, sifted, smoothed, and felt with curiosity and pride what he'd produced over the years, and as he's now imagining his machines grinding to a halt, a shy, melancholic smile is flitting over his face: guess this will be it, he thinks, and with a soft sigh he gets up and leaves his office.

It was early in the year, January or February. I wasn't allowed to go to school because I was sick with mumps. And a man was dying on the stairs to our house. But I didn't know that he was dying. Nobody had seen him coming. He was half sitting and half lying, to rest, only to rest. His wide gray coat was cascading down three steps covering most of his boots, which proved that he still had two feet to walk away, because they shivered, both boots, intermittently trembled and then stood still again as if to rest, yes, to rest. He seemed to have made sure that he wouldn't prevent anybody from leaving or entering our house, because he had folded his body almost at right angles with his back closely snuggled to the wall near the doorframe, and his legs following the path of the handrail's iron posts. A considerate man under a heap of gray fabric. The collar lounged over much of his face, a woolen bonnet covered his head, kept it warm. It was such a cold winter day! I was standing at our dining room's bay window staring at him. I was wondering if I should go and tell my mother, who was getting ready to go out. Or should I go and bring him coffee? His feet shivered. I have to run, sweetie, I hear my mother yell in the hallway, too rushed to come in and properly say goodbye. Through the window I see her opening the door. She steps out and as she is closing the door she briefly pauses. With one heel of her pumps momentarily hanging in the air as if in search of an untroubled landing place, she looks shocked or possibly pensive—or am I just expecting her to halt and look at this man, take care of him or call someone to do so? But only fleetingly she seems to notice this shadow at her side, perhaps too rushed to capture the imperative of a dying man. On she hurries down the stairs, and off she drives in her car. Incapable of deciding what to do, I keep standing at the window looking at this man. His feet tremble less and less. Maybe he's falling asleep? Then a flashing blue light. A police car stops in front of our house. My mother or someone must have called them. Two officers come up the stairs. They don't even bother to ring the doorbell, which would allow me to finally come out and be close by. Maybe my mother told them that nobody was home. The first officer taps the man's shoulder. When nothing happens he turns the body around. Now the man is lying flat on his back, his arms and legs sprawled over the short flight of stairs. I can't see his face. Hovering above without further touching him, the two officers talk with each other. Then one takes off a glove and holds his fingers to the man's neck. A moment later he straightens up and says something to the other officer, who then takes his walkie-talkie and speaks into it. I guess they call an ambulance. The first officer lights a cigarette. They wait. I wait. Then an ambulance comes down the street. No flashing light. Two medics come up. They hunch over the man, lightly slap his cheek, flash a light into his eyes, check the pulse at his neck, briefly wait and then straighten up again. They talk with the officers. They shake their heads. They leave the man lying in this uncomfortable position! While the medics go back to their ambulance, the police officers search the pockets and the insides of the man's coat. Then the medics come back with a black plastic bag, put it around the man and zip it up. Now it looks as if he's been small, thin and light, but the bag seems to be heavy! I can see it when they put it on a stretcher, drag it down the stairs, and hoist it into the ambulance. The medics close the doors and drive off. One of the police officers goes back to his car and stops the flashing of the blue light. The other remains standing at our door as if lost in thought. Finally he grinds his cigarette out on the top stair, turns around and looks into the window, right where I stand watching him. He looks at me, and I feel caught and ashamed.

Meanwhile, four workmen have managed to take the big window out of its fixture. A cool morning breeze has filled the lobby. You have to leave, the hotel owner tells me, we're removing all the furniture to make room for your mother's art show. I get up and retreat but continue standing next to the elevator, because it's so interesting to watch how the sofas, armchairs, tables, and rolled-up carpets are carried to the window, lifted through the open space and then pulled onto the floor of the truck. Amazing how much they can fit in. It's moving day! Enna and I cannot be in anybody's way. Mother has parked us on the kitchen's windowsill, each with a butter pretzel for lunch. Our apartment is emptied out. We'll move to a big house, father had announced months earlier. I like it here, I'd countered. Nobody listened. Now Enna claims: we will have separate rooms! But I don't want to sleep alone, I object. She gives me a pitiful look. I'm already done with my pretzel and gaze at hers. You can finish mine, Enna says, because she knows what I'm thinking. Mollified, I accept her offer. When the last chair is heaved out of the window, I take the elevator to return to my room.

It's so quiet here, and dark. I slip out of bed. My naked feet curl when they touch the cold stone floor. I don't remember where the light switch is, where Enna sleeps, or where my parents are, because we are in a hotel, that's what I remember, and we got a babysitter to watch over us, but she is nowhere either. Light is shining in through the doorway, that's where I go, because the dark silence makes me anxious. I can't reach the doorknob, it's too high up. I'm trapped! Enna, I whisper, and when she doesn't respond, I call louder: Enna! Enna! There is no answer. Suddenly the light comes on, and a strange woman sitting in a wing chair next to the bed squints at me. What's up? She wonders, yawns, and struggles herself out of a big blanket that's wrapped around her, chin to feet. Where's Enna? I ask. She's with your parents, the woman responds, they are at the reception down in the hotel lobby. I want to go there too, I demand. It's only for grown-ups, the woman claims. No, I insist, Enna isn't a grown-up either. True, the woman says, and smiles a bit. Take me there, I order. I'm supposed to make sure that you stay here, she counters, but she comes and picks me up, sits me on her arm, next to her big bust, and holds me tight as she opens the door. She smells of strawberries. I don't like to be so close to her, but she can open the door. When we enter the hallway the lights come on. I hear music coming from a lower area of the hotel. Look, she says, and places me on the balustrade securing me with her arms all around me, there is the reception! And I look far down where lots of people are mingling, the music is playing, and something exciting is going on. I can't see my parents or Enna, but I'm mesmerized by the crowd swirling around the bar and the dancefloor like petal-dotted water in a whirlpool. For a long time I sit there and watch. If I had the right outfit, I'd go there too, but I am in my pajamas, and that's why I eventually agree to go back to bed.

How would she deal with all the attention? For all her life Marlene has craved to be somebody noticeable, but she also has liked to be secretive in unchallenged ways. And now all these people are looking at her! Or are they? Many don't even seem to register that she is the artist. They greet and hug each other, stroll along, a drink in hand, chatting with friends or standing in small groups discussing something, but not necessarily her art. Marlene looks at the crowd, a bit alienated and disappointed, even angered, yet also relieved. The thought of being almost invisible tickles her. She can spy on people, eavesdrop on what they say about her pictures. She also plays with the idea of slipping out, escaping through the back door, being where nobody can ask her questions like: how do you feel about coming out as an avantgarde artist so late in your life; who do you consider yourself most akin to or influenced by; are you making a feminist or an octogenarian or an anti-minimalist statement, since your paintings are so exuberant, provocative, maybe even sexually explicit, indeed very female – here for instance, where it looks like blood gushing out of a marble triangle, and here, the black mass, which seems to be engulfing the pink, light as skin, on the other side of the canvas, and this face, or what could be seen as a face, in purple, in pain, shrill and beyond…A tall man in a tuxedo approaches her, a smile on his face, a price list in his hands; he seems to want to talk with her, the artist, but what would she say? I see Lilli, small but feisty, her cheeks red and round, yet I also see Marlene, who is anxious, feels overwhelmed, insecure, and she therefore turns away, as if she hadn't seen this potential buyer – he would have been the first had she let him – if only she had! Instead she roams through the crowd as if alone, unrecognized, and forgotten, familiar only with herself. As a sign of respect for her quirks, not even the hotel owner dares to be at her side. The tuxedo has disappeared. Everybody has someone to talk with except for her, who experiences all of this like the strange start of a dream.

I have nothing left to do. Why am I still here? I could leave and meet Sam at home. This long trip home…I open the balcony door and step out. It's windy and cool. Gray and rough, the moor stretches to the horizon. Out of sight the sea is belting the coast. Maybe this has been my life, calm, steady, good, and now at the end of my journey, the sky is as close as the ground. Scaled up to the balustrade and sitting between two empty flowerpots, I may just accidentally become unbalanced or fly out with the buzzards, oblivious of the weight that life has put on my heels. If only I could get myself to flap my wings, but my arms are heavy, and my editor-in-chief remains silent when I fall through the empty hours of this morning, this morning without Sam. It doesn't have to be that way. There is always more to come. And yet! I leave myself before the rush ends. I look down from the balcony at this sorry spot. It was a mistake! I cannot feel myself touching the ground. I land with a thud. I break through and through but look like I'm curled up on velvet cushions. All motion walks out on me, one by one, and starts swirling around in a crazy dance. The chauffeur runs over. He looks up to my balcony and down to these shattered bones and shakes his head. The man from the reception desk joins him. He feels for the carotid and can't get a heartbeat. He returns to the lobby to call for an ambulance. The chauffeur shrugs his shoulders and withdraws to the garage. The place is quiet, the winds have calmed down. The cockatoo eyeballs me from the hotel's flagpole. The sky is red, and the air is full of music. And there is the little girl, crouched down next to me. She wears a yellow dress, pale like the moon, and even though she wants to go to her party, she stays and watches over me.

This silence feels suffocating. Sam, I say, I'm so glad that you are here. I don't know what I would do without you! He gives me a concerned look. What's troubling you? He asks. I can't tell him, and I keep my eyes closed, pretending not to have heard his question. I hope I can fall asleep, because I don't want to face it, not now and maybe never. Sam slightly shakes me, saying: tell me! And so I want to tell him, but the words betray me. I tremble, I stammer just incomprehensible stuff. Sam interrupts me: shush, he says, calm down, you can figure things out. Yet desperation hits me, and I claw my fingers onto the plank of our boat that is shaking in the storm as if about to break apart at any moment. How did I get thrown overboard? I'm wearing a lifesaving vest, yellow and red and puffed up all around me, the water is icy, froth whips my face, the currents try to wrench me off the plank, to wash me away, they pull and punch me, but I hold onto the ship, I splutter, gasp, and cough, going up and down, with every wave-breaker banging tons of water on me…And finally, there is Sam's hand stretched over the edge of our boat, and holding on to the reeling as he leans out as far as he can and grabs my hand and pulls me, pulls, and I flail and scream and struggle, and he holds my hand, doesn't let go, and finally he is able to drag me onto the ship. There I lie, a heavily breathing, shivering, whimpering chunk of wet cloth, still in the middle of the storm—but safe again, safe with Sam.

They put me into a box. It's made of birch tree, raw planks unadorned, which pleases me. Even though it looked rather narrow, I feel quite comfortable in it. Right hand put above my left. The hotel owner stares at me and smirks for unknown reasons. Next to him the Chairman of Pinpoint Pharmaceuticals appears. He wears a big woolen scarf around his neck, his nose shines red, his eyes are swollen – obviously he's still sick with his cold. What happened to her? He asks. She fell from the balcony, the hotel owner responds, sheepishly grinning and rubbing his hands. I want to object but decide to keep my mouth shut. Meanwhile a limousine has been slowly crackling over the gravel. It stops only a few feet away from my coffin. The chauffeur gets out and opens the back door. Maybe Sam has arrived? Instead I see an airy veil of tulle rising above the black car's roof, then a hand holding a bouquet of white flowers, and finally the whole bride gets out. They're having a wedding here, I think, and feel a bit excited as if I were invited. Now the other door opens and an apparent groom disembarks, black suit, silver tie, and a fitting silver pocket square elegantly arranged with one corner sticking up, two others casually hanging down. He looks over to my coffin. I'm surprised. It's the guy from Randy's Roadrunner Rentals! He buttons up his jacket and hurries around the back of the limousine towards his bride. Slowly, as if reluctant, she turns around, and now I can see it: she is the waitress from the coffee shop in Watertown! How strange, I arrived only a few days ago, and already I know the whole place! The chauffeur makes a bow in front of the bride and groom, gets back into the limousine and drives off. Randy offers his arm, the brides takes it, and together they stride to a lawn in front of the hotel, where some of the lobby furniture has been arranged into a long table set for at least 20 guests. Before sitting down, the bride struggles to reel in her long tulle veil, which had run behind her over the dirt and is now carefully piled up behind her chair. Randy has already taken his seat. He is reading the menu. And here comes Lilli, dressed in a lovely summer suit and high heels, her long curlers beautifully arranged – she looks stunning! Next to her, Peacock in brown cords and a sweatshirt, somewhat unfitting for the occasion, but obviously in high spirits; he carries two bottles of wine, which he places in front of the groom. I'm glad that it's not their wedding. And then the guests come running from all sides, swarm around the table, haggle for a good seat, snatch a chair and sit down after placing their gift-wrapped wedding presents in front of them between the wine bottles and bread baskets. It seems to me that I've seen some of these people before, maybe in the greenhouse or during the congress or at the market hall, I can't quite remember, but they all look somehow familiar. And amongst them, to my surprise I also discover the man with the binoculars, which are now hanging down on his hairy chest. He has left his tree to attend the wedding party? Cocky grumbles: can't we close the coffin – I don't like how Sine is staring at me. My mother shakes her head and reassures him: She won't do a thing, let her be. The waiter pours wine in the glasses. An old musician plays compositions of Nino Rota on his accordion. I wonder about the wedding cake. The bride smiles.

Sam is lost in thought, but if he were asked, he wouldn't be able to say what he's thinking about. Light is swimming by. From afar a siren wails. His throat is clogged. The last he remembers is waiting at a police station to make a report. A long time ago. He was told to wait. Two officers keep mumbling in what seems like a random conversation. The wooden bench hurts his back. He sits and waits. He is tired, feels hot, his joints ache. It is past midnight. And as Sam is looking over to one of the officers while trying to formulate a succinct complaint, he realizes that he can't say for sure what the color of his rental car was. Was it gray or silver or taupe or beige? Maybe it doesn't matter if he knows the license plate, which seemed easy to remember when he first read it, but now he isn't sure about that either. The rental company will know, he just has to give them the name…Sam feels weak and feverish. He closes his eyes, just to rest a bit, the officers will tell him when they're ready. But what was the name… and he strolls along this small street considering…he did the right thing, and now he's ready to travel back home to Sine who is waiting for him. Someone shakes his shoulder, Sam lifts his foot to sit up straight, but instead he slides down a green slope, an endless lawn, but they grab him in time, and he wants to apologize, but he has no air to exhale the words. They lift him onto a stretcher and secure him with bands all around him, safe and tight. No idea, the officer says, he just came here, that's all. And Sam wants to say something but drifts off in a fog of pinkish mesh, slips through heavy air without oxygen, flies or falters and ends up between two white barriers that prevent him from running away – if he still has it in him to run…

Now a toast for the bridal couple, the hotel director proclaims, and gets up from his chair to give a speech, not noticing or minding that he has his napkin stuck in the collar of his shirt. He harrumphs and solemnly says: I'm honored and proud that my dear friends, Ran & Rose, as we call them, have chosen my hotel for their wedding party. A wedding, that's serious business! Heaven knows! When you marry you join forces, sort of merge them, and soon you can't tell them apart anymore. Congratulations! I was there once, believe me! When my dear wife left – or should I say: when she chose to run away with one of our hotel guests before he'd paid his bill – or maybe she only ran after him to collect the money he owed us (a comforting alternative I entertain) – anyway, when she ran, and she'd hinted at that in the preceding days (in retrospect I had to admit that to myself), well, to say it plainly: in her pursuit of honesty or happiness she hurried, couldn't wait – patience never was her strong suit – and so she may have taken a dumb shortcut and perhaps drowned in the moor, poor thing! The terrible truth is: she just disappeared, never came back, never turned up to this other guy either (I checked with him), never sent a postcard from Australia or wherever…To make a long story short: when that happened, years ago – yet it still feels like yesterday – I experienced first-hand how weak I was without her! I'd joined forces with her, and then I lost them all…Moved to tears by his own account, he honks his nose, raises his glass and concludes: Be strong, be together, be strong together! To the bride and groom, to the new couple! Everybody claps as he sits down. The Chairman of Pinpoint Pharmaceuticals bellows: "Now it's your duty to have many children!" Everybody laughs and cheers. At the other end of the table the chauffeur gets up and shouts: My wedding present is ten free rides, wherever you want to go, and be it around the world! All laugh and applaud. The bride blows him a kiss. The night porter hollers: Take him up on that! Now an elderly woman next to Randy gets up, taps a spoon on her glass, and when there is proper silence she says: Hello everybody! I'm Randy's mom, and over there (she points across the table), this is his dad. We invited you all, so welcome to this festive occasion! And a hearty welcome to you, my dear Rose, welcome to our family! Randy tried many times to get married and always failed. Don't know why, but the ladies took off, one after the other. Not you though! I'm glad he finally made it. He's a good guy, sweet-tempered, and with a little oversight of his father, he runs the bike shop quite well. Rose, eventually you may decide to stop serving coffee and rather join me in the office to take care of the bills and orders and phone calls. I can introduce you to it all, it's not too complicated. But take your time, no pressure from our side. Anyway, my husband and I have thought of a meaningful present for the two of you, and here you go – Jack, why don't you get our present…? And a short, portly man across from Randy's mother jumps up, hurries over to the garage, and only moments later he shows up with a tandem, red and shiny. Merrily he activates the bike-bell. The guests scream

Oooh! and Ahhh! Randy gets up, walks over, and shakes his father's hand. He seems touched; sheepishly smiling, he eyes this parental gift. His father passes him the handlebars and returns to his seat at the table. Randy tests the air pressure of the tires. Then he beckons Rose. Immediately Rose takes off her bridal veil, stuffs it under her seat and joins Randy. There they stand, a young couple on their wedding day, and everybody is looking at them. The treeman, having exchanged his binoculars with a photo apparatus, rushes over and takes their picture. Randy blushes, briefly hesitates, but then he turns to his young bride and loudly says for everybody to hear: Rose, you are the bloom of my heart, you make my life blossom, may we flourish together! The audience laughs and applauds. The bride whispers something into Randy's ear, and he nods. They mount the tandem, she in front, he behind her, and together they start riding off; a bit wobbly it looks as they slowly struggle over the bumpy grassland, but as soon as they reach the road to Watertown they gain speed and in perfect harmony they smoothly glide into the twilight of this day, a flower garland flapping behind them. *Goodbye* crows the cockatoo. The guests are swaying to the soulful tunes of Fellini's *Amacord* – maybe dreaming about getting married just once more. Lilli and Peacock are dancing. I sit up, get out of my coffin, and without further ado return to my room.

DEPARTURE

At the hotel they change the sheets every day. Lying on my bed I inhale the fresh laundry detergent and miss the scent of Sam's shower gel, his aftershave, even his sweat after workouts. I miss Sam. When he gets back, we'll have to seriously talk. We are in the last third or even fourth of our life: How do we want to spend it? What is important to each of us? That's what I want to bring up. Pensively he looks at me. Good question, he finally says, and after a while: I'm not yet done with work. I think I can push my research still further. There is one more step I want to take. If I retired now, it would feel like giving up. Others would take over and make it. Maybe I'm too vain to grant them that. But there is also this: what else would I do? My work is such an important part of my life — you and my work — that's all I care about. He shifts a strand of his hair out of his sight, and I see the dark circles under his eyes, which I had noticed before but had forgotten about not wanting to realize how tired and stressed he'd felt before going to this conference. Softly I say: At least Peacock will step down from his post at the university and be a cook. Peevishly

Sam looks at me and grumbles: He's said that for years, and I don't care about him. No! It's about this idea: I want to give voice to those who can't speak. I believe it's possible. Right now I have a great team. We work well together. I don't want to let my colleagues down. I shouldn't even have considered joining this company in California. This was a mistake. They just want to grab my results, market ridiculous gadgets, and run profits. I think I'll continue where I am now, try to refine the algorithm for our speech-neuroprosthesis, make it work faster, better…Oh, I interject, and realize that I had completely forgotten about it, the monitor, right? Yes, Sam confirms, and his voice sounds slightly impatient, the monitor's communication with a neuro-chip, that too needs improvement. It would help so many people, for example people with A.L.S. or cerebral palsy, a device which can read and vocalize what these patients want to say. And then maybe along the way there will be an algorithm that could tell us what we have forgotten, fragments of previous thoughts, started and left hanging, prescient thoughts that didn't make sense at the time but would now, or what we were dreaming at night, a key to our unconscious, our memories, there is so much going on in the brain…Wouldn't it be interesting if we knew more about it?

The monitor! Where is it anyway? I jump up, open the closet, rummage around in the drawers, almost blind from a sudden panic for no reason as my hands feel through the soft tissues of socks, shirts, and scarves, lift blouses and turn sweaters, but there is nothing. How strange that Sam didn't take his monitor on his trip, I think, and want to blame him for putting me in the position of having to guard and now lose it or be responsible for not having paid attention. Had he asked me to make sure that it is always loaded? I hadn't plugged it in for so long. I hadn't heard it beep or hum. I kneel down to check under the bed. Nothing. Maybe the maids had helped themselves to it, because it gave them so much to giggle about. Or the little girl took it when she was here, just wanted to play with it? Or had the monitor played *me* the whole time, and I hadn't noticed? Why hadn't I given it a closer look while Sam was gone?

Here, Sam calls, and throws the little prototype he has been tinkering with over to me. I catch it and throw it back, which surprises him, but just like that he returns it, and for a short while we play shuttlecock in our living room. The doors to the garden are wide open, the sun is shining in, it's Saturday, Mikki is with a friend for a sleepover, time is ours. Okay, I eventually suggest, I win, and you have to take me out for brunch. I will, Sam replies, but first I'll ravage you a bit, and he takes me in his arms and starts kissing me all over till

I'm out of breath. Laughingly we roll on the carpet. Puck comes running, tail wagging, excitedly barks, he thinks we are playing and wants to be part of it. Well, Sam suggests, breakfast first. And we put Puck on the leash, take the big basket and go to the farmer's market, buy apples and peaches and big blue plums, salad, parsley, and radish, and at the end sunflowers, small and sturdy, a big bunch, they'll look nice in our entry hall! Sam carries the basket. Hand in hand we stroll over to our favorite coffee shop and take a seat at one of the outdoor tables that gets the full morning sun. I have cereal with berries, Sam orders a scrambled eggs sandwich, and we both have cappuccino. Puck gets a little treat. He sits at Sam's feet and watches the scene, maybe looking out for other dogs. I wonder if I should stop writing, I say. Sam peers over to me. Why would you do that? He asks, surprised, playful, just taking this conversation lightly. I'm not sure, I reply, it's so hard to find a publisher for the things I like to write. It's discouraging. To write just for the fun of it doesn't seem right. Sam puts his hand on mine and slightly squeezes it. I like what you write, Sine, he says. And Enna likes it, and your friend Linda enjoyed your short stories, you got good feedback. Yeah, I say, but still – shouldn't I rather engage at Mikki's school, help with their theatre productions or sit on the school board, do something more productive...? You can do both, Sam gives back, the one doesn't preclude the other. But you shouldn't give up what you enjoy most. I see it when you are writing:

you are fully focused. I like that you get so involved in your stories. It's your passion! Sam has reassured me before, and I'm grateful that again he holds this space open for me. Still I'm reluctant. My father always wanted to write, and now he runs his wallpaper factory, I demur. Yes, Sam gives back, he wanted to be the breadwinner for his family, it was his choice, but does it make him happy? Puck barks and for a while we watch him trying to make contact with an old lab that has settled next to its master at a table nearby. Eventually I resume: Is being happy the decisive criterion? Not the only one, Sam emphasizes, but yes, an important one. He lets go of my hand to pull out his wallet and pay the bill. The shadow of the big chestnut tree has reached our table. We decide to go home. Getting up, Sam says, maybe you can get a degree and teach creative writing; then you'll be doing what you like best and feel socially connected and productive in the common sense; it may even give you access to some publishers…

Something whispers in my ear, but when I open my eyes, I can't see anything, our bedroom is dark with scant light shining in through the curtains from the streetlamps, but I'd heard it so clearly, it was Mikki's voice, saying something with an urgency that worries me. Sam lies with his back towards me, calmly breathing. Was it a dream? I sit up and look around. Our bedroom door is closed, but as my eyes adjust to the dark I see Mikki sitting on the fauteuil in the corner next to my bedside. Mikki, I whisper, what are you doing here? She doesn't respond. Gazing at me with big stern eyes, her blond curlers springing off her little face like a halo, she looks like a china doll. Mikki, I call her again and slip out of bed, but as soon as I'm on my feet, she's gone. Relieved, I realize it was a dream, only a dream. But since I'm already up I decide to go check on her. The hallway boards softly creak as I go over to her room. I hear the grandfather clock ticking in the living room. It's like in a movie, I think, and slowly turn the door handle to Mikki's room. Her comforter is mounted up, her stuffed bear has fallen to the carpet. Where is she? Cautious not to awaken her I surround her bed, thinking that as so often happens she may be curled up at the foot end. But when I lift the cover, the bed is empty. I'm shocked! Mikki, I call, Mikki? There's no answer. In a panic I rush over to our bedroom to awaken Sam, tell him that Mikki's gone, kidnapped, lost…I push open the door, I'm ready to shake Sam awake – but then I see Mikki, dressed in Sam's flannel shirt, sleeping on my pillow, her hand snug under Sam's shoulder. Holding my breath I stand there watching the two, my whole world wrapped in this night's dream. How I love them! How I want to protect them! They are everything to me! A nightingale chirps. Happily I tiptoe over to the fauteuil and nestle down in its soft cushions to spend the rest of the night.

There is a soft knock on my door. Who may want to come for a visit? I open and can't see anything. The movement detector that used to turn on the lights in the hallway whenever I stepped over the doorsill had stopped working a few days ago and hadn't been fixed despite my repeated complaints. Only the Emergency Exit sign sends its red beam through the empty silence of this place. But now I spot the hotel director leaning on the wall opposite my door. He looks disheveled; his striped bathrobe barely covers a loose T-shirt over sagging sweatpants; a flashlight hanging down from his hand flickers onto his sneakers. I say Hi, and he shuffles closer. He smells of beer and cold smoke. Excuse my unseemly appearance, Madame, he offers with a hoarse voice, I caught the cold from one of our guests, and it got worse since the heating in my chambers was cut off. We are out of season, you know, and I meant to request, if you don't mind, to let me know the date of your departure. I don't want to throw you out, by no means! However, you may want to know that the movers will be coming in the next few days. Of course they will take the smaller items first, pictures, mirrors, chairs, etc., but there will be some commotion, which might disturb your peace of mind. I've put them on hold to adjust to your plans. You are a valued customer, and I respect your needs for flexibility… His announcement shocks and frightens me. Can I stay till Saturday, I rush to ask him and explain that I have to reorganize my travel plans.

But actually I didn't have any plans, I never meant to leave, and now I feel rudely forced out. The hotel director takes a fulsome bow and artfully smiles. Of course, Madame, he whispers, Saturday it is.

The help, a young woman in a plain gray dress, who has just explained to me with unnerving patience the rules of the house and the functioning of the various items and call buttons at my disposal, gives me a friendly smile and asks me if there is anything else that I might need right now. Absently I shake my head, stunned that I have arrived here, albeit by my own choice, here at this place, which will be my last residence – can that really be? The aid softly closes the door. Many times she may have sensed how alienating it is for a new resident to move into assisted living, even if the contracted assistance is only part-time, and the senior still is, as they say, semi-independent. Now here I am in my bedroom-study-kitchenette with bathroom and partial service expandable to full time care. Little could I take to this place. Mikki and I had carefully sifted through my belongings. Each item had brought up memories and the question of whether I still needed to hold on to its physicality or could content myself with thinking of it – each item a pinch in my heart. Mikki had taken some pieces of furniture, photo albums, and a small sculpture, the rest went to charity and will enter the lives of others who will weave their own stories around it. And the things I did bring along now look strange in this strange environment, recognizable but deprived of their familiar contexts – as if not mine any longer. They placed my walker next to the door, which makes sense. My laptop on the small desk is still closed and plugged in to recharge. The bed is covered with the Crazy Quilt that Sam had given me for our tenth anniversary. Looking around I tell myself that it's alright, it's how it ends. I need help, I can't deal with everything on my own anymore, and I don't want to. I will be here, they'll take care of me, cook and clean for me, and I'll write till my last glimmer, why not! It's just inevitable. Will you be okay? Mikki had asked me, and I could see how much it pained her to leave me here, but I had insisted, I wanted her to live her life rather than take care of mine. Absolutely, I had said, and she had hugged me, trying to hide the tears in her eyes, but I had seen them and felt grateful for her empathy. I'll call you tonight, she had reassured me. I had thanked her for all her help and waved as she left and kept turning to me after each step as if to indicate that she could easily stop and undo everything. Slowly I walk to the window and sit in the chair, which I guess will be my favorite. Next to it on a small book stand there is a lamp well suited to reading. The window offers a view out into the park in front of the main lobby where the sign Aurora Assisted Living is surrounded by flower arrangements all year round, even in winter, as they had prided themselves. I sit down and look over the big lawn, and a deep calm arises in me. Here I am in the last stretch of my long life. It was a good life. I'm okay with making these last adjustments that are required now. Beyond that I can end my life as I please with maybe some more good years still to come. I nod to myself. I would like that.

In the late afternoon I decide to take a walk. When I step out of the lobby, the little girl joins me. She takes my hand like a duck takes to water. Silently we walk along the road and then veer to the moor land. I notice that she leads the way, gently nudging me towards the hills, and since I have no particular goal in mind, I let her guide me. Soon I will leave, I say to her, and she nods as if she already knew. We won't talk about it. Anyway I'm not sure when I will leave for real, because I dread the lone way home. To my surprise I hear myself asking her: Do you want to come with me? Did I say or only think this? The little girl doesn't react. She seems focused on a small hill in front of us, a nice knoll over-grown with red heather sitting among the gray stones like a child's ball, deflated and useless but still shining. It hadn't been there before, I think, or I hadn't noticed. With a jar the girl breaks away from me, runs towards the hill and at its foot she turns right and disappears behind its slope. She seems to know her way, but does she? Isn't it dangerous to run around here? Anxiously I speed up, unsure about the muddy ground, concerned about myself and her, but I want to see where she went. I turn around the mound – and look: there is Maddy, a white calf at her side! Both stand as if on display on a green moss patch just fitting their size. The little girl kneels next to the calf and pets its shaggy fur. Maddy moos and runs her long pink tongue over her newborn's eyes. I'm stunned! At some distance I sit down to watch the scene. The calf now stumbles ahead, latches onto the udder and eagerly drinks from the teat as milk is drooling and dripping down from its chops. We all gaze at it in wonder. I'm getting goosebumps. Mikki and I struggled so much before we finally figured it out. She was born early and so small, I was anxious, it hurt. Finally, Sam got a nursing aid who covered my nipples with cabbage leaves, which calmed the inflammation. Eventually we made it, and then I enjoyed every bit of it. What a peaceful time we had, long hours musing and humming, just she and I, sinking deep into the dark blue of each other's eyes…Maddy looks at me and smiles.

Well, I have to get ready! I open the closet doors and the drawers, throw my luggage onto my bed and separate the shoes and clothes I still want to use till Saturday from the rest that can be packed now. It's much easier to fill the suitcase at the end than at the beginning of a trip. Since most will go to the cleaner and into the laundry, I don't have to worry about wrinkles. I hear the movers in the hallway calling each other, banging, dropping, and dragging stuff across the floor, opening and closing doors. What a noise! The hotel seems filled with life. All of a sudden! Now my phone would ring. It hasn't rung in days, and since I wouldn't recognize the number on the display I'd be reluctant to pick it up. Because if I did someone would tell me that they have Sam in their ICU, that he came in on Monday with a sepsis, that he's not out of the woods yet but better, and that they think he'll make it, they're taking good care of him. No! No! I would drop everything and try to get to him, but how? He's so far away, so far…! Why would I think that? Why this shocking fantasy? I take Sam's flannel shirt, my favorite, off its hanger, bury my face in it, and take a deep breath, sniff it…Long ago it lost its scent, but it is as if it were about to come back any moment.

This is the moment he'd pictured and played with many times. Lukas, upright in front of his desk, picks up one piece after the other, all these figurines he'd received and collected over the years, the utensils he'd used a million times at work, all these items, which now are scattered over his desk as if waiting for his call to muster, but instead of lining them up, as had been his habit, Lukas just grabs and drops them into the black hole of his briefcase. He had signed the contract in the morning, by which he had sold his company. All of it. How had he gotten to the point of doing this, after it had been steadily growing since his grandfather had founded it in 1895, his father had taken it over against all odds at the beginning of the Great Depression, and he, Lukas, had successfully expanded and modernized it, in such a way that Camber Wallpaper Inc., employing now more than a thousand people, had developed into a prosperous firm, an even culturally valued institution, giving scholarships and awards to writers, artists and musicians—and still he had to sell it, because neither Enna nor Sine wanted to run it, which was good, no doubt, so someone else needed to take over. That's how it goes. Lukas feels tired and unsure how to think about these last moments in his office. Is there relief, remorse, or merely resignation? He wavers a bit before taking a small oil painting off the wall. It shows his grandfather sitting at his desk, the very desk he's now cleaning out. Lukas wraps the painting in a sample of wallpaper that had been brought in just yesterday. His eyes scrutinize his desk, this piece of furniture that had suited his grandfather, his father and himself – all of a sudden it looks shabby. Shabby! What a surprise! The simple design and simple wood of this desk used to radiate his family's tradition, modesty, dignity and design. The luster is gone. In fact it looks so run down that Lukas knows the new owner will immediately discard it. No one will want to sit at it any longer. He stops picking up what is his. All items look dead, are dead. All will be cast away. With a vague smile on his face he closes his briefcase, and as he turns to leave his office, his former office, he sees a little indentation in the desk's top drawer, this sharp nick that Sine once when she was little had stabbed into the wood with his scissors, because she was so mad at him for staying at work and not joining her at her birthday party. Throughout the years it had always made him smile when his eyes touched upon this little nick, his daughter's mark. He puts his finger on it, covers the little hole, senses its raw edges. A sharp pain rips through his heart. How could he leave this desk? He feels like picking it up, slipping it into his briefcase, carrying it home, and sitting with it for the rest of his life...Lukas walks out, walks through the long hallway as he has done so many times before, past his employees—his former employees' doors, these doors that are open as they usually are. He already said goodbye to them in his farewell speech, and he doesn't feel like saying goodbye again to any of them individually, even though he considers some of the older guys his friends. They all hear my steps, he thinks. They are looking through their doors to see me go by. Some are standing in their doorways. He knows they are grateful for having been secured in their positions by the contract he'd hammered out with the new owner, yet they may still feel abandoned or sorrow-stricken by his leaving. They may want to hug me, he thinks, but they understand that I might crumble at the slightest hint of affection. As if lining a funeral procession they silently watch him go. Lukas, cotton-wrapped and upright, looks straight ahead and walks, still there but already nowhere, and when someone calls his name and another mumbles *Bye!* – or was it just a thought – he slightly nods into the open air, steadily striding along. Along and out. Some moments in life are unique, he thinks while riding down the elevator, and this, he knows, is one of them.

Because of the moving commotion they don't serve breakfast any longer in the lobby. The receptionist sends me to the milk bar. When I enter I see the innkeeper sitting with Marlene who is sipping with a straw at a big glass of milkshake. Immediately she waves me over, and as soon as I sit down, she says, we were just talking about you! I feel almost assailed by her remark, but the innkeeper quickly chimes in: only good stuff, and she offers to get me also one of these milkshakes, which, she says, turned out particularly delicious this morning. So I stay. I'll be leaving soon, I think, and who knows when I will see Marlene again? Hence I can put up with some discomfort. What's there to talk about me, I ask. Wistfully Marlene looks at me and says: We were talking about aging. You don't understand, you are young and beautiful, at your age all seems easy, all is possible, you don't think of growing old, you can't imagine how everything that once was naturally there, all of a sudden starts seeping out, shrinks, fades, your skin wrinkles, your flesh sags, your breasts descend, your hair thins out, you see the strands in the bathtub where they end up clogging the drain, and while previously you could eat everything without putting on weight, suddenly you pack all that fat around you, on your belly, buttocks, legs and all, and you try to undo it with these elastic shirts, which at first seem to make most of the excess disappear, and you look again close to how you used to look, but the longer you wear them, the more they pinch you, they squeeze all confidence out of you – I've seen your scornful smirk when you saw these things hanging in the laundry room – and in particular in summer when it's hot, you sweat and smell, and everything becomes a drag, you become your own burden…I started to watch young women with a feeling of awe, their bodies were so beautiful, yes, and I envied you for being young, Marlene says, and looks so lonely that despite being put off by her descriptions I feel like hugging her, only briefly, but I don't. Shaking her gray head she says: I tell you this, because my mother never told me. Maybe she was right not to tell me. Back then I may have thought, it's her fault, it wouldn't happen to me, certainly not. And when you became a teen eventually hitting twenty, I looked at you, how airily you went your way, totally unsuspecting of what lay ahead, and a deep trench opened between us, but you had no idea…I didn't want to tell you then, I was ashamed, I rebelled against it, but I also didn't want to burden you. So I kept it for myself…All in thought, she moves her milkshake back and forth. I'm not young anymore either, I softly say to my mother, I know what you are talking about, at least some of it. I've had similar feelings when Mikki went to college…

Sam calls. Finally! He is in an upbeat mood. I'm at the airport, he says. I'll be boarding in a few minutes. Tomorrow I'll be home. I can't wait to see you! In the background I hear the boarding announcement. My heart is beating. Really, I ask, you are coming home? My question seems to puzzle him. There is a short pause, and then he emphasizes that yes, of course he's flying home now, what could prevent him from doing that? See you soon, he says, I love you. And I respond by saying it too: I love you. The line breaks off, and we both board the plane, because we want to be together on this flight, this particular flight that will bring us back home, where we belong, where we've spent so many good years, productive years, challenging at times, but we always managed. Our home where we raised Mikki. Good times, few clouds, a life lived. Yes. And I squeeze his hand to let him know how much he means to me, and how grateful I am for his love and for all he does to keep our little family up and running.

This here, Marlene says, vaguely gesturing at herself, this here, and she nods in bad blood, indicating that she'd been the victim of wrongs, always. This here, and she stops in search of the right words, any word that could fathom, at least roughly fathom her hurts and the bravery with which she's carried them through time. Her eyes cast down looking at nothing in front of her, nothing other than her life that keeps showing its old loops, images all out and up to accuse her. But she'd done nothing wrong. Nothing. And still her sister would say: you've ruined our Christmas party! You came to ruin our Christmas party! She'd only come home to be home at Christmas. No, her sister charges, you didn't like that we all had a good time without you. Oh what to say! She only wanted to be home on Christmas. Her hands shiver, these hands that used to be beautiful and kissed, kissed by her officer, the officer on duty. Let me kiss your hands. Hands she gave him and more. Let me kiss all of you, let me kiss you. So what?! You hurt our family, you bitch, the officer's wife yelled at her. Bitch – yourself, or what could she say? Her thin legs are too short to reach the floor. Dangling them in the air like a child, at age 98 slouching on her bed, too high for her—everything was too high, too much and too little, for all her life it's been that way, always. Yeah, yeah, she softly whispers and feels the warm urine running into her diaper. Nobody knows, nobody will notice. One day when nobody was there to drop in and look after her, she'd taken her walker and had shuffled over to her secret cabinet in search of…she'd meant to find and destroy this thing…something she should have destroyed long ago, and why hadn't she? Oh so many memories go with it, her only token, how could she ever destroy it? But where was it and what? And now she's shaking her head, over and over, and she can't decide if she already destroyed it or not, then or earlier or even later? Nobody was supposed to find it, nobody. Oh nothing matters anyway, once I'm dead, she thinks, pushing her lower lip ahead and scratching her knee. Who are they to judge me? All my life I was on my own. Why would I care? She bends forward in a sudden interest to see her toes, her warped toes protruding out of her puffy feet. And by doing so she almost loses her balance, almost falls off her bed, but reflexively she jerks back. Who cares and what for anyway, she thinks, discarding a thought with a throw-off move of her hand. Then there is nothing, a standstill of time, no thought, nothing. Again she shakes her head and softly swings back and forth. Yeah, yeah, she thinks. And I don't care! But the dogs are barking, and her mother is yelling, and the dogs cling to the chair they are sitting on, supposed to stay on the spot and wait for their master to come home. He said so. He told them. Goodness gracious! Her mother is unnerved. Work has to be done, bills have to be paid, the customers are waiting in line in front of the store, and here she is dealing with stubborn dogs, two black and white terriers, for heaven's sake! Ha, now you can see that you can't always get what you want! A gleeful smile blazes its trail through her wrinkles. You always want to order people around, but my father left without telling you where he went and when he would come back, and his dogs refuse to follow your orders. Far away she hears the church bells ringing. Soon Enna will come to remove the tray with her breakfast. I won't have it, I won't eat up everything any longer! For a moment she deeply savors her triumph. Nobody can order me around. I do what

I want! And then she slowly lifts up her legs, helps with her hands to lift them up, and lies down on her pillows. Footsteps are coming towards her door. Grabbing the comforter and quickly covering everything up to her chin, she pretends to be sleeping. Motionless she lies on white sheets with her eyes closed when the door opens. Then there's nothing, silence, no step inside the room. Obviously Enna's just looking at her, seeing her sleep, or so she thinks and wonders if she should address her, wake her up, or leave her alone? After a while Enna softly closes the door. My mother unveils a sly smile.

One sunny afternoon Enna goes out, and even though she is feeling a bit in a maze, immediately she notices the crisp air like a long sought-after relief. The door falls shut behind her with this soft sucking thud, so familiar, but now so new. Sleep, she thinks, sleep well, and she slowly tucks a strand of hair behind her ear – her long, still shining hair that falls like a curtain when she bends over her mother to feed her, or to smooth the sheets over her pillows, or to check if the thin transparent tube from the oxygen machine goes straight into her small encrusted nostrils, or to find out if she's asleep—all these things, done a million times, but now no more, she feels, she can't do them anymore, and she descends through the open staircase that is cluttered with leaves and small branches, since this early fall storm had washed over the area in an unexpectedly furious assault. She won't suffer. Enna knows a restaurant not too far away. Years ago she liked to go there for dinner. Does it still exist? Would she see anyone she knew, just by chance? The doorbell rings, bing-bang, when she enters, and through the smoke and steam of folksiness she notices that her preferred table is free, this small window table in the corner between the coatrack and the bar where she can see everything that's going on in the restaurant while remaining nearly invisible to others. So she thinks. She orders an Irish coffee! At home her mother is breathing. The waitress puts a small plate with two cinnamon cookies next to her coffee. Fresh from the oven, she says with a smile, and Enna thanks her. I haven't seen you in a while, the waitress adds, and Enna feels grateful for being recognized. Not being forgotten! Still she feels like a stranger, like an intruder into another kind of life, like she's stealing the pleasures of a mundane social moment, a pleasure that still can be hers — but not her mother's. Oh do sleep, finally sleep and fare well. But what is so desirable about coming here and sitting at this table? Looking around, Enna feels gripped by a sense of normalcy that is almost alienating. This kind of normalcy has been seeping out of her days in an unperceivable trickle, and now it seems to rush back as if with a vengeance! Enna straightens up and smiles. I'm not lost, she thinks, not yet! The Irish coffee melts on her lips. She orders rack of lamb with baked potatoes and red wine. For a while she doesn't think of anything; she just watches what's going on in the restaurant. The food is good. The light is agreeable. On the TV they're showing an old movie with Gregory Peck, whom she liked. There is no sound, but she remembers enough of the story to get lost in its shifting images. Ice cream for dessert! With all these treats Enna feels satisfied, somehow fulfilled – and yet a sudden emptiness asserts itself, like an onslaught on all she'd worked herself up to, really, to the point where she thought she could leave, really could leave. It felt right, it did. For a decisive moment this new belief had replaced all she had held on to for all her life. She could close the door from outside. That was before, but not now, not anymore! And with a sense of panic rising from her stomach and flooding her heart with guilt and shame, Enna demands the check. At first she wants to wait for it, but then, feeling unable to contain herself, she just throws a bill on the table, more than she owes, for sure, and leaves in a mad rush, runs in a frenzy all the way home, up the stairs, and arrives at front of the door. All is quiet. An anxious smile flitters across her lips. She opens the door and enters. In the hallway she turns on the light that casts its faint shine into her mother's bedroom. She sees her lying in her bed just as before; she hears her snoring. Slowly she goes in and turns the switch of the oxygen machine to *On*.

My bags are packed. I hope they still have a porter who can carry them down, because the elevator too is out of service. I called the reception desk and let it ring, but nobody answered.

If they can't bring my baggage down, I may just leave every-thing here. When I open the door, I see Jules standing in the doorway unsteadily, it seems, a pale shadow on the brink. Come with me, I say lightly as if we once had agreed about it, come back, it was a mistake, you know. He doesn't move. I go past him, proceed through the hallway leaving him behind. Yet I still see him in front of me, looking at me from afar, desperate or angry, I can't tell, or is he more resigned than determined? He stumbles, fails – and I missed it. Could I have stopped him? I'll never know, I'll always wonder. It's only now that his old mother may have come into her own. Left by her husband and son, by her relatives and the few friends that occasionally spotted her life, she's sitting in an outdoor coffee shop at the Kurfürstendamm watching the tourists stroll by like figures in an advertisement, a video without a story. The populated emptiness of the moving images dissolves the loose threads in the void of her busted soul. Nobody is looking at her. Maybe one day a stroke will fell her some-place between here and there. She may drop at a street curb in Charlottenburg or under the falling leaves in Grunewald. Passersby will make the necessary calls, tardily an ambulance will roll over the crackling gravel path and stop in front of this misery wrapped in a once fancy coat. Having deter-mined that she isn't alive anymore, they will lift her on the stretcher, still careful as if trying to not hurt her. And slowly the car will leave with some flaneurs quietly looking on as the vehicle disappears in the dusk. Only weeks later, after the landlord has finally started doubting that the lady from the fifth floor is visiting with her son, and tentatively puts the police on notice about her disappearance, will they be able to solve the mystery of who she was. Or a remote relative, who believed that she was living with a friend in Jakarta and had no idea that she owned a condo in Charlottenburg, only three bus stops from where he was running a small rare books store, will see her photo published in a public notice. They'll wind their way to the morgue, open the cabinet, roll her out of the freezing slot where she's been lying for weeks still in her coat and next to her small Coco Chanel purse, in which she'd carried an ordinary set of keys, a valet with some cash, and a photo of an old woman holding a little child on her lap – which will be identified as being her little self on her grandmother's lap. Her relative will point the authorities to the family grave at the Weißensee Cemetery and stand by when the mother is finally buried next to her husband's and her son's ashes – while somewhere on the opposite end of the world a baby is crying in the dawn, as his mother is picking up the pieces of their shattered life, sad, brave, and determined.

In the evening my father reaches Acheron's shores. The sun is still shining, spreading orange particles all across the sky – soft it looks and wide like a shell, this sky above and beyond. He sits down and leans his back against the trunk of a white cottonwood. Good old tree. All is quiet, which makes him smile. He feels relieved after the long hike. Having reached the end of his trip seems sweet. Yet melancholy tugs at his heart. What a journey to come here! Having seen the sun rise over the ruins of Machu Picchu, heard the night chatter of Africa's wild forests, felt the smooth waters of the South Pacific, and been gripped by the majesty of the Andean Highlands… Even within the small circle of mundane life: Sine, his little girl, beaming at him when he came home; Enna snuggling close to him on the sofa; and Marlene, how beautiful she was, how exciting, and her voice, her voice… My father draws circles in the sand. He feels tired and far away, yet also close. What will come? For a moment a wave of nausea washes over him, then ebbs away. A boat's approaching from the horizon, black against the paling heaven, slowly moved by Charon's calm hands. He will come. My father looks ahead, his heart empty for a moment, then gripped by a sudden fear. What will come, what? Will it hurt? Will he notice? Then he relaxes again. There is nothing he can do about it. There is nothing left to yearn for. He just wishes it would be over. He closes his eyes and feels a slight breeze on his face. A last dream, he thinks, one more dream…and Sine comes with a bowl of black cherries, his favorite. She places it in his lap and sits down next to him. How was it, she asks, how? And he knows she is asking about his life. He ponders, wants to focus on something particular, but all seems equal, all's indifferent now, nothing's there to hold on to. Good, he then says and thinks, this is right. Sine smiles. How is it for you? He wants to ask her, but something holds him back. So he only looks at her, sees her graying hair still falling long over her shoulders. She seems to tremble. I can do this, he says, and she nods. She's gone. Charon pulls the boat onto the shore, all slow motion. He knows what to do. It is cold. My father shivers. His mother, standing nearby, waves her hand. He cannot wave back. Where is his father? His father is nowhere. Or is it Charon? Charon wears this long black hooded coat, as they portray him on stage. Nobody can see his face. He has no face or merely the face of everyone. His bony fingers tackle the rope. Someone throws a ball towards my father; it hits the sand and rolls around to his feet. Come, it says. His mother waves again. Charon straightens up and looks at him. Still my father wants to rest, cannot summon the energy to get up and walk over. There is no urge. Everybody calmly waits. My father looks on. He knows he has to get up, one last time, up and over to his ride. Someone touches his shoulder. My father looks up. His father is next to him, emaciated but unbent, his vision transcending the horizon. Father, my father murmurs, and he feels alive. He takes the old man's hand and gets up. They both stand tall in front of each other, my father slightly taller than his father and so much younger, hardly a young man though, and yet...He lifts up his father, or is it the other way around? So it is, his father lifts him up. Yes, the old man carries his son in his arms, walks slowly with steady steps through the dunes and the grass, over shelves and stones, walks and walks, and my father's head leans on his father's shoulder, his eyes closed, his sight ceased, his hands holding onto the old man, hugging him, warmly, tightly and so tenderly. Sunset's last gleams expire. Everyone boards the boat. Small waves roll on the shore. The water is black, the sounds subside.

My bags are packed and lined up close to the door. While I'm waiting for the porter I look around this room, where I've been first with Sam and then on my own, all these days, a long time. I'm ready to go home. I look forward to getting back to our house, our garden, our daily routine, the start of the next semester, my students...Hearing steps approaching in the hallway I open the door, and there is the waiter, who obviously now also must function as a porter. Is this everything? He asks, looking at my baggage, and when I confirm he lifts the biggest bag up and says, boy, that's heavy, what do you have in this bag? My whole life, I respond. He looks at me and laughs. That's funny, he says, that's exactly what my grandmother used to say. We would be in a hurry to try to get her out the door, and she would rummage through her things, and we would say, you don't need to bring anything, what are you looking for, and she would say: my whole life! She was stubborn, he adds, and starts walking ahead of me to the stairwell, huffing and puffing. I realize that I have to up my tip and check my pockets for some more change. When we come down, the lobby is empty, but the receptionist in official attire is standing at his usual now deskless spot as if waiting for me. We emailed you the bill, he says with a friendly nod. Thank you, I respond. The hotel director comes out of his office and states: You are leaving! And when I confirm, he adds, it was a pleasure having you here! He walks me to a side exit apologizing that the revolving door doesn't work, and as I'm about to step out he suddenly grabs and shakes my hands with unusual affection wishing me all the best and a safe trip. The waiter drops my luggage in front of the door, takes his tip and steps back into the lobby. I hear him locking the door from inside by turning the key twice. It's a beautiful morning, the sun is shining, a fresh breeze tussles my hair, the air smells of sea. Soon Mikki will arrive. I wonder if I still have time to take a walk around the hotel, but then I see Mikki's car, the new red car she had told me about, approaching on Watertown Avenue, and I decide to stay and wait for her. The cockatoo comes flying by, sits down on the lamppost and looks at me. I'm going home. That's all I can think about. I'm going home. Mikki stops her car right in front of me and jumps out. Sorry I'm late, she calls and gives me a big hug. No, you are not, I was early, I respond. Together we haul my bags into the trunk. When I open the back door to get into the car, Mikki asks, why don't you sit in the front next to me, I have a lot to tell you. Oh you can, I give back, but I want to sit in my usual place, next to Sam in the back. She looks at me funny but doesn't object, and I get in. *Goodbye*, screams the cockatoo. A nice car, I say to Mikki, very comfortable even in the back seat! I'm glad you like it, she responds, I like it too, it's all electric, imagine! Slowly we drive towards Watertown. I have exciting news, she then says, watching me through the rear mirror. Oh, I say, what is it? Hank and I will have a baby, she says, in December! How wonderful, I exclaim! Yeah, we are over the moon! And you'll be a grandma, she says and briefly looks back to me. On the seat next to me the monitor hums.

www.ingramcontent.com/pod-product-compliance
Lightning Source LLC
Chambersburg PA
CBHW052027220726
48293CB00015B/416